At first she thought she'd badly misjudged the time, and that dawn had slowly crept up. As the shadows grew sharp and unnaturally clear, she dared to move her head and saw the landscape cast in a harsh blue-white light. Her eyes followed it up; she saw great beams breaking the night, and high in the air a ship hung, bathing the ground in three moving spots of luminescence.

The Prl'lu were on the prowl.

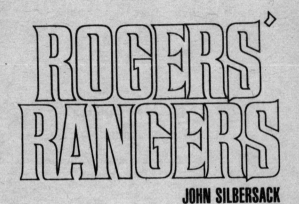

ROGERS' RANGERS

JOHN SILBERSACK

ACE SCIENCE FICTION BOOKS
NEW YORK

*To my brother, Jim Silbersack,
and with gratitude to
Susan Allison and Charles Platt.*

"Buck Rogers" is a trademark of Robert C. Dille registered
with the U.S. Patent and Trademark Office.

ROGERS' RANGERS

An Ace Science Fiction Book / published by arrangement with
the author

PRINTING HISTORY
Ace Original / August 1983

ISBN: 0-441-73380-8

Ace Science Fiction Books are published by
The Berkley Publishing Group,
200 Madison Avenue, New York, New York 10016.
PRINTED IN THE UNITED STATES OF AMERICA

Prologue

Those were some of the best years of my life. And I haven't been precisely suffering since.

They began on a planet, a green sort of friendly place, that Tony Rogers called Blackjack after some old friend of his from before the time he woke up to fight the Second American Revolution. At least that's where I think of it as beginning, but by then I was already an adult woman, thirty-five, practically middle-aged by the standards we had then. I'd had the same sort of upbringing any child of that day had. Those were the years of respite, remember, between the defeat of the Han Empire and the reappearance of the Prl'lu. We had nothing to fear. The cities of man were once again being built in the open and, with Tony's help, humankind's lost science was being slowly recovered. He had only to describe the inventions and discoveries of the twentieth century and our scientists would begin their research to recover the golden era. It was exciting and, like a thousand other children, I grew up fascinated by science. It became my field and, until I met Tony, my devotion. Nothing unusual. As I say, there were a thousand others like me and I was no smarter than the rest, but I was in the right place at the right time.

I suppose it really began a few months before we got to Blackjack. I was one of the project heads on the construction of the *Wilma Deering*. Just one of them mind you, and not the most important. But I was a generalist. I guess I still am today. Anyway, I had a pretty good grasp of most of the technical work that went into designing our first spaceship and I suppose Tony appreciated somebody who could keep him informed without trying to make an expert of him. He was marshall then

---

Excerpted from *Notes to My Life* by Dr. Ruth Harris.

and he'd clearly had too much of experts. Anyway, we were good friends.

The *Wilma Deering* was nearly complete when we got our first warning that the Prl'lu had surfaced again—literally surfaced: the first attack came from the sea. We might have handled that, but more Prl'lu kept coming, from the West, the Antarctic, and then—this is what did us in—from the Moon. We didn't know what hit us at first. You know now that we were being pummeled by rocks from the Moon. That might have been the end of the war, maybe of the human race, if the *Deering* hadn't been near complete, *if* Marshall Rogers hadn't insisted on taking the fight to the Moon. If.

If this and *if* that. History seems a funny thing if you've lived it. Anything might have happened, the wonder is that every little thing leads to something else.

I went along with Rogers and a crew of the best men. . . . Even now I've got to shake my head; I'll probably never meet their like again. With a handful of men and women, most scarcely out of their teens, we walked into the Prl'lu moonbase and wrecked the place. I'm sure that most of us saw our mission as simply an honorable alternative to suicide.

Well, I suppose any fight you walk away from shouldn't be blown up that way, but I can tell you that none of us had very high hopes. Things would have been very bad indeed if I hadn't blundered into the teleportal system. No fault of my own, and no credit either, but it saved all our lives.

We know a lot more now about the Prl'lu setup than we did then. Hell. I guess I use the word advisedly. We thought of the Prl'lu as Hell and the Devil wrapped up in one and we couldn't begin to sort one kind out from another. For most of us, excepting Tony, the only good Prl'lu was a dead one. I suppose you've heard the phrase.

I'm doing a lot of supposing here. Times have changed and I don't know what I can count on you to know. "Rogers versus the Prl'lu" seems to be about what you're taught in school, as though the whole thing was put on like a boxing match. There was a lot more to it than that, I can tell you. For one thing there were umpteen different kinds of Prl'lu. Actually they call themselves Prl'oi. It means *the Great Race*, and I guess by some lights they have a claim to the title. They conquered most of a galaxy and came close to exterminating us. Enough to make you hate all of them, right?

Wrong!

Prl'oi, that's the species name. Prl'lu make up sort of a subdivision of warriors and technics and middle-level administrators: Prl'an—well, I wouldn't want to be a Prl'an on a bet; they took care of the dirty, boring jobs, sort of like servants to the rest of the Prl'oi. The whole thing was arranged like a beehive: Prl'oi all start out the same, but some get brought up as fighters and some get brought up as worker bees.

Some, I should mention, are queen bees. Wrong sex, this was clearly a patriarchy, but one out of a hundred thousand more or less was bred a Prl'arek, the ruling elite. And I don't want to forget the scum. At least that's how they were treated by the pure-breeds. The scum were our saving. Half-breeds, human-cum-Prl'oi; because of their half-Asian ancestry they were known as *the Han*. If it hadn't been for the Han, the third revolution might never have begun.

Of course Rogers was the catalyst. Tony Rogers. I don't know if I can make you see him as I did then. I thought him the greatest man who ever lived, and indeed through an accident of Prl'lu science, he'd lived as no man ever had, born in the nineteenth century, grown up in the twentieth, then accidentally put to sleep by Prl'lu science until he woke in the twenty-fifth century to lead the Second American Revolution. You know all that, but did you know that even then he was more than a hero? He was a mythical figure to most. But when I was growing up, he was an old man. The twenty-fifth century was drawing to a close. He had initiated an old order in which he seemed more a relic than a man. Plenty of people wanted to lock him away into retirement, like an old museum piece. When a man enters history it's hard to allow him the privilege of making it. That was Tony's dilemma.

And then he was revived. Don't ask me how one man can be so intimately involved with fate that by pure luck and good deliverance he should be awarded a second and then a third life. Tony's just like that, I guess. Anyway, Prl'lu science came through again, and again by accident. Suddenly Tony was young, and simply by being clumsy enough to fall *for the second time* into a rigged-up, alien hole in the ground. Today, owing to the same science, nobody grows old, but then it seemed a miracle.

We became lovers.

Strange lovers, I suppose. I had dedicated myself to science. Tony, though young in the flesh, was already six hundred years old, give or take a few decades. Still, only seventy-odd of those years had been spent wakened. So we were unlikely and sometimes dispassionate lovers. . . .

Enough of that! Tony'd never forgive me if I dwelt too much on past sins. On the past.

The fight was on the Moon, so there we went. Tony wouldn't have it any other way and I was bound to follow him. We pretty much put an end to that nest of rats—before they pretty nearly put an end to us. We found out later that Shak't'kan did his best for seven weeks to get the moonbase reactor back under control, but the damage our raiding party had done was irreparable. At the time though, he had us running to catch up with our feet! Give him credit, Shak't'kan was a great general; misminded, and on the wrong side, but he knew what he was about. Would have caught up with us too, but we took a blundering blind shot, right through a door to another planet. The kind of thing you couldn't credit unless you were fool enough to be there.

We burned our bridges. Actually they were burned for us. The teleportal was shut behind us, and though we didn't know it then, there was to be no going back along that route. I might have been worried but I didn't have time. We were on a new and unfamiliar planet and the only thing we knew for sure was that in some way it lay within the Prl'lu dominion. I thought it very likely that we'd stepped into a bigger mess than we'd left behind.

Well, all that sorted itself out later. For the moment what we knew to be sure was that Prl'lu science had spirited us mercifully away from Shak't'kan and his boys—and stranded us in the damndest building *I'd* ever seen. A big pyramid, chock-ful of anything a Prl'arek might want to keep the humans in their place. It was an armory, a repository, a com center, obviously a link in the teleportal system, and much more. Pretty soon it became clear that it had been empty a long, long time. Thousands of years, at least. In a queer way that was very encouraging, it suggested that the Prl'oi weren't an ubiquitous evil; that they'd suffered a few setbacks here and there. And most definitely here! I'm sure that building held the key to Prl'oi history, if only we'd known how and where to look.

At the time all we were looking for was a way out. We were in retreat, mind you, and not paying a lot of special attention to the scenery. So I bumped, curls flying, into big blunder number two.

Looking back it all seems kind of interesting and, well, bright of me to have had all these adventures. That's how it is, I think, with the kind of people who always seem to pop up in the nick of time, assess the situation, meet all the right people, save the day, and live to tell about it; it's just fine in retrospect, but when you're young and worried about surviving to live to a ripe old age it's ruing the day and a quick prayer before the ''here-we-go-again'' impulse shoves you off into some other piece of stupid danger.

And then there's always the worry that if you go and get yourself killed you're apt to take someone you care about along with you.

Which is just what I nearly did. I was poking around, looking for a way out of this Prl'oi stronghold and not very pleased with myself, I can tell you. Fact is, I was miserable, and I just *knew* that I was in over my head. And then, don't ask me how, some Prl'lu contraption that freezes your body and plays games with your mind just sort of stepped up and bit me. It goes to show you that a doctor's degree doesn't necessarily confer common sense. Of course it was up to Tony to come get me out.

Well I can't tell you too much about what happened in there. It didn't make much sense anyhow, just a lot of dreams and imaginings that you'd better believe I'd sooner forget. It's hard to be much clearer than that. The operating principle of the thing was that whatever you *believed* had its own sort of tangible reality. And, like a goose, I believed that it was nearly all up with me. A Prl'lu warrior behind every tree, that sort of thing.

It nearly *was* the end of me, and Tony too. There were aliens gadding about in there; two of them. These were Blackjack Prl'lu, mind you, and they didn't know what humans were. I think it goes far to disprove the theory of species antipathy that one of them showed no hesitation at all in joining up with Tony and me. The other one, well, she couldn't help herself. I mean, she nearly did get us killed, there was no mistake about that. And in her own queer way she was going about the killing quite deliberately, but in another sense she was blamelessly unaware of what she was doing. That's rather obscure, isn't it?

Her name was Aquintir, which means *Mother of Some Strength*. I can well believe it. The poor unfortunate had been relegated to this solitary dreamworld, unable to act, to sleep, or even to die, for more millennia than there have been years in my life. No wonder she was as crazily vicious as—I confess, words fail me. Still, she had her share of strength. If you've ever spent a lonely hour by necessity, then you'll appreciate what I mean.

What I felt at the time was that something utterly strange and scary was happening to me. In the world of the mind you can literally feel someone's pain and fear. I was feeling pain like waves curling over my head. It was hard to keep my feet on the ground, it so nearly bowled me over.

Looking back, I don't see how I could have other than mixed feelings toward Aquintir. And then of course the business with Rogers.

Even in her madness she was formidable as an enemy. Madness, really, was her best weapon. Tony was the first to see that and turn it to advantage. I don't exaggerate when I say that Tony has saved my life several times over, but getting me out of there was the greatest thing he ever did for me. To live forever in limbo!

Tony fought Aquintir's madness on her terms with memories of the past, the episode in his life that he calls the Great War. You can't imagine what that was like. I can't and I caught a glimpse of it; I'm surprised that he can live with it. From what I saw, the twentieth century couldn't have been a picnic, and I've seen hard times.

The fight would have gone against us if fate hadn't delivered to us a companion, Jak't'rin, as sane and as rational as Aquintir was not. He too had blundered his way in and I'm sure he was as shocked as we were to encounter such a troubled mind. He and Tony fought side by side to subdue Aquintir's dangerous fantasies and to make sense of nonsense.

I'm afraid that even so the fight was going against us. In the world of the mind, dementia can be very resourceful.

Tony and Jak't'rin were pitting their minds against Aquintir's, allying their thoughts, focusing all their will against her insanity. I've got to make you understand; their wills were like a double-braided whip and when it reached out at her she flinched like an animal. *Nothing* I've seen was ever like that. She flinched and recoiled! The blow came fast with all her fear behind it. I fell to the ground, Tony staggered, Jak't'rin was swallowed up—lost!

And then that whip flicked out again and I could sense that it hadn't diminished—in a sense it was stronger than ever—perhaps because one "man" wielded it. Tony and Jak't'rin had merged!

It was a grand fight. *Epic* seems the right word. And it was the first time in long memory that human and Prl'lu had stood side by side against a common enemy. Side by side, and then . . .

They won. We won; but at such cost! In order to win

a victory, Tony had to entirely dominate what was left of Aquintir's mind. When we walked away from that alien trap, Tony Rogers was no longer quite human. He shared his mind with two aliens, one whom he had sought to vanquish and one whom he had sought to save.

Does that make sense? If it doesn't, it's not for lack of trying. I've spent a long time mulling over what happened that day and I'm still not sure I've got it right. I content myself with the thought that Tony, though wholly himself, had yet another part of him that was not himself. A part he could call upon in need, and one which exerted itself only in times of sleep or stress; times when Rogers' conscious mind slipped from control.

I suppose I should have been grateful, maybe even thought Tony fortunate. I didn't. It frightened me, but I tried to put a good face on it. After all, Tony's alter egos *had* saved me. They were to do so again.

All the time Rogers and I were fooling around downstairs—my fault, you'll remember—our men were having troubles of their own on the surface. By then they'd found a way out, in the process demolishing most of the pyramid's interior and bulldozing out an exit. It was something to see, But I wouldn't care to see it again. Enough to give you claustrophobia.

The trouble began when they got to the surface. They ran bump into the Blackjacks, the Prl'lu indigenous to the planet; under normal circumstances they might have been quite friendly really. Problem was this pyramid thinggummy amounted to their holy-of-holies and it didn't do much to endear us to them when our men shoved a hole in its side and started pouring out. Think of it from their side, will you? A bunch of short, mealy-looking humans scrabbling out of their temple like termites out of an altar.

They were good and mad. And our boys weren't exactly predisposed to Prl'lu either.

The battle was nearly over by the time Rogers cum Aquintir cum Jak't'rin got to the scene, and of course saved the day. I was there too, Johnny-on-the-spot.

With the new authority vested in him by being part

Prl'arek—a ranking one at that; turns out Jak't'rin was the hereditary wallah in those parts, or so Tony put it—Tony was able to make the peace. He parted the sides like a visitation, which I suppose he was. There were casualties, though. A lot of them. Maybe it was fortunate they were on both sides: As it was, I know that Tony's strength and concern (I shouldn't leave out *justice*) were the main things that stood between the Blackjacks and our boys in those early days.

It took Tony some time, but he got us working together. He wanted badly to get back to Earth and settle the fight there. And he did get back, and I came along with him and the men he called his Rangers!

PART ONE

1.

Rogers strode confidently over the scattered girders and piles of rubble. Overhead, metal beams caught the sun as they were swung into place by men wearing jump-belts. Excavation was going well, he felt. Before long the Prl'lu teleportation portal would be uncovered and his men would be free to take the fight back to Earth's conquerors. In the warm alien summer he was feeling just fine.

Before him stretched out the open valley and in its center lay the shattered remains of the Prl'lu installation that housed the portal, which had brought his kind here from Earth's moon, fighting a hard-won retreat from Shak't'kan, the Prl'arek hereditary commander. Behind him stretched the dark forests of this alien world. Rogers drew a long breath. The forests reminded him of a place long forgotten, of the forests of the Ardennes where he had served in another fight under a hard task-master. Privately Rogers thought of this world as Black-jack. General Blackjack Pershing. That had once been a name to conjure with.

Grunts and barked shouts from the construction site shook him from his reverie. With a slow grin, he saved himself from sloppiness. Wouldn't do to start acting my age, he thought. Wouldn't do at all. Smiling broadly now, he struck his way toward the new human settle-ment. Temporary, he hoped.

It stood at the head of the valley, perched above a rivulet that clumsy human feet had already turned into a small swamp. Solidly built lean-tos and huts lined the edge of the forest. His men were good, competent engineers, Rogers thought, but they had hardly an ounce of artist in them. The encampment would weather anything from a native attack to a hurricane, but it clearly wouldn't stand up to a woman's close scrutiny; and where had Ruth wandered off to?

He picked his way to the largest hut and ducked under the doorway. There, waiting for the midmorning conference to begin, sat two of his lieutenants, McNab and Douglas.

"Morning, Marshall," Douglas drawled. Easy familiarity with their chief was something Rogers encouraged. His men weren't parade-smart, but they had the guts and conviction to respect themselves and their commander without a lot of regulation twaddle.

"What's on the agenda for today?" He always felt it was a stupid commander who issued orders without first consulting the men responsible.

"The settlement's virtually completed, sir," Douglas said. "A few men are still knocking together a smokehouse so our provisions won't spoil, but that's all that remains to be done. I've arranged for three of our men to haul water and see to camp hygiene; the rest who aren't on excavation detail are off with Captain Jackson's natives, hunting fresh meat."

"And where is the captain this morning?" Rogers demanded. "I trust he isn't too busy to honor us with his presence?"

"Sir," McNab spoke, "it seems he's just that—which brings me to my own problems this fine morning. Sir," McNab looked at his commander with some apprehension, unusual enough in itself to quicken Rogers' attention, "not all the men have your faith in these native heathen Prl'lu, begging your pardon. Down at the excavation site there's been some trouble. Nothing I haven't been able to handle yet, and I'll grant you the natives make fine workers. Once you explain what's needed to them, they can do twice the work of a man.

Lord! They're strong enough, but they're Prl'lu, sir, and the men don't feel right working alongside them."

Rogers looked vexed. "Do your men feel this way, Mr. Douglas?"

"Well, Marshall, I can't say they're entirely easy with the situation. A lot of them feel we should be mounting a guard on the settlement instead of traipsing about hunting with Prl'lu. I can't say I really blame them. Those out in the woods must feel pretty vulnerable."

Rogers sat studying his lieutenants a long moment. They were good, forthright men but they had their eyes uncharacteristically averted. He knew what they must be thinking and he decided to meet the challenge head on. At this juncture nothing but open confrontation would suffice.

"It's no secret," he began, "even to the men, that something happened to me while Dr. Harris and I were caught in the Prl'lu stasis machine. *Something*." Rogers grinned wolfishly to show he wasn't going to mince his words. "I walked into that machine human, I'm sure they're saying, and I walked out something else. More than a man? Less than human? Or," his voice steeled, "your commander. I need your complete confidence, so let's thrash this out here and now!"

His two subordinates moved restlessly in their chairs. Neither was prepared to answer first; the growing silence was broken by a new voice from the door. Dr. Ruth Harris stepped into the room confidently and took a chair next to Rogers. Her steady gaze took in the two lieutenants' harried expressions and she ventured a cool chuckle. "I heard some of that. You two needn't look so woebegone. Your doubts are perfectly natural; Captain Jackson and I shared them. Indeed, so did the Marshall, a point you should list in his favor."

"Now Ruth . . ." Rogers began.

"Nonsense, Tony, of course they'll be weighing the evidence. Doesn't it make sense to trust them with the facts? After all, you're asking them to trust you."

McNab spoke up. "And the facts are, Doctor?"

"While rescuing me from the stasis chamber," Ruth flashed Rogers a close look, "Marshall Rogers pitted

himself and his will against the Prl'arek entity Aquintir.
Purely a mental confrontation, though I assure you it
seemed real enough to the marshall and me at the time.
Aquintir is insane, even by the standards of her species
—perhaps especially by their standards. Her ego is un-
checked. I assure you, though, that hers is a formidable
and cunning mind.

"We were joined in our struggle by a Prl'lu tribes-
man, a leader of the faction that Marshall Rogers has
since made our ally. His name is Jak't'rin, and without
his assistance doubtless both the marshall and I would
have been lost for keeps. During their telepathic struggle, the marshall exerted his full power of human reason
to communicate with the Prl'arek—not to kill or subdue, but to understand.

"In short, their minds merged. The Marshall seems to
have absorbed the alien entities with, as far as our military position goes, entirely beneficial results. We "won,"
Aquintir "lost," and the marshall and I emerged in time
to stave off your massacre by the native Prl'lu. You may
regard the marshall as either fit or unfit for command. I
remind you though that without his augmented abilities,
we would not be here doubting his humanity today."

The two lieutenants dropped their eyes at that quiet
reprimand, but it was evident that they weren't through
just yet.

"Doctor," Douglas asked, "can we be sure that the
marshall is not being influenced in any way by these
Prl'lu minds?" He looked at Rogers while he spoke.

Rogers felt it was time he stepped in. "It falls out like
this, Lieutenant; either I've remained human despite the
two Prl'lu mentalities I share, or I and my motives are
alien, in which case you daren't trust me. I submit,
though, that my actions since the incident have been
completely in the human interest. The Prl'lu mentalities
lie buried in my mind; they do not control it. I have
access to their speech, their memories, even their per-
sonalities, but I cannot control their thoughts, just as
they are powerless to influence mine. For the most part
I'm not even conscious that they're there." At this,

Ruth looked carefully at Rogers. She knew that she could best support him by hiding her concern, but it was there, beneath the surface, just as the two Prl'lu minds ticked away in Rogers' subconscious.

"If," Rogers went on, "I can communicate with the Prl'lu native to this planet, fine. If they will follow me, even against their own kind who enslave Earth, better yet. If this will win Earth's freedom, I'm for it, though even I find the present situation a trifle disconcerting. Still, need I remind you that this is not the first time I've benefited from Prl'lu science? In my day"—he grinned again—"we had a saying, 'Don't look a gift horse in the mouth.' "

Ruth leaned forward and caught the table's attention. "My examination, conducted with Captain Jackson, entirely substantiates what the marshall has said. His condition, whatever it may cost *him*, is to our benefit. His mind remains unimpaired."

As she spoke, the three men at the table, even Tony Rogers, visibly relaxed. Strange, she thought, how willing we all are to accept reassurance.

At that moment a commotion was heard outside. A gasping youth, pale with exhaustion, burst through the door. "Marshall Rogers . . . a message . . . from Captain Jackson . . ." he managed before Rogers was on his feet, leading the boy to a chair.

"Ruth, please get us some water!" Ruth rose to obey, knowing full well that Rogers welcomed the interruption. Water was to be had right outside the door, but she made as much of a production as she could of getting it and nursing the messenger. If this would help McNab and Douglas's lingering doubts slip away, she was all for it.

Between draughts of water, the boy spurted his message. "Captain Jackson, sir! He needs you at the Prl'lu campsite. He says to tell you that Prl'lu from tribes in the hills are wandering into camp. They're curious about us, sir, and suspicious, the captain says. He needs you to tell them what for."

"I heard a hint of that this morning from the

hunters," McNab spoke up. "Prl'lu from the hills just aren't willing to believe you speak for the Shapers unless they see you themselves."

"You see," Rogers said mildly, "my new skills have their uses. McNab, Douglas—if we're done here, I'll be off with Dr. Harris." He cast an appraising look around the room and was apparently satisfied; he crossed to the wall rack and took down two jump belts from the supply there. Handing one to Ruth, he belted the other around his waist.

The boy, somewhat recovered, was looking worshipfully at Rogers. "Sir," he asked, "can I go with you?" Rogers caught Ruth's eye and she nodded. "All right," he ordered. "Belt up and show us the fastest way back. You'll find it's easier than running." So saying, he ushered Ruth and the boy out the door, checked their belting, and on his command the three took a running jump toward the sky.

The forest stretched forever, a verdant, fresh green. The trio were practiced jumpers; Rogers and Ruth would try for high parabolic leaps, launching themselves from every branch and treetop. The boy leapt in low, controlled military style. His motions were efficient, effortless, but above him Ruth and Rogers gamboled, somersaulted, and made general havoc while the sun shone in the sky.

"Ruth," Rogers called, "do you think we convinced them?"

The question floated in the air while Dr. Harris steadied herself eighty feet above the ground. "If we didn't convince 'em we gave them food for thought!" she shouted back. "I think the only thing that'll satisfy them is an actual military action. Our Prl'lu against Shak't'kan's. We have to make a convincing try for Earth!" She called this over her shoulder while her jumps took her ever higher into the sky. Behind her, Rogers could only shake his head.

"It's not going to be so easy," he said. "By now they must have Earth sewn up. We're going to need to be something pretty special if we want to make a dent in their forces. Something more than a division of men and a few tame Prl'lu anyhow.''

The two were side by side now and the alien sun was high in the sky. Underneath, the forest was unending, a dense green broken only occasionally by a rivulet of blue. ''I thought these Prl'lu had an agrarian culture,'' Ruth prompted. Despite her confident words in front of Douglas and McNab, she was curious to see how thoroughly Rogers had assimilated his alien consciousness.

''They do,'' Rogers answered. Landing for a moment's rest on a sturdy branch, he waited until Ruth joined him. The boy hung back, too, anxious to hear whatever was on Rogers' mind.

''These plants.'' He pointed to a species of vine clinging to the tree's trunk, high enough to feel the sun's strongest rays. ''They produce a kind of nutritious sap, in all seasons, in whatever part of the vine catches the strongest sun. The Prl'lu tap them, like we used to harvest maple syrup when I was a boy.''

''Maple syrup?'' the boy asked.

''A staple we used to use with Sunday morning flapjacks,'' Rogers answered, to no one's great enlightenment. ''When I was young a great many people on Earth lived like these Prl'lu. Peaceful, isolated . . . great Indian nations. A man named Ernest Thompson Seton wrote a book. . . .''

With a frown, Ruth called him from his reverie. ''Tony, I wish you would tell me what it's like for you when you know things about the Prl'lu that you couldn't, shouldn't. . . . What precisely happened when you answered my question?'' At Ruth's tone the boy looked embarrassed and walked by himself to the end of the branch. Rogers and Ruth stood as they were, eyes locked.

''You still don't understand, do you, Ruth? No, I suppose you can't; I hardly do myself.'' Rogers' voice was low enough so that only Ruth could hear him, but the words carried a sad loneliness that prompted the doctor to take back her question.

''If you really don't . . .''

"No," Rogers insisted. "There's something you have to know as chief science officer: While I can control myself, my human half, there is no other weapon we have as important to our survival as my ability to think like a Prl'lu. But if ever I can't control myself . . . well, I want you to be on the lookout for that. Because if I lose it, god help us."

"Tony, surely you don't think there's a chance of that?"

"There's always a chance and we both know it. It won't do discussing it with McNab and Douglas—they wouldn't know what to look for anyway, and it would frighten them. But I'm asking you and Captain Jackson to keep a weather eye out. Don't jump to any conclusions; sometimes to get what I want I have to sink pretty deep into my Prl'lu psyche. But you've known me long enough and well enough—you'll know the change for what it is if you see it.

"And now I think it's best that we get going. Jackson isn't one for idle worry." So saying, he leapt from the branch, leaving the boy and Ruth to follow.

It wasn't long before they reached the Prl'lu encampment. As ever, Rogers was struck by the resemblance to the great Indian cultures of the American northwest, a resemblance Ruth or his men, born in the twenty-sixth century, could never know. Longhouses of stout, shaped timber, more than a dozen of them, ringed the miniature meadow. Smokehouses and wicker weirs in the brook spoke of a small but efficient fishing industry. Well-constructed fire rings were near the principal lodges, and already male and female Prl'lu, sharing the tasks equally, were roasting meats and preparing grain in simple mortars. Laughing children scurried underfoot like youngsters anywhere, disrupting their elders' conversations and cookery. Everywhere humans and Prl'lu both were engaged in homely and happy activity. The camp was so much more orderly and congenial than the hastily constructed huts his men had built by the excavation site that Rogers had to shake his head ruefully. The comparison was not lost on Ruth either. Summoning a winded grin she said, "You know, I think I could get used to this—particularly if we're stuck here for good!"

This was indisputably an alien culture, but for all that not so alien that a man or woman couldn't warm to it. That was in Rogers' mind as he looked about him—and it didn't take his Prl'lu mind-share to see it. On Ruth's face, on the faces of the men he saw about him working side by side with aliens who back on Earth had been sworn enemies, he saw the beginnings of acceptance. His face darkened. No such acceptance though from the men back at the excavation, the men who hadn't had to live side by side with the Prl'lu during the last fourteen weeks. They lived by a truce, but it hadn't changed their minds or hearts at all.

As Prl'lu villages went, this was pretty large—more than a hundred men, women, and children gathered together in an economy that took from the forests and the plains in about equal measure. During the last few months a number of Rogers' men had been detailed to the village, assigned hunting and farming chores. A new longhouse had been added, expertly built by Prl'lu hands. Rogers' men had made their contributions too. A water wheel and slew irrigated the local equivalent of a kitchen garden; beside the Prl'lu-built and very efficient kiln, the men had erected a well-stocked forge. Girders and metal plates gathered from the excavation site were piled beside it, ready for use as rough stock. Inside, finished tools and utensils attested to willing industry, and Rogers was grateful to see it. As he knew better than any, human and Prl'lu collaboration had never been so necessary.

"Marshall!" The excited cry carried across the compound. "Marshall, over here!" Ruth grabbed Rogers' arm and pointed. "I see the captain over there," she said, craning on her toes. Once Rogers was pointed in the right direction, he saw Jackson without difficulty; he was waving his arms inside a knot of excited Prl'lu. Together Rogers and Ruth started across the yard. As he walked, he called greetings to the men and Prl'lu he passed; they responded with warm grins. Even the usually composed, habitually stolid Prl'lu faces cracked a smile.

"Hullo, Jackson," Rogers drawled. When he saw any of his crew acting impatiently, he tended to behave —deliberately and infuriatingly—as if he hadn't a care in the world. Ruth knew it was intended to put his men at their ease, and it seemed to work: no one ever panicked with Rogers in charge. Still, his country-bumpkin act had its limits; *she* wasn't prepared to stand around exchanging pleasantries while something was obviously wrong.

"Something's the matter, Captain?" she demanded.

"I'll say. The place is falling apart and—begging your pardon, Marshall—it wouldn't be happening if you were on the spot. The only person these Prl'lu want to hear from is you."

"So, Jake, I didn't come up here to hear how you missed me. You have a problem. What is it?"

Jackson seemed to relax a bit. If his commander wasn't worried, neither was he. Ruth had to admit that Rogers always seemed to handle his men right.

"Well, Marshall, during the last week a number of Prl'lu from the hills have been drifting into camp. Didn't pay much mind at first; they're good workers and god knows we've got work enough to do. But the last day or so the hill Prl'lu have almost outnumbered ours. Stak'by here has been trying to keep them in line, but absent authority isn't a concept very well understood around these parts, if you get my meaning. The newcomers want to hear direct from you, sir!" By now Jackson was shaking his head despondent as ever. In evident mimicry, his companions, Prl'lu unfamiliar to Rogers, were shaking theirs too.

And now that he looked about him, Rogers saw that there *were* more Prl'lu in the village than he remembered. His own men had stretched camp facilities to the breaking point, or nearly so. Any visiting Prl'lu were bound to be a problem, and an influx of newcomers from the hills, Prl'lu from neighboring and distant tribes, was bound to crowd the camp dangerously. More than that, Rogers knew that his hold over the peace, through his mind-sharers Jak't'rin and Aquintir, was unnatural at best. Would these "wild" Prl'lu obey him, an alien?

"I think introductions are in order, Captain," Rogers prompted.

Jackson jumped to order. Protocol clearly was not one of his fine points, but he could see that a better show was needed for his commanding officer.

"Sir, I present, T'Leep, Trak'tim, T'Erris, and The'guavra. But I don't precisely know what their designations are. *Tribe warrior* is as close as I can come."

The Prl'lu stood as rigidly and as proudly at attention as any earthly military men and, despite their pelts and barbaric ornaments, no one could mistake them for other than officers and gentlemen—to borrow from Earth's perhaps outmoded usage, Rogers thought.

He paused a moment and closed his eyes. His face fell expressionless, and Ruth hastened to grab his arm. Solemnly, in flawless Prl'lu, he declaimed, "Men of war from the hills, I greet you as does my tribe. I am Jak't'rin. I share this body, this mind. Give credence to me and this man of Earth. With me is a Shaper. . . ." The small company of hill Prl'lu gasped. "We have found common cause with the earthlings," Rogers continued.

2.

The storm had been struggling to merge sea and sky for three days and nights. Seas that should have been high were driven flat by the gale-force winds. This wasn't a hurricane yet, the captain knew, but some said a white squall was worse—and a great deal less predictable.

Four days before, the crew had taken the last sight; since then the schooner had been trailing log and dead reckoning. *Reckoning for dead*, its captain thought sourly. His ship had no business here. No ship did. Four hundred years ago these seas had fairly bristled with electronic navigational aids. Today they were largely unvisited and unknown.

Still, the important thing was the longitude. And *that* was the only element of the position that the captain felt comfortable with. As far as the latitude went, they could be 400 miles north or south of their reckoned position. The antique charts were accurate enough in spots, but the intervening years and a nuclear war had turned much of their detail into fiction. On the old HMSO chart, the Californian coast might just as well have borne the word "unexplored." Even if they were lucky enough to find the right bit of coast, San Diego harbor was an unknown quantity. All these old military installations were. The possibility of lingering radioactivity, not to mention unexploded conventional weapons, kept all but the foolhardy away from the ruins of Hong Kong, Pearl Harbor, Brisbane, Sune Chaw, and San Diego. No doubt the world was littered with such danger spots, but they were easily enough avoided if you wanted to do so. Trouble was, the people who had cut his orders didn't want him to.

The *Freelance* held its course. The lead had been registering "bottom" these last two hours. The bottom was sandy and shoaling in fits and starts. After midnight the captain thought that the wind was beginning to hold, though it was from the foggy point, south sou'-west. He ordered sail crowded on. With luck they'd cross the track of the old 'cans before daybreak. If the maps were good, a big "if," the bay would yawn open, a dark spot on a lightening horizon.

They were running free along the coast, the wind still blowing fresh, when the passenger climbed up the aft gangway and joined the captain by the small light of the binnacle. Holding out a steaming cup of coffee to the captain, the passenger braced herself and buried an exposed face into her own mug. She swung there, in motion with the boat, eyes bright above the cup's rim, waiting for the captain to finish his coffee. When he did, with a sigh, she asked, "Well, skipper? Are you going to be able to deliver me or not?" Her face was small and her mouth set in a tight grin, but the squint in her eyes was measuring.

The captain stared back a long moment. He wasn't used to being questioned aboard his own ship, particularly not while breasting a gale. Besides, he had some pretty strong feelings about this doxie, not very friendly feelings either.

"Well, ma'am, it's 'yes' to your question if my crew and the *Freelance* hold out and the weather's with us and the harbor's still there. And if we don't come up against any Prl'lu patrol to ice the cake. Then it's 'yes' to you and be damned but I'll say again I think landing at Santa Barbara's a safer bet."

The woman—hardly a woman in the captain's eye— stood more firmly and said flatly, "Orders are orders, skipper. And its precisely to avoid patrols that San Diego was chosen. Now," her voice raised itself against the wind, "are we going to make it and when?"

Obviously containing his anger, the captain answered "yes" to the first question. To the second, though, he shrugged deep in his frame and pointed to the East.

"Can you catch that sound, ma'am? Those are breakers piling up the coast. When we hear the sound ebb, that'll be the gap with the lagoon behind. No gap, no harbor."

"Will that take very long, Captain?" Her words were placating now, but her expression betrayed impatience.

The captain shrugged again. "It's God's guess," he answered. "I'm tacking close in with the land so there'll be no chance of missing the anchorage, and its only good luck that'll keep us from grounding. How long? Soon enough and not a moment too soon, is my answer. In truth, a coral reef or half the antique navy might lie under our bow; either will do us in quite neatly. So, soon enough. And if we're caught standing off this shore after daybreak, heaven help us; the Prl'lu won't."

He turned his back and fought his way forward

against the wind and spray, leaving his passenger standing next to the mute-faced helmsman. She stood a long time, absorbed in her own thoughts, staring absently toward the darkened shore, picking out the flashes of light thrown up by the sea as it broke and piled on the reef.

The dawn was standing hard above Point Lobos. The ship slipped through the calmer waters of the bay, two lookouts and a soundsman posted at the bows. The wind was still fresh, but this close inshore it carried with it the baked taste of the desert country. It sped the *Freelance* too swiftly for the captain's liking though, and on his order the ship was pointed close up to the wind and the luffing sail heaved slow rhythmic claps.

As the sky brightened it was evident that care was indicated. In the ghostly light the ship slipped past half-submerged relics, rusting and shapeless with age. Crags of broken concrete lifted above sea level and torn girders stretched under water. The captain stood by the helm, his face dark with strain. Men were posted the length of the ship, ready to push off any object their boathooks could reach.

The still, heavy seas made their passage difficult and dangerous. By the sternsheets, the passenger finished a last cup of coffee, utterly self-contained. Even in his worry, the captain had a thought for her, a woman he didn't much like. Still, to be put ashore in this desolate place, and for what reason? His orders hadn't revealed that.

The *Freelance* made for the southern extremity of the bay, where the weather would be less raw, the sea less severe. The captain was looking for a moorage that would give him more than safety from the elements, though. He wanted a bit of wreckage or a narrow cove that would hide his ship and its raking masts from Prl'lu eyes until the sun set and they could go from this place, leaving their passenger behind.

He found his spot in the ruins of a trestle bridge; its twisting girders effectively masked his ship's presence. With a creak of tackle, the sails were lowered and the

Freelance made fast. One by one his crew repaired to the fo'c'sle, grabbing a day's sleep before their journey continued. Only the captain and his passenger were left on deck. Without a word he unshipped the tender and drew it by its painter to the ship's side. Just as silently the woman stepped aboard. Together they rowed toward the shore.

The shore they came to was crested with sand and sea spittle. Once it must have been several hundred feet inshore—the center of town, in all likelihood. Now the only sound came from their boat grinding into the sand and the raucous calls of sea gulls disturbed in their endless search for food.

With a splash the passenger was over the side and wading the last feet to the beach. The boat, suddenly lightened, bobbed a few feet offshore. In it the captain slowly unshipped his oars and called good luck. In response, the woman shrugged a small pack onto her narrow shoulders, gave a wave of her hand, and began to disappear across the top of a dune.

"Wait!" the captain shouted. "What's your name?"

The woman turned back and shrugged. "You can call me Falstaff," she shouted back, "Falstaff Jones."

Later, when the dusk fell, the *Freelance* cast off from its makeshift dock and in long reaches made its way out of the bay.

The going wasn't bad, she thought. The first bit, across the dunes, had been almost restful after the long journey by ship. Further inshore, California's climatic vagaries had baked the air dry and ahead she saw the sun breaking through and shining on a range of foothills; hills which, with any luck, she'd be climbing by nightfall. Back in Australia she'd been warned about California's sudden changes in weather. She was reminded to check her canteen.

For the moment the ruins of a city surrounded her. "Ruins" was perhaps overstating it, she thought. In another hundred years it might be hard to detect anything here at all. Only concrete and warped steel remained, thrusting above scrub vegetation. One of the

tragedies of all time, she thought, that so many of
mankind's greatest achievements should have crumbled
to nothing since the World Wars and the Han invasion.
The secrets of the Pre-Collapse world, secrets which
could have yielded a weapon for use against the Prl'lu,
had disappeared in an atomic blaze or been trampled
beneath alien feet beyond recovery by the scientists and
historians of her age.

She checked her map, another antique, and pondered
her bearings. She had a small compass and a lightweight
sextant such as they had used on the *Freelance*, but she
planned to use the map as far as it could guide her. That
meant traveling the cracked and broken path of some
ancient highway. Before she had left on this trip,
strategists and historians had planned her route, a
bewildering array of roads and numbers marked in red
on her map.

It wasn't going to be easy. And unless she got unex-
pectedly lucky, she'd have to trust to shank's mare for
the bulk of the trip—at least until she got in touch with
one of the guerrilla groups along the way. Pity, she
thought, that her pack didn't run to a jump belt, but
this was an area where Aussie science took a back seat to
North American technology. She shook her head and
studied the map again. Interstate 5 up the coast to
Anaheim and 15 northeast to Las Vegas. In all about
four hundred miles. The names were strange, but such
Pre-Collapse maps were familiar enough, and blessedly
detailed. Towns and cities might disappear, but whoever
had drawn the map five hundred years ago had seen fit
to include elevations; they'd be all right, and, god willing, the water too.

Her job was to reach her destination as quickly as
possible; most certainly she had to be there by May fifteenth, when the conference was set to begin. Still, if the
opportunity to encourage a little creative mayhem along
the way presented itself, she saw no reason to pass it up.
On her map, three or four spots were marked by sigils
drawn in ink with a careful hand along her route; these
were the locations of North American holdouts identi-

fied by the Aussie authorities prior to her departure.
Pitifully few. Other marks, showing the locations of
Prl'lu installations, all but crowded them from the map.

The courier posted by the surviving guerrilla bands in
North America, the first link in the chain that led to her
presence here, had filled in some details, answered some
questions, but left others unanswered with a shrug of
the shoulders or a shake of the head. The courier had
been sent to establish contact with the Aussies and to
notify them of a last-ditch conference to determine the
world situation. The important thing was this: Aussie
representation at the May 15th conference was crucial if
mankind was ever going to win freedom. Whatever else
might occur was of secondary importance. Her superiors had impressed *that* upon her and, with a wry grin,
she had to acknowledge the force of their authority. She
had very few superiors indeed.

She decided to stretch her legs and set out with what
she hoped was a fair show of blithe spirits—it wouldn't
do to give too much thought to the miles stretching
before her. The path she took was almost due north. In
a mile or two she should strike the road that was to take
her a hundred miles north nor'west, up Interstate 5
toward Los Angeles—a city once so huge it was still
remembered her side of the ocean. By then she would
have problems. L.A., or whatever might be left of it,
was known to be heavily patrolled by the Prl'lu. In all
likelihood one of their underground cities lay nearby.

The broken country was deserted but still dangerous
for all that. The scrub land was littered with debris
and pits. For the first time, she began to have an inkling
of the ruin visited on this continent. Australia had
reverted, yes, like the rest of the world, but it had never
been occupied by the Prl'lu. There was nothing like *this*.
And she'd seen it all, been part of every Aussie action
for nearly twelve years. Now she was twenty-eight and a
tried veteran, but this trip was something completely
outside her experience. She made her way carefully,
once nearly impaling herself on a broken girder hidden
in a pit. Small animals, rabbits mostly, a reminder of

home, had left their spoor everywhere. The ground was littered with their pellets, and sometimes with their bones.

A half-hour later she heard the predator baying close at hand. Actually, "predators," she thought. Since the Collapse, dog packs had become a study that survivors were carefully schooled in.

She took to the bush, like an animal, in turn. She dodged and stooped like a rabbit herself, quivering with adrenaline, leaving the bush shaking in her wake, hunting a hole to hide in. The baying had ended. The heavy crashing of the pack through the brush raised her hackles, but just as surely it started awake her feral streak, the animal alertness that had more than once saved her life.

·She broke through the brush into a clearing. A sanctuary hole, probably an abandoned basement, broke the ground a hundred yards away. Behind her the pack was already snatching at air. She cut the earth with her heels racing for the edge, but the lead dog, a grey mastiff, lunged at her back. Without time to think, she launched herself toward the hole; at her back she felt the tearing, clinging canine paws.

They fell and scraped their way to the bottom, dog and woman fighting for control, but they hit the ground together. The wind was knocked out of her, but she was conscious of the jaws hanging greedy and open over her head. With more anger than strength, she balled her fist and planted it deep into the dog's open mouth. The teeth gripped her wrist instantly. But in their struggle, as the dog relaxed to renew its hold, she drove her fist deeper into its throat. Soon it was gasping for air and she still lay near paralyzed with effort under its paws. But the fist pushed itself farther and farther up its larynx. With her free hand she fought off the raking claws and batted its vulnerable nose. The dog died, her arm buried in its mouth up to her shoulder.

Later she examined herself closely in the failing light of the pit. The dog's teeth had raked her skin from wrist to biceps but hadn't penetrated dangerously; if she'd

been an aborigine, she'd be pleased as punch by the
markings. As it was she didn't care for them much one
way or another. She cut off a strip of lining from her
jacket and made a bandage. Then for the first time she
took a close look at her surroundings.

The walls of the pit towered above her, nearly vertical. They were made of soft stone or rotting concrete,
dirty brown, pocked and chipped. She began to look
around her for something to pound footholes in it.
She'd made good her escape, assuming that the rest of
the pack had left. At least she could no longer hear them
prowling the edge.

In a corner she found a decayed bit of iron, which she
pounded against the pit's side until she'd exposed it's
solid core. That, she thought, should bring the bastards
to attention if they were still around. While she scraped
out footholes she heard nothing. Maybe the dramatic
disappearance of their comrade had frightened them
off.

By the time she reached the top, the afternoon was
already long gone. The pale sun was tingeing the sky
with its first bit of pyrotechnics. She would have to keep
going until dark, her step steady and sure even in the
broken country.

Long after she'd begun to worry that she'd missed her
first bearing, a broad ribbon of concrete spread itself in
front of her. As she hastened nearer she saw that its
flawless length was cracked and dimpled with age and
stress. The sun was glowing dark red as she dragged herself up the embankment and stood on the threshold of
Interstate 5, her road to the north.

During the next few days, she rationed her speed and
energy carefully, pacing herself as long-distance runners
do with a steady, almost unconscious, count. A quarter-
mile jogging, a quarter-mile walking, repeated again
and again until her second wind gave way to her third. A
meal and the road again. A Spartan camproll at night.
During the first four days the routine altered only when
she had to search for fresh water. After the stock of
dried foods ran out, an hour or more each day was

wasted grubbing around for food. The country she was
traveling through was dry, almost a desert, but it had
once been under cultivation. Near the infrequent springs
she found shoots of lettuce and radishes gone wild—the
remnants of gardens—and rabbits were fairly easy to
trap.

On her sixth day she approached the ruined city of
Los Angeles, twenty-five or thirty miles distant. She was
careful to travel at night, marking her progress by dead
reckoning and a nightly star-sight. The terrain held
nothing unfamiliar or out of the ordinary, just desolation and scrub, until she reached Anaheim. There,
crumbling but still erect, marked plainly on her yellow-
ing map, Angel Stadium prompted her turn to the East.

She was worried. In the two nights she'd traveled
since leaving Interstate 5, she'd made little enough progress. This was a different sort of country and she was
unused to it. It was different even from San Diego's
weathered ruins and the rolling country she'd encountered on her trip up the coast. For an Aussie,
Anaheim's urban sprawl was a disaster that time and
war had only imperfectly blotted out. Her impatience
was complete when she was turned for the hundredth
time from her course by the all-too-solid ruin of a building fallen across her path. It was immense, taller even
than the masts of the *Freelance*. It completely blocked
the street she was crookedly following and in the moon-
light the pitched holes of its broken windows resembled
predator's caves. She perched for a moment on a clump
of rock while she rested and looked carefully around.

As she saw it she had two choices. Either she'd have
to find her way around the ruin, which meant scaling
what amounted to the walls of a canyon built of broken
buildings and debris, or she could find her way through
the building, trusting to her compass to pick a more or
less direct path through its darkness to the other side.
The small of her back itched at the thought. So far in
her travels, she hadn't seen or heard anything to worry
her, except for the wild dogs, though to be sure she'd
been living more like the hunted than the hunter. Still,

to cold-bloodedly enter this collapsed mausoleum of the ancient Amer-continentals seemed like deliberate folly. Snakes, dogs, anything could be lurking in its dark. And an inborn warning prompted her. Although the ancient Aussies had not fought the Prl'lu with nuclear weapons, others had, and she and all of Earth's unhappy survivors lived five hundred years later with the daily horror of radiation poisoning. It was normal caution, taught to her in the cradle, to think twice before entering an ancient place full of isotope-retentive metal.

She had more or less made up her mind to attempt the canyon walls when a change in her environment, some subtle scent or sound, registered on her mind. Instinctively she threw herself to the ground and rolled into the shadow of a small hill of broken masonry. Only when she'd wriggled into a protective ball was she able to think back and examine what had gone wrong. For a moment it puzzled her and she felt almost foolish enough to emerge from her cover, but then the lone call of a prairie dog rescued her memory. It was silence that had startled her; suddenly she had heard the sounds of the night stop. Not peter out or shift in the wind, but stop completely: the crickets, prairie dogs, all the barely audible sounds of a summer's deep night. That was reason enough to lie still and small until whatever predator had chanced here either produced itself or disappeared and let things get back to normal.

She lay quiet and concentrated on the night around her. After five full minutes, and ten, nothing. After twenty, her back hurt and she longed to scratch her nose, but still the night continued weirdly silent. After forty minutes she was longing, actually longing, for something, any sign of the unfriendly presence, even if it meant exposure. Before she decided to move though, a subtle but noticeable change caught her attention. Granules of sand, only a few inches from her face, began to cast tiny shadows. At first she thought she'd badly misjudged the time, and that dawn had slowly crept up. As the shadows grew sharp and unnaturally clear, she dared to move her head and saw the landscape cast in a harsh blue-white light. Her eyes followed it up, saw great beams breaking the night, and, high in the air, she saw the ship hanging, bathing the ground in three moving spots of luminescence.

The Prl'lu were on the prowl.

Without more thought, she had made her decision. If she could make her way the hundred yards to the collapsed building, she would have a chance to escape. It was clear the Prl'lu were looking for something, but not her, she thought. It seemed hardly probable that they'd been aware of her progress and yet waited until this moment to pick her up—or exterminate her.

No, the Prl'lu were searching for something else. All the more reason that she reach the building undetected and stay that way.

She waited in her crevice until she was sure the Prl'lu ship wasn't budging. Moving as little as possible, she tugged her pack off her shoulders and lashed a length of rope to its straps, so she could drag it behind her as she inched and crawled her way across the open space. As long as the ship was directly overhead in this broken country, her only chance was to keep a low profile and especially to cast no shadow. She took off her boots and made them fast by their laces to the pack. Their angular shape was a dead giveaway in the open. As an afterthought she blackened the soles of her feet with ashes from the crevice and stripped off her jacket. She held it open between her arms to help make her figure irregular, inhuman, against the ground. With this last precaution complete, she began to inch toward the building, now thrown into brilliant relief by the Prl'lu searchlights. The light did not make the building look less forbidding, but the blackened windows gaped as empty as ever.

A steady crawl took her halfway across the ground, but there a beam of light pinned her, unmoving, on the canyon's floor. She didn't think she'd been spotted, but the moments that the light hung on her seemed long. She lay still, firmly a part of the rock and soil under her, ever aware that a dis ray or projectile could at any moment burn her shadow into the ground. After long minutes, the light played farther on, against rock and gully, and in the comparative darkness she hastened the last few feet to the nearest fissure in the building's side. As she scrambled, the ship's beam seemed to jerk and caught her legs sliding out of sight. Fearing that the brief glimpse might have been intelligible to the Prl'lu, she didn't stop just inside the building as she had planned, but blundered her way deep inside where no light could penetrate. There she paused and wiped the sweat from her forehead. With a shiver she forced herself to consider her situation calmly. It seemed unlikely that the Prl'lu would land and follow her inside, especially if they'd caught no more than an ambiguous glimpse of her. No, they would stay aloft and wait to see what, if anything, emerged from the tumble of girders. If nothing drew them away, they might hang around for days before they gave up and left.

Until then she was trapped.

3.

He was tossing violently in his sleep. Ruth sat by his side and wrung out a cool rag to place over his forehead. She drew it from a basin of water the boy fetched hourly from the spring. That was the only way it could be kept cold.

The dream was bad this time. She could tell it was very bad because Rogers sometimes gritted his teeth and the trapped moaning sounded cavernous in his chest.

Joaquin stopped in sometimes. Ruth discouraged all the others. If they saw Rogers this way it would frighten them. Sometimes when he spoke in his dreams it was with his old familiar drawl and he recalled Earth and old friends; but other times, most of the time, his voice was unnatural, harsh and guttural, his human throat shaping the ancient Prl'oi speech.

Tony wouldn't want them to hear that; wouldn't want them to see him wracked and feverish. He'd made that clear to Ruth that day in the trees. Still, she couldn't hide his illness. Something was obviously up when the Marshall didn't show his face two days at a stretch, but she could do her best to hide the symptoms.

She only wished she could hide from them herself.

The dream went on and on. Legions of marching Prl'oi, an empire won and slowly lost; flitting forest shapes; immense, shadowy machines of war; fleets of ships flashing in alien suns; worlds laid bare and devastated; a royal palace; a crying child. Individually, the images seemed sharp and staccato, but in Rogers' fevered mind they merged and blended one into another, shaping themselves to the shapeless, frightened imaginings of his human brain.

He could feel himself swept along, caught up in a current of alien desires and fears, fierce ambitions and gentle moments. It was all real enough to cause the convulsions that kept Ruth at his bedside. But Rogers knew nothing of that; he knew nothing of the world around him, just this deep, turbulent, painful dream.

Yet he was conscious. Conscious, maybe, as men never are. In the welter of conflicting thoughts, the amalgam of man and Prl'arek, man and Prl'lu, the assemblage of Rogers/Aquintir/Jak't'rin was minutely aware in all its vast detail of the functions of the spinal cortex, the neural chassis, the protein-potential pre-wired into each individual energized cell.

Ruth sat quietly, holding, sympathizing, sometimes understanding. She shared as she could.

Even when the words made sense, their meaning was obscure.

"Frank," he called one night, "how far?"

"I don't think it's as far as that. God it's wet."

"Do you hear something?"

"Frank, Frank? Oh god, are you there? Frank?"

Sometimes he spoke clearly about things Ruth had heard him talk about. The American Expeditionary

Force, for instance; that was the War, the one he called the Great One.

"Johnny, get your gun . . . on the run . . .

"every son of liberty. Hurry right away, go today . . .

"make your daddy glad to have had such a lad . . .

"sweetheart, sweetheart . . . not to pine. Boy's in line."

The ramblings never ceased. When he was under one of these spells Rogers never properly slept, he ran and tumbled through memories. And not just his own either. Sometimes when the Prl'arek Aquintir and the warrior Jak't'rin spoke through him, Ruth would call for Joaquin. Together they would listen and try to make sense of the Marshall's ramblings.

"*Wyrd oft nereo unfaejne eorl, ponne his elle. Aldrum nepdon. . . .*"

They took copious notes, recording and searching for clues to the Prl'oi, to the history of the Great Race, and searching too for any useful bit of knowledge that might surface.

And all the while Ruth miserably prayed that the Marshall would wake up.

One night Ruth and Joaquin listened to something new, something in the old language, a chapter in the history of the Great Race.

"Oh, the ships, oh, they were large, fine ships. They carried the Race to many stars.

"Yes, past the big planets the worlds were cool, healthy, worthy incubators of the Race.

"The one she chose was blue from space. Blue and swept by cool wind. Ice was strong on land.

"A world for the sleeping and the begetting.

"A world to incubate, our time until we were called.

"I stood a last night before leaving, staring at the single gray moon and feeling the glory of our Way."

Ruth took it down as Joaquin translated. It didn't occur to her until later that Rogers in whatever guise was talking about Earth; Earth a hundred thousand years ago. Or some other planet, some other Earth. It made no difference, could hurt no more; it was too long gone for that. But strange to think that she might be participating vicariously in the distant past of her planet.

"Hullo? Ruth, Joaquin?" Rogers shuddered. "That was a bad 'un."

Ruth smiled for the first time in three days. "What do you want for breakfast?" she said.

4.

"Get it adjusted, you fool!"

Everything in the chamber shone a reflected blue. Shak't'kan glared at the screen. Earth filled it and on Earth the North American continent bisected two oceans. There were two eternal and incompatible views from the Moon: the brilliant Earth and the empty pit of space. Moonbase had been specifically built to take advantage of the former. Unfortunately, from this vantage point the Prl'lu empire looked insignificant indeed.

The image on the screen wavered again and Shak't-'kan gave an uncharacteristic bellow. "Keep it steady!" His corpsmen hastened to comply.

The picture didn't look good to his practiced military eye, but in truth there was little he could do—except anticipate and worry. With a flick of a switch he superimposed Prl'lu strongholds, steady orange lights, on earthly coordinates. The wavering screen suddenly filled with a tenuous necklace of light, a band that stretched from Hawaii to Los Angeles, Denver, and Providence. Old and convenient names for the new order—the Prl'lu Empire. Another switch and captive humanity flickered into view: prison camps scattered across the continent, under his direction, willing workers for the Prl'lu order.

Pity, he thought, that another switch would not reveal Earth's remaining outlaws.

His reflections were interrupted by a messenger doffing vacuum gear. *Another trial*, he thought sourly. Moonbase would have to be evacuated in short order. Marshall Rogers' sojourn on the Moon had nearly ruined everything. As hereditary commander of the Prl'lu race, Shak't'kan was probably the only corpsman with access to all the pertinent data—militarese for knowing how nearly the Great Race had come to defeat. He didn't trust anyone else with the knowledge.

Obedience, dependence, and fervor were built on conviction. Not failure!

After properly saluting the viewroom staff, the youngster spoke up, "Commander. Chief Engineer Tashlar reports a building power imbalance in the generating system. Sir, he requests you visit him—*immediately*. He says, sir, that the reactor cannot spare him."

The messenger looked almost stricken by the last part of his mesage, as well he might be. Prl'lu did not summon their commanders, particularly officers of Shat't'kan's importance, except under the most dire circumstances. And universally it was the bearer of ill news who suffered first. Chief Engineer Tashlar knew this well and would not lightly have sent this stripling here. In the last six hours the situation at the reactor must have become grave indeed.

Obedience, dependence, and fervor were built on conviction. No doubt.

"As I expected, Corpsman," Shak't'kan snapped. "I'll attend to Tashlar myself," he said firmly to the room before leading the stumbling messenger into the airlock. As he expected, not an eye wandered from its screen as he took his departure.

If one had, the miscreant corpsman would have been tried and condemned on the spot.

Obedience, dependence, and fervor were built on fear. Nothing else.

"Tashlar! Report!" Shak't'kan's tone was imper-

ative. He was sure Tashlar hadn't summoned him for
other than the most dire reason, but still it would be
fatal to show a subordinate, even the chief engineer,
that he was concerned. To emphasize his impatience,
Shak't'kan stamped his foot. The two guards who followed him night and day at a proper, inferior pace
sprang forward and drew their dis guns. It was well that
his troops be reminded that his whim had the force of
law. It was· well to show Tashlar that immolation by
reactor meltdown was not the only, or the harshest,
death.

"Lord Commander." Tashlar's tone was completely
lacking in the kind of subservience Shak't'kan expected
and, while outwardly contriving to bristle, he sunk in-
wardly. The situation must be worse than he thought.

"Commander, I have been completely unable . to
staunch an embolism in the nucleonics system. As you
know, the earthling's attack on this base successfully
penetrated Level Four. . . ."

Shak't'kan knew all too well. Rogers had led his
troops right through moonbase's best corpsmen. The
damage they had done was irreparable—very soon the
whole place was likely to go up in a nuclear fireball.
And he didn't dare let any of the surviving Prl'lu carry
their story of the superhumans and defeat back to
Earth.

". . . their activation of the teleportation system
severely overloaded nuclear capacity. When they broke
contact from their end—and I confess, sir, that we have
not been able to trace their location—an infinite loop
was prompted in the system. . . ."

Rogers and his men were a definite menace. He could
only hope that they had stepped out of the portal system
into empty space. Still, with the system's complete
dysfunction on this side . . .

". . . inability to maintain· atmosphere, and very
likely gravitronics will fail before . . ."

The base was a shambles and only his inability to admit defeat kept Shak't'kan going through the motions.
Obedience, dependence, and fervor were not built on

defeat. Shamed warriors could not be allowed to return to Earth. . . .

". . . complete meltdown within four solar hours." Tashlar stopped his running report of disaster and faced his commander in chief stolidly. He knew something of the commander's thoughts, but a warrior of the Great Race did not plead. For some moments the room was silent.

Then Shak't'kan exploded in a sudden fury.

Coldly he began. "Did I understand you, Tashlar, to say that nothing could be done or would be done?"

The engineer was calm in his response, "It is much the same thing, my Lord; what could be done is as sure a death as to do nothing." He beckoned to his four assistants who stood, immobile, at their stations. "There is no point to sacrifice these . . ."

Shak't'kan's hand leapt up and the engineer died on the spot where the guards' dis rays met. The game was being played out, Shak't'kan knew, according to logic and necessity, but still he regretted the loss of a key player. Another would have to be found to fill the role. He eyed Tashlar's assistants. They had not let their attention so much as dart from the consoles. Either they were exceptionally dedicated technics or even Tashlar had underestimated moonbase's danger. They too would have to be sacrificed. Almost negligently, he made the circuit of the room, staring without really seeing over each technic's shoulder at the colored lights and controls that spelled out nuclear conflagration. When he reached the last technic, he laid his hand on the corpsman's shoulder and pulled him, protesting, from his dials. Meltdown was imminent then; under normal circumstances no technic would so disobey the commander in chief. He ordered the assistant engineer to take control and with his guards he resuited and left the compartment. It wouldn't be long now.

On Level One, an atmosphere of general and badly hidden panic hung over the warriors. Shak't'kan was not accustomed to the feeling, and its import took several minutes to penetrate. When it did, his rage was uncontained. The Prl'oi, the Great Race, were not to be permitted such defeatism.

He made his way to the airlock joining moonbase with his flagship, *Rhodopis*. In any event, even at full complement his ship could not carry all of the moonbase crew safely back to Earth. No, most would have to remain. Even had there been the space, these troops were too beaten to be allowed to mix with his troops on Earth. *They were polluted by defeat!*

At the lock he snapped the names of key personnel to assemble. Two who arrived improperly uniformed he ordered to fall out. They would remain behind. The rest suited in silence and, at his bidding, filed through the airlock into the ship. He followed and made his way to the bridge. In seven hours the ship would deliver him to the blue globe below.

As the ship lifted from the Moon's surface, the four hundred Prl'lu left behind began their own funeral service. They would die, bravely he hoped, before the day was out. Shak't'kan's mind was already on the problems he would encounter on Earth.

The voyage was uneventful. Shak't'kan spent it reviewing the strategic data his technics had collected from their vantage point on the Moon. The Prl'lu goal of world domination was as yet far from complete. His immediate problems lay on Earth. The surviving guerrilla armies were the major menace. Comprised of feral humans and renegade Han, particularly the traitorous Princess Lu-An, they were more than a nuisance; they had so far managed to forestall consolidation of his Empire. It was a situation which could not be allowed to go uncorrected. He had ideas on the subject. When he reached Los Angeles, they would be implemented.

His crew were preparing for their descent into the atmosphere. Several miles above Earth, their speed required expert control, but in the hands of his trained men there was nothing to worry about. The virtue of an Inertron ship was its ability to seemingly defy the laws governing conventional aeronautics. The airship could accelerate or stop at the flick of a switch; the force that propelled it, the protodimensional substance Inertron, was the same force that powered their dis rays and jump belts. They were forces not of this world, a science imported by the Great Race from its empire beyond the stars. Unfortunately, Shak't'kan realized, knowledge of this science was no longer confined to the technics of the Great Race; it had been first imitated and then adapted by the most intractable of humanity's remaining holdouts. Their scientists, he knew, were researching day and night, hunting after new and more formidable weapons for use against the Great Race.

If they but knew it, humanity's forceful ingenuity was the most effective weapon they had. His plan was to turn it to task against them.

When the warning lights for the final leg of the descent came on, Shak't'kan strapped himself in to his largely ceremonial seat at the pilot's console. Others would control the splashdown and conduct the ship in its submersible mode.

From his seat he could barely see the gray coast of North America. This area of the Pacific was wreathed in summer storms. Their targeted position was several miles west of Los Angeles proper, almost midway between the coast and the Fieberling Guyot. Their city had been built on the submerged steps of the Monterey fan. From there Shak't'kan coordinated activities on a worldwide scale. Most of the important Prl'lu strongholds were similarly defended by the world's great oceans. The continental cities had proved too vulnerable to attack. More than a few still stood exposed and it was very much in Shak't'kan's mind to correct that situation, but on the great continental shelves of the Pacific and the Atlantic, twenty-three cities hosted a combined force of several million of the Great Race—

Enough to conquer a world.

For a brief moment as the ship hung over the swollen seas, Shak't'kan surveyed his crew. They were of the Race and they would know no defeat. With a sharp command he ordered the ship down. Their progress had been until now entirely silent and neither space nor atmosphere had buffeted the craft; but, as it floated momentarily on the surface, the ocean swells skewed and threw the vessel. Shak't'kan could feel the ship shudder as it slipped below the surface. The motion became less violent and then disappeared as the ship gained depth, headed deeper and deeper toward the ocean fastness of his Race.

When the ship closed with the lock, he was the first out the door.

"Commander, events have progressed as you predicted!"

The groundside crew were sycophants, but they had their uses. Shak't'kan marched on toward his quarters.

"No one has been more cooperative than the human Holcomb. And human stragglers flock to our doors. Not only does Holcomb keep the imprisoned humans in proper accord with . . ."

He passed the com center with its hundreds of technics and clerks. The hum grated on his ears, but it evidenced the growing scope and power of his realm.

"We've opened up seven more acres of the Los Angeles Human Station without introducing a single new guard from the company stocks. The humans are largely self-governing, at least. . . ."

The news was good to hear, but not unexpected. He'd followed this man Holcomb's career, conscientious *and* unimaginative. He made a perfect lackey.

"Three buildings finished. An infirmary in the works. These humans should be grateful to get out of the hills. . . ."

Shak't'kan had heard enough of this puling talk. As he reached the portal of this private quarters, he waved aside the minor clerks and aides-de-camp. He could still hear their yammering after the door slid firmly shut. With a gesture of impatience, he fiddled with the com controls under the private screen in his room. Only the ranking Prl'arek in any given city had private access to the communications network, sound *and* sight, but instant access was crucial to running a worldwide empire. As the foremost ruler of the Great Race on Earth, Shak't'kan's access was the most extensive of all. It was also the only com unit equipped with certain features that he believed to be secret. Their efficacy, he hoped, was about to be demonstrated.

The screen grew blurry with movement; the image wavered, then cleared. In it the spare ascetic image of Sataspes, his hereditary second-in-command, reclined unawares in his private quarters. For several minutes Shak't'kan watched, gazing intently at the hard, bony face, looking for a clue to its thoughts. None came. Sataspes's character was as impervious as ever—a quality much honored among Prl'arek, he wryly thought to himself. In this case though, Shak't'kan knew, he'd have preferred a less perfect subordinate.

His attention quickened when a light pulsed by Sataspes's couch. The Prl'arek got to his feet and cycled his portal. There was a faint look of expectancy on his face as he admitted two visitors into his chamber. Shak't'kan watched as the two walked into the focus of his scanner. As he thought, one of them had accompanied him back from moonbase. The other stood just outside his vision in a dark part of the room. He adjusted the controls for sound and sat back, settling comfortably in his chair while his eyes studied the screen stonily. He found their conversation extremely interesting.

"Shak't'kan has returned, lord Sataspes." The one who spoke was Teaspes, his airship's commander, an ambitious man in the Prl'arek ruling elite. "He has heard reports about the Los Angeles retention camp and has withdrawn to his chambers."

"What then do you report?" Sataspes's tone was sharp and his question was addressed pointedly to Teaspes. The subordinate officer hung in the background.

"The moonbase, my lord, is in shambles. It has not proved possible to repair its energy source. I fear that it is lost—a meltdown cycle . . ."

"I know all this, you fool!" Sataspes barked. "What can you tell me that I don't already know?" His tone was scornful. He turned his back and stepped across the room.

Teaspes followed him eagerly across the floor. "Only

that his plans are evidently very near completion, my lord. The Commander spent the last several days on the Moon examining Earth schematics. Indeed, despite the danger, he ordered that we remain on the Moon until his plans were finished. His only reason could have been . . ." He broke off hurriedly when Sataspes swung around to face him with a scowl.

"Facts, Captain. I want facts, not speculation. But I see you've brought a technic with you. Is it possible he has what I require?"

For the first time, the inferior officer stepped forward, fully into the scanner's focus. Shak't'kan leaned forward to see his face. It was the petty officer who had been on duty in the Moon's Command Room, who had helped him program the scanners to run strategic schema of the Prl'lu position on Earth. More than anger at this further treachery prompted his undivided attention now. He was curious to hear how much of his plans had been deduced; he wanted to hear what this young technic thought of them. One of the disadvantages of command was the impropriety of asking advice.

"My lords," the young technic was hesitant.

"Get on with it!"

"Lord Shak't'kan has decided to devote his attentions to the situation on Earth itself, now that the moonbase and our position in space have been lost. I believe he feels our installations on Earth are much more vulnerable than is generally supposed. The problem of all these attacks on our continental bases seems to occupy a great part in his planning and seems to be causing him much unease." The youngster stopped, evidently awaiting further direction from Sataspes. For his part, Shak't'kan was ruefully admiring. The youngster had got it right. Or most of it; there was more. And time to see if Sataspes could get it out of the fledgeling.

"Well go on! What does he plan to do?" As ever, Sataspes was impatient, a quality Shak't'kan knew well in his second-in-command. Sometimes it produced results; somehow he didn't think it was the right approach to the boy, though.

"Well, my lord, the Commander repeatedly had me do correlations between the human retention camps and what he thought were the most exposed of our cities. He seems to regard all of the land cities as more than ordinarily vulnerable to attack, but he took a special interest in the cities in the interior. Whether or nor a local retention camp could provide a work force sufficient to transport the city, and so on."

"Transport?" Sataspes sounded incredulous. Shak't-'kan rather expected that. In many respects Sataspes was a model officer, and a model Prl'arek was accustomed to think of offense, not defense, and advance, not retreat. What Shak't'kan proposed to do would amount to retreat in Sataspes's eyes. Little matter that it was a strategic and tactical necessity. What he proposed was to move all above-ground cities, or all the underground cities in the continental interior, to the Earth's great oceans, where they could rebuild and grow on the protected continental shelves. To do that, enormous work forces were needed, millions more hard laborers than the Prl'lu could summon themselves. That was why the position of the retention camps was so important. Humanity had become willing slaves under Prl'lu domination. Or rather, most of humanity had; the rest posed a ready threat; but he had taken that into account as well. The question was, did the young technic have any inkling of his further plans? Evidently not.

". . . to reposition them on the continental shelves. I gather he envisions a complete withdrawal to the oceans, utilizing pneumatic tubes for access to the land. Four cities in the interior of this continent, one of which he proposes moving into a great lake. Seven across the sea in what the humans call 'Europe.' Six more in the landmass to the south, and in Asia another nine. When all this is accomplished, I gather he anticipates an assault on the southern continent, Australia. . . ."

As was to be expected of a technic, the facts were accurate enough—but could he reproduce the strategy?

". . . I assume that Shak't'kan envisions using human labor for all this. That explains his insistence on these retention camps. Afterwards, well, the labor force is expendable once the work is completed. I imagine that the interior lands will be relegated to the survivors. The coastal lands will be ours. . . .''

NO! And it was a crucial omission. The youngster had done very well, but he'd missed the point, and as things stood Sataspes and his fellows could be left a while longer. They had their uses and, if Shak't'kan kept his eye on them, he should be able to forestall any bid for the ruling seat. Their dissatisfaction with his management of the Empire could be made to work to his advantage. He waited for Sataspes's response.

The boy droned on a while before Sataspes cut him off. He asked Teaspes for his comments and was awarded an uncomprehending series of pointless cautions. Impatiently, Sataspes bid them leave his chambers. They would be rewarded, he said, in good time. After they left, he returned to his couch, impassive as ever.

With a mixed feeling of accomplishment, Shak't'kan switched off the scanner. Despite the need, he didn't much enjoy spying on his only son.

An hour later, after a brief rest, Shak't'kan was to be found in the Command Center. It was the largest technic hall in the installation. From there all of the city was regulated and beyond it the Command Center maintained links with all the cities scattered around the globe. In this room, Shak't'kan was not merely a lord in name, but was able to directly administer daily life in its most minute public detail for every Prl'oi the world over. In this room he commanded absolutely; out of it he commanded by delegated authority.

Usually the room teemed with technics and warriors intent on a hundred thousand tasks. In moments of alert, the room held a thousand practiced and drilled workers. Tonight it held only thirty.

On the huge screen hanging over the assembled officials, two grainy pictures vied for attention. On the left, a greatly magnified picture of the Oceanus Procellarum shimmied in black and white. On the right, in color, a single warrior held his place at the com controls. He was on the Moon in an emptied command room and for the moment at least he absorbed all their attention.

"Lord Commander, the funeral service has been concluded here. The crew are gathered in their quarters. I'm sure we'd all appreciate a benediction." He paused, seemingly embarrassed. "That is, we all hope, request, that you will deliver one...."

The circumstances were unusual but, before the gathered officials of his Empire, Shak't'kan stood by himself and coldly said, "No."

Around him, even amongst this group of jaded hereditary infighters, there was a sudden cessation of all sound. He knew what that meant. He hadn't conformed to expectation. His men had expected him to weaken, just this once. The only other mute vigilant was his son, Sataspes.

At that moment the image on the right side of the screen skewed and blackened. The young man's face was twisted and removed from the screen. On the left a sudden tiny burst of light marked the lower quadrant of the map. Most missed it; their attention was on the wrong crater.

Even the ambitious, Shak't'kan thought, *seldom have their eye on the right spot.*

The moonbase was no more.

5.

"I don't know when I've seen more accomplished in less time," Ruth said.

The ranks stood against the foreign sun. Their martial splendor was a little disturbed by their lack of costume, but Ruth thought they looked quite fine indeed. Rogers paced the troops relentlessly and Captain

Jackson led them in their training, straining alongside them. "Tame" Prl'lu ranked shoulder to shoulder with "wild" tribesmen from the hills, and men stood beside them. The lines were a little ragged, the assembled soldiers a little rough and ready, but, after only three weeks of training, this was a company that could achieve genuine miracles in battle, Rogers knew; a company that surpassed anything Earth had ever offered, either in his own day or in the twenty-sixth century. As a special operations force, this combination of men and Prl'lu couldn't be equaled. Rogers thought back to his own war, to the Great War, the war they had all thought would end war for good. And he thought about the war of conquest he had fought in the twenty-fifth century against Earth's Prl'lu overlords. That had been titled *The Second American Revolution*.

Both wars had been misnamed. The Great War, the war *over there*, had been followed by world wars two and three. The Second American Revolution had been undone by a second, even a third invasion of the Earth. To win this one, always assuming they got back to Earth at all, he'd have to do more than just send in the Marines. It was a happy irony that he'd found the very troops he needed in these country cousins of the Prl'lu who enslaved Earth. But if he was right, the combination of the men and Prl'lu, this special force, would be the extraordinary catalyst necessary, the forerunner of a true revolution that would set the world on fire. After his namesake of the very first American revolution he called them his *Rangers*.

The men didn't know the reference, but they answered to the name with a will, as they did now.

"Raaan-geers!" Rogers' command was an extended bray, the kind of tone designed to carry to men in battle. This time though, the note carried a hint of pride and a more-than-deserved well done. "At ease!"

The troops stood properly in place until Captain Jackson signaled them to relax. Then the rough, home-made pipes came out and men and Prl'lu threw themselves in small friendly groups on the hammocks that lined the parade field. Very quickly, Ruth thought to herself, men preparing for war became comrades, despite the differences in their backgrounds. And what difference could be greater than that between human soldiers and tribe Prl'lu, now reclining side by side on the grass.

"Jackson," Rogers called the captain to him, "how do you think we're progressing?"

"Well enough, sir. I wouldn't want to brag prematurely, but we have a fine group of men here. Sergeants Harburg and Appleby have been doing a fine job; and I might say, sir," Captain Jackson's voice dipped diffidently, "they seem pleased, and that's not a usual occurrence, sir, if you get my meaning."

Rogers laughed. "I understand all too well, Jackson. I've had run-ins with sergeants that should have gone down in history. I'm often surprised they didn't."

"Well sir, as you say, sergeants can be hard on the troops, but I kind of get the idea that there'll be no such problems here."

"And any problems between the Prl'lu and the men?" Rogers was clearly shifting the topic to a subject that continued to worry him. "As you know, I've been concerned about reports of friction . . ."

Jackson hastened to set the record straight. "Nothing of the kind, sir. Since you began training all of us together, things have gone—well—swimmingly. Nothing to be worried about."

"Well I'm glad you feel that way," Rogers replied, "but where's Joaquin? I'd like to sound him out." The Prl'lu captain had left the field when his men were ordered at ease. It had been he that Rogers and Ruth had come up here particularly to find. This afternoon Lieutenant McNab had arranged that they be shown about the excavations. Rogers particularly wanted Joaquin to be there to settle some problems that had come up with the Prl'lu working at the excavations.

"He'll be about somewhere," Jackson said vaguely. He was already anticipating the next trial he was going to run his men through. All morning he'd had a detachment putting together a suitable obstacle course; if all went well, that was to be the afternoon's entertainment.

He rather relished the grunts and groans he was sure to hear. Once a company was confident enough to complain to their company commander, rule one in the unofficial bluebook said they were ready for battle. If he had his way, these troops would not only be ready, but willing!

Jackson grinned. Rogers mistook his amusement. *Even Joaquin*, he thought bitterly.

During the weeks since he'd begun organizing the Rangers—at first, largely in an effort to improve human-Prl'lu relations—his biggest unforeseen problem had been the Prl'lu penchant for independence. Their warriors hadn't been brought up in an atmosphere of teamwork. When a job was to be done, Prl'lu warriors fought among themselves to be the one to do it. To a man they were mavericks, and, like humans of their kind (Rogers had to admit he'd often been accused of the same), they drank all night and fought all day. And it was only by hook and crook that he'd persuaded the best and most independent of them to show up and *behave* during training. By hook and crook and the indespensable aid of Captain Joaquin.

And now Joaquin had let him down. "I hope he'll be fit for our inspection," he said, a little stiffly.

Ruth and Jackson laughed when they caught his meaning. "He'll be all right," Jackson said. "He sneaked away to see his wife and new daughter. We got word earlier that she gave birth about noon."

Ruth chuckled. "And I delivered. Not without a great deal of help," she hastily added.

Rogers grinned and admitted to himself that life didn't begin and end on the parade field. "All the same," he said, "I think we're making progress. And," he added, "I gather from Lieutenant McNab that we'd better be. The portal system is almost completely excavated and pretty soon we'll have it in working order. And then, with luck, we'll be able to get back to Earth. At least that's the present scenario. But I'm forgetting, how's the baby? Isn't that the proper question?" His grin was wider than ever, and yet Ruth thought it included her alone.

"A healthy, gray-eyed, bouncing girl," she responded. The grin didn't fail to work its charm on her and she teased, "And she looked a great deal like you!"

You old dog, she might have said. At one time Rogers had been notorious, and Ruth kept reminding him of his past. It was one way to keep him at least partially at bay.

"I only have eyes for you," he quipped back. At that moment Joaquin hustled up and saved Rogers from Ruth's response. Together the three left Jackson with his men and, deep in conversation, strolled across the field. "Well, Joaquin," Rogers asked finally, "now that congratulations are out of the way, I'm very concerned about your feelings regarding the Prl'lu recruits. Things going well? And no trouble between the Prl'lu and the men? Jackson seems confident on that score, but you're clearly the expert here."

Joaquin's expression was, as always, studied and careful. "No difficulty as yet, my lord. Certainly not among the troops. I gather though that Lieutenant McNab has experienced some problems on the mixed excavation crews."

"*That* I'm only too well aware of," Rogers said ruefully. "But I sense some hesitation? Something is worrying you."

"My lord, it is only that which you yourself have commented upon. My men are primarily warriors, not soldiers. They train, yes. But in battle they are likely to act without direction, according to their courage and resourcefulness."

"That, Joaquin, is precisely why we need them!"

"True, my lord. But have you considered that in battle they will be facing, as you have told us, their own kind? Beings who, if no longer like us in spirit, retain our shape? And you ask us to fight alongside those who bear comparatively little resemblance to us—in short, an alien race, *your* race my lord. We have agreed to do this. But in the heat of battle. . . ."

That had always been the problem, Rogers thought sourly. He had his own ideas on the subject, ideas prompted in part by Jak't'rin, the Prl'arek lord who shared his mind and body. He could only hope that their joint conclusion was correct—and persuasive. In short, they had decided that Blackjack's Prl'lu had no choice. Their culture had stagnated here since the Prl'oi Empire had packed up and vanished, leaving their hundred-times great-grandparents behind. Collaboration with humanity was the obvious solution, and it took virtue in being of benefit to both sides. But it did mean a fight, and that against an aggressor related by race to these Prl'lu. Very distantly related, Rogers kept assuring himself, but obviously related and physically similar, nonetheless.

There was nothing for it but to face the issue squarely.

"Captain Joaquin, I'm counting on you to see that the Blackjacks don't have any misplaced loyalties. The Prl'lu your men will be fighting on Earth would no more acknowledge your kinship than . . ."

He groped for an expression suitably damning, gave it up and started fresh.

"You know, Joaquin, that I've already told you more of my personal history than most of the men know except by hearsay—particularly about my life in the twentieth century. I've done this to try and give you some perspective on humanity so that you and your men won't feel that you're blindly following me alone. You've been a good listener. In fact, you probably take more stock in my tales of the days before Earth was invaded than even Ruth here."

Hearing this, Ruth made a face, but she knew it was probably true. Having grown up on the planet, it was awfully hard to accept as gospel most of Tony's stories about an Earth brimming with people—and *they* hadn't even heard of the Prl'lu. It all seemed too idyllic, and not a little pie-in-the-sky. No, Joaquin *was* probably a lot more believing than she was.

"So you know that when I woke up from my Sleepy Hollow snooze . . ." Ruth and Joaquin looked a little bewildered and Rogers brushed the expression aside with an impatient wave of his hand ". . . I found things very much changed in the good old U.S.A.; and, if you ask me, not a whit for the better. New York, Chicago, everything all gone. I know it doesn't mean anything to you, but accept it as evidence, the evidence of my own eyes that among the good guys and the bad guys, the eminently bad guys are Shak't'kan and his buddies. That's my argument in a nutshell, but consider this: You and I don't have such a hard time seeing eye to eye. Why do you think these Earth-born Prl'lu can't sit at a conference table and talk peace? They'd like to see *both* our kind dead, that's why!''

Having pronounced his impassioned speech, Rogers stalked a little way ahead of Ruth and Joaquin, and the two, left in his tracks, looked each other in the eye and smiled briefly. In many ways these two understood Rogers better than anyone else did. And they thought well of him too, despite his little theatricals.

Rogers wheeled around, stood dead in his tracks and boomed out, ''Well?'' in such a tone that they both burst out laughing.

After some thought, Joaquin answered seriously, ''That accounts for everything, my lord, if reason alone would decide the matter; but it will be Prl'lu faces we'll be bringing our war to if we follow you to Earth—what if they reflect our pain?''

More than once, Rogers reflected, Joaquin had shown a gift for probing to the unpalatable heart of the question. Equally seriously, he answered the Prl'arek chieftain. ''And will your people not answer Jak't'rin's command?'' More than he could have wished, Rogers' hold over these people was through his intermittent mind-partner, Jak't'rin, hereditary chief of his tribe and well known among all the Blackjack Prl'lu to be a brave and honorable warrior. His command carried weight that the slightly more democratic Rogers found onerous, not to say downright scary. Still, if it was the only way . . .

Joaquin replied very seriously, ''Yes, that counts for much and may sway the balance. But there will be those who wonder whether My Lord Jak't'rin's judgment and . . .'' he and Ruth held a brief, whispered conversation ''. . . uh, *karma*, can remain unimpaired in such a body as yours. If you can be convincing in this matter, then I foresee no further problems.''

After a pause, Rogers observed drily, "We'll have to trust to my karma then, won't we?'' His tone was even enough, but there was an unfamiliar timbre in his voice. Ruth and Joaquin both felt more than a little that they'd received a stern reprimand. Evidently on some subjects their chief wasn't about to be balked.

To break the silence, the Prl'lu flashed an uncharacteristic smile and beckoned his fellows into their jump belts. Together the three friends launched themselves aloft toward the skytrail that reached back to maincamp and the excavations. It was an unusually silent trip.

They splashed to a landing in a muddy field that Ruth grudgingly admitted was no more wet than the next. They took a few minutes to extricate themselves and trudged, rather grubbily, up to maincamp's ignoble nerve base, the foreman's hut. In front of it, pacing nervously, they found Lieutenant McNab. He'd obviously been there awhile; the mud was churned and scuffed into a minor gully beneath his feet.

"Marshall! Ruth! I must say, it's about time!'' McNab sounded angry.

"Not too late, I hope?'' After the brief jaunt, Rogers at least was back to his cheerful self and Ruth gave McNab a look of commiseration. She knew better than most how irritating Rogers' bulldozing good humor could be.

"No, no.'' McNab shrugged and started off toward the excavation sight, the little company in tow. Five or six yards later, he noticed the silent Prl'lu: "Oh, hello, Joaquin. Sorry—didn't see you were along.'' Mumbling, McNab plodded on.

"Before we get down inside,'' he suddenly continued, "I want to make sure you understand the situation here. It's been a week or more since any of you've been below the surface and . . .''

"That's what we're here for, Lieutenant,'' Rogers cut in. "You point out the sights and we'll tourist it up.''

"Oh, well then, see for yourself!'' McNab threw out

his arm to encompass the whole valley, but obviously
his preoccupation lay at its center. When the three
newcomers took a closer look, it was immediately clear
why the note of frustration had crept back into Mc-
Nab's voice.

Even in its broken state the golden pyramid dwarfed
everything near it. It was incalculably old; certainly
many thousands, even hundreds of thousands of years
old. In any time or place it would have been a spectacular sight, but measured against the crude shanty-
town the work crew had erected in its shadow, it was
more than that. Its sheer bulk made the work crew's efforts seem puny. Fire-blackened and torn though it was,
its golden fabric was still brilliant and bespoke a technology and craft far beyond human capability. Only
long, arduous months spent digging their way through
its broken interior cut short the crew's superstitious awe
of so imposing an alien monument.

When Rogers and his men had first teleported to
Blackjack, they were fighting a dangerous but well-
known enemy at their rear. Shak't'kan's overpowering
force of warriors had taken back control of moonbase,
or what was left of it, and hounded Rogers' men into
retreat. The Prl'oi commander had conquered Earth
and swept aside all opposition and then had forced
Rogers and his men into the unknown, to blindly trust
their lives to an alien teleportal system that might have
deposited them anywhere. It had left them shaken but
unharmed, deep in the warren of passages and installations that formed the core of the golden pyramid.

They soon learned the fight wasn't half over.

Ruth and Rogers were the first to take the leap. The
men followed, fighting a rearguard action. Once
through the portal, they scattered and sought a way up
and out. When the first man reached the surface and
discovered an exit for his fellows, he was greeted at the
door with a fatal barrage of arrows and stone-tipped
javelins. Rogers' men faced a new and unfamiliar
enemy.

These were the Blackjack Prl'lu, simple and primitive
descendants of the warrior race that had conquered a

galaxy. As racial cousins of the Prl'lu warlords who now mastered Earth, they weren't inclined to lightly pass over this invasion of pale and spindly aliens—especially since they accounted the gold pyramid their most holy and revered ground.

Their warcraft was crude but effective—particularly against the exhausted and demoralized humans. Arrows and slings, stones and knives—the weapons were crude but the carnage was especially vivid. Twenty-fifth-century humans weren't used to it; quick and bloodless disintegration by dis ray figured more in their experience. The fight was carried back into the sacred pyramid. Once again, Rogers' men were in retreat. So the humans died, bloodily and horribly, and it looked as though the savages would win.

Until Rogers fought his own private battle with the hereditary chieftan of all of Blackjack's Prl'lu clans. They fought to a stalemate in the labyrinthian confines of the alien repository. They were barehanded; their only weapon was the power of mind and purpose and conscience. Rogers won—in a way. But Jak't'rin now shared his mind, shared his body.

With the resources of a Prl'lu mind and conscience, Rogers was able to win the savages' peace and eventually their trust and respect. He no longer accounted them savages; he could not, when Jak't'rin's and Aquintir's minds were part of his own. He could not help but have a unique insight into an alien culture that most of his fellows had branded an enemy.

Of course, he had the advantage. A child of the twentieth century, Rogers had no cradle-born hatred for the Prl'lu. His hate was for individuals, not the whole race. It was different for his men.

It was with this in mind that he had formed the racially mixed cadre, his Rangers. In unity, strength. Strength against what the golden pyramid stood for.

Against the might of a Prl'lu Empire, vanished here but still taskmaster of Earth.

Against superstition.

Against prejudice.

Against any and all threats to individualism and freedom. Rogers didn't quite know how to put his feelings into words. He doubted if the children of the twenty-fifth century would understand anyway, but he knew what he felt: That by uniting friendly Prl'lu and men, not only here on Blackjack but also back on Earth, by establishing and strengthening ties of mutual advantage and esteem, by plumbing this holy pyramid and solving its mysteries, and by excavating and repairing the teleportal system, he could reestablish the lost era of his youth.

It was enough to keep him going.

"Lay on, Macduff!" Rogers took the first step into the tunneled excavation. McNab couldn't have known the reference, but he caught Rogers' meaning. He hastened forward and began the underground tour.

"You'll remember," McNab said, "that most of the fighting was contained in the first two levels. At least, that's where we began to regroup and bring heavy artillery against the Blackjacks. So that's where we sustained most of the damage to the building—and, as you'll remember, most of the casualties.

"Consequently, it was on Levels One and Two, and this, the ground level, that we've had the biggest job so far. It's been damn hard work, I can tell you. Not like digging a mine, you understand, where all you've got to do is move a lot of hardpacked earth from one place to another. This job isn't so much digging as shoring up. It's like a game of pick-up-sticks; you pull one out and if the sticks on top budge a bit, you're out. You lose your turn. Except if something budges during our excavation, we're apt to lose three or four men."

"Any more accidents since I've been done here?" Rogers asked.

"Only minor ones; Tabeling broke his arm."

Ruth was indignant. "Why wasn't I notified?"

"We've stopped bothering about minor accidents," McNab said stiffly. "We're getting close to our goal and the men are beginning to feel the excitement. They're not letting these kinds of things slow them up."

"Well," Ruth began. Rogers shushed her up and McNab continued. "When we reached the dropshaft to

Level Two, we experienced our first real engineering problems. After all that solid digging, it was a relief to break into a clear area. All the debris above the shaft had fallen to its bottom and there was quite an area of free space. Thought we had it made, but dropping down the shaft was out of the question—it was obviously out of operation. So we lowered men on ropes and jump belts down to Level Two, but they found that blocked up, too. The problem was, it was impossible to do any real work just floating around there in space . . ."

Rogers was getting impatient. "So you blasted."

"Could've brought the whole place down!" McNab sounded shocked. "No, we got the Prl'lu working on it. Man, those guys are strong!" He sounded admiring.

At least McNab's won over, Rogers thought to himself.

"They pulled the stopper out of the entrance to Level Two like a cork out of a bottle. After that, we began to make better time," McNab continued.

By now Rogers and his little group had begun to navigate the timber catwalk strung up and down the dropshaft McNab had been talking about. Obviously work here had been progressing smoothly.

True, the tunneled areas were dark, at least by Rogers' standard; McNab didn't seem to be bothered. True, they were lit by an unlikely collection of pitch torches and chemical lamps—and, Rogers thought wryly, the crude Prl'lu torches put out by far the best light. And true that only a few passages had been opened up in a building that covered, by McNab's calculation, thirteen acres at ground level alone. No telling how much more the building spread out underground. *Like a bloody iceberg*, Rogers thought. Still they were approaching the teleportal station, and that, if it was in working order, was the important goal. The rest of the pyramid would just have to await Lieutenant McNab's leisure.

Unfortunately, Rogers had plans and they didn't include anyone's leisure.

Their descent was slow and Rogers was itching to hurry on ahead. As an ex-mining and chemical engineer,

even though of twentieth-century vintage, he was well
practiced in the little tricks of gait that made subterranean travel an efficient exercise. McNab was all right,
he'd had a lot of practice lately, but Ruth hung behind
to make sure of her step and Joaquin, who, like most
Prl'lu topped six and a half feet, was careful of bump-
ing his head on the low ceilings. As they made their way,
McNab called out observations about the excavation.

They weren't all encouraging.

"Right along here," he pointed to the ceiling, "we've
been having problems with cave-ins. Timber just isn't a
suitable shoring-up material and we haven't been able to
salvage half the alloy girders we need. Some nasty accidents have been pretty narrowly avoided and we're getting more than our share of minor ones. But," he
paused until he was sure of everyone's attention, "it's
down below Level Three that we've got real trouble. A
lot of the machinery we're digging out is still alive. So be
careful what you get into," he cautioned unnecessarily.

Ruth was quick with a question, though. "Lieutenant? If some of the machinery is still operable, wouldn't
it be possible to put some of it to work for us?"

"I wish we dared to. But it's been messing around
with the live equipment that's caused all the fatalities so
far. It's best left alone."

Rogers wasn't willing to let the subject drop that
quickly. Something, perhaps a subconscious thought
from his Prl'lu mindguest, was itching at his mind.
"Lieutenant, have you been able to identify any of the
machinery you've come across so far?"

"Very little, sir."

"Well, I think it'd be a good idea to inventory it in
any case. And I think you might arrange for Ruth as the
only scientist in our lot to take a look over it. And I'd
like to be given that tour as well."

"Now, sir?"

"Well, point out what you can along the way and
we'll arrange for a fuller sightsee later on." Rogers
turned to Joaquin. "It's encouraging, though. If any
machinery is still operating, there's a chance that the
teleportal will be working as well.

"That reminds me, Lieutenant, you gave me to understand we were close to finding the teleportal. How close?"

"Could be any time now, sir. It depends on whether the teleportal chamber has caved in or not. We're digging in the passage leading there right now, but it's slow going. We can't afford to dislodge another section of ceiling; it could fill in the chamber and wreck the teleportal. If it isn't wrecked already," McNab concluded gloomily.

They were far enough into the pyramid now that they'd begun to encounter workmen busy at the job of excavation. They passed three of the crew, two humans and a Prl'lu, hoisting a ceiling support into place. It was a hewn-out log and, as large and thick as it was, it looked barely equal to the task of holding up the sagging ceiling. It was obviously heavy, too; much heavier than a comparable alloy girder. The two men lugged it into rough position on the corridor floor and the Prl'lu, without pausing for breath, stooped and lifted the log into place. Quickly the men pounded wedges top and bottom to secure it and they were done. Ruth was frankly amazed at the operation.

"The Prl'lu seem to come in handy down here, Lieutenant."

"Yes, we've found them very helpful," McNab said, "despite the problems."

Rogers and Joaquin exchanged a look.

Before long, they passed through another dropshaft leading to Levels Three and Four. Down here the work was going on apace. As the little group made its way through the newly excavated corridors, they were frequently jostled aside by busy workers. Somewhere deep in the inner corridors of the pyramid, a low rumbling sound suggested unleashed power; presumably, the powerful hum of alien machinery pointlessly droning on through empty millennia. Just overhead, the ceiling creaked and rustled with the sound of shifting debris; hardly a reassuring sound. And it was getting hot down there. Sweat was clearly visible on the humans' brows, and the air was too muggy to let it dry.

"From here on, look out," McNab said. "This has all been only recently dug out and we've reached the level where we can expect unpleasant surprises."

"Why's that?" Rogers asked.

McNab pointed to broken ends of cables hanging from the corridor walls. "Some of those are bound to be live. And there's some gas leakage. Every once in a while—*kapooey*! The whole thing could go up." He shrugged to show there was nothing to be done about it and continued down the corridor. Twenty minutes later they reached a cavity that showed the first evidence of the pyramid's unfettered energies.

It was a room full of machinery, blinking lights, and the stuttering hum of power. These gave every appearance of purposeful activity, but whatever purpose moved them remained obscure. They were of alien design and possibly, quite probably, their purpose would prove just as alien and unfavorable.

Ruth found the whole thing unnerving.

"I just don't like the way they keep *on*," she said, "as though we weren't here. How can they keep going like this without something to control them?" She glanced warily around the room as she said this and it was clear to her companions that she was uneasy lest the something or the somebody in question suddenly appear.

Rogers took the situation in hand. "This, I take it, is one of the installations you mentioned," Rogers said to McNab.

"Yes, sir."

"And do you have any idea why it's still working and just what it's doing?"

McNab looked around as though willing an interlocutor to appear from the walls. He found one in a young man whose torso had all but disappeared in a partially disassembled console. "Is that you, Carberry?" he called over. The legs twitched and a muffled voice sounded from the cabinet. McNab steeled his patience and tried again, "Carberry!"

The legs twitched again and then slowly the boy's body began to appear out from under the gray metal housing. When he finally disentangled himself, they

could see that the voice and legs belonged to a slim, wiry
young man, barely out of his teens. His red hair was
cropped close to his head and he held a soldering iron
and voltage meter in either hand.

"Yes, chief?" the boy said. He was evidently pleased
by the interruption, because his freckled face could
barely suppress a wide grin.

"Can you tell us what all this machinery is for?"

"Well, I wouldn't go that far, chief," the boy's grin
broke the surface. "This stuff is a little out of my
league. But it's plenty interesting," he added.

McNab turned to Rogers. "You see, sir, we haven't
been able to make much headway in this side of the
investigation . . ."

Young Carberry broke in. "I can tell you one thing,
though, this machinery hasn't been operating long—
five or six months at the outside. I'd guess it's only been
juiced up since we got here."

Rogers looked the youth over. "And how can you tell
that it hasn't been clicking away since this place was
built? And won't still be when we're all in our graves?"

"Well," the boy answered seriously, "the basic
mechanisms are electronic and, barring some breakage
in the power source, I suppose they could be kept going
a few thousand years—always providing the machinery
can automatically correct for worn out parts, that sort
of thing."

"Then—" Rogers began.

"Wait. The basic machinery is electronic, but there
are plenty of moving parts and there is just no way those
can be kept working for centuries without wearing
away. And there's no way you can circumvent something like that. No, I'd say that we tripped the starter on
these things when we entered the pyramid through the
teleportal linkage."

"Do you think you'll be able to identify any of it?"

"With time and some help, I think we may be able to
puzzle some of it out," Carberry replied.

"Right. Well, you have right up until we leave the
planet for that. And Ruth." Rogers turned to the
woman. "When we're finished with the tour, I'd like

you to work with the boy here and see what you can
make of this stuff. What we learn now could be crucially important later.'' Rogers turned back to Carberry.
''How is it you're up on the electronics? I thought Dr.
Harris had the only technical training here.''

The grin appeared again. ''Well I guess I've just been
interested, sir. And I've fooled around with machinery
quite a bit back on Earth, read the books, and all that.
Things being what they were, though, I never managed to finish my training. And when the war broke
out. . . .'' He didn't need to continue. They all knew
that school wasn't the only thing the war had interrupted back on Earth. It was a grim thought.

The group tried to make better speed down through
Levels Four and Five. The deeper they penetrated into
the pyramid, the more signs of subterranean activity
were to be found. Then too, as they approached the teleportal level, sweating workers were everywhere. Despite
the heat and the stale air, the sight of so much willing
activity cheered them all up.

Most of the trip was spent in a seemingly endless suc-
cession of corridors and connected rooms as barren and
as meaningless as any mine shaft. Three more times
though, they passed through rooms full of live machinery and stood quietly by while other young men probed
and investigated their workings. Once they had to run
through a corridor where falling masonry had broken
one of the live cables that lined the walls. It spat a
shower of sparks at them as its energy did its best to
drain out into the air.

Finally, on Level Six, they reached the deepest point
of the excavation. It was a corridor like any of the
others they'd passed—full of debris, dust suspended in
air, madly tilting planes where the ceiling and floor had
rushed up to meet each other. At its mouth a small knot
of men were gathered. Evidently they'd interrupted an
argument.

''Ridiculous,'' the tallest of the men practically
shouted. ''The only way to make sure it doesn't collapse
is to tunnel in from the side. If we broach the tunnel

we're sure to bring it down."

A lean, grizzled little man interrupted him brusquely. "Sorry, Rauber, but that's all wet. If we don't go in now, there could be further cave-ins on the other side of the tunnel, *in* the teleportal chamber. We can't waste the time. What we should be doing now is shoring up the tunnel's collar, instead of standing around and jawing," he added angrily.

Rauber was about to answer back in kind, when he noticed Rogers and McNab leading the others down the shaft. Shaking his head, he went to meet them. "Overhear any of that?" He looked Rogers frankly in the eye and said, "We've got a real difference of opinion here and it's just as well you've come along to settle it."

"Let's take a look." Rogers led the way back to the blocked passage and asked if this were certainly the entrance to the teleportal chamber. He was assured that it was. For long minutes then, Rogers shone his flashlight over the fallen debris, investigating the crevices and the sharply tilting ceiling. What he saw didn't please him, and he took a long-handled steel job from Rauber to try and shift some wreckage obscuring his view. "Won't budge," he grunted. "This fall is in hard!"

One of the crew who had been working on the break spoke up. "That's what we've been breaking our backs on, sir. It's packed and that's a fact. Won't be any safer round about either," he added bleakly.

Rogers turned to Rauber and the short man, Fischer. "And you can't decide whether to go around the hard way or straight through?" The two nodded. "Well in that case, my recommendation is to go under." The crewman shot him an approving look, but Fischer, Rauber, McNab—even Ruth and Joaquin—were looking at him incredulously. "Can't you see it?" he said. "We can't cut through; that tangle of junk and rocks is tougher than a solid wall. You'll break your drill on the cross-grain; it's like plywood. On the other hand, if we simply tunnel in alongside, the pressure from the ceiling will spread out over the enlarged area and squash the new tunnel flat. You'll only weaken what little support the ceiling has left. But if we go underneath the caved-in tunnel, we've got all the support we need and the plug will act like a spring damper above us.'' Gauging his audience, he thought he'd better add, "Remember, I used to build these things for a living."

The hard-faced crewman broke into a grin. "You've seen it, sir. That's the way to do it. Why I've done some mining myself, and that's always the way with it: 'When in doubt,' they say, 'dig a little deeper.' ''

"Won't that take a long time?" Ruth asked with a frown.

"Not if we dis through." Rogers was thinking quickly. In their retreat from the Moon, Rogers' men had only been able to carry lightweight personal arms. And most of the dis weapons they'd brought with them had had their powerpacks exhausted during the battle with the Blackjacks. He'd been hoarding the few remaining weapons, but he was impatient to reach the teleportal. It would be dangerous, though, to attempt to cycle the portal back to the Moon without any modern weapons. He made his decision on the ancient principle of first things first. "McNab, have the dis guns broken out and brought down here!" While the lieutenant went to retrieve the pistols, the group waited in the underground chamber and Rogers silently reviewed the position.

Once they broke through into the portal chamber, they'd find out where they stood. If the teleportation device was working, there was no reason that they couldn't plan to attack immediately. The troops were trained and ready and although there was a worrisome lack of weaponry, there was no lack of spirit. Besides, fighting on the moonbase end was likely to be hand-to-hand. There was no room in its closed corridors for any other kind of warfare. That's why he'd trained his men so relentlessly in guerrilla tactics. Quickly and quietly in—and then hopefully a bloodless victory.

The first job would be to send in a reconnaissance team. Joaquin and two of his men had already been picked and trained for that. Once on the other side of the portal, they'd masquerade as moonbase crew, collect the information Rogers needed, and return as quietly as they'd gone.

From the Moon—well, they'd have to trust to luck.

McNab hastened up with the dis guns and some men trained in their use. Quickly Rogers outlined what he wanted and the men got to work. Rogers and the group stood back and, when the order was given, watched the floor silently disappear. As ever, Rogers marveled when he saw solid matter vanish beneath the dis ray's beam. The sides of the new tunnels pointed in a 45-degree angle beneath the old one. They were perfectly smooth, three concentric shafts dropping out of sight somewhere below the blockage.

There was no need to wait for the tunnel to cool. When the soldiers moved aside, Rogers' group simply grabbed up a few lights and jumped into the open hole. The pitch was steep but by no means difficult. Seventy-five feet below the corridor level, Rogers ordered the process repeated and a new tunnel pointing up and toward the portal chamber instantly opened. Rogers led the way into the chamber. Scrambling up the incline, he could feel the excitement mount with him. This was it!

The teleportal chamber was just as they had left it—how many months ago? In the fighting and in the general destruction of the pyramid's interior, it had gone unharmed. In front of Rogers, the teleportal console cast its own winking illumination. Needles in dials swung smoothly. The curious opaque emptiness that was the actual portal looked as steady and unchanging as ever. It was a heady moment, but all Rogers did was silently grab Ruth's hand and hold it tightly for a moment before swinging his arm around Joaquin and giving the Blackjack a good pounding on the back. "Looks like we're in business," he said.

The next hour was a hectic one. Support apparatus was brought to the chamber and young Carberry was summoned to give the teleportal system a look-see. Presumably the machine was still attuned to its counterpart on the Moon.

The moment neared for a test. Joaquin wouldn't be ready to attempt his reconnaissance for some hours yet, but it seemed wise to try out the machine right away. As a precaution, Rogers ordered a group of soldiers to stand ready. He and Joaquin took the two all but exhausted dis pistols themselves. When they opened the portal, it wouldn't do if some curious Prl'lu on the other side sauntered through. Finally they were ready.

Ruth stepped up to the console and, on a word from Rogers, punched in the opening sequence. The machine responded slowly—presumably to give the operator a chance to walk around to the portal entrance. Instead, Ruth had time to draw back and join Rogers' side. The screen shimmered and disappeared.

The portal was open!

And suddenly the room was torn with the sound of air rushing violently toward the open exit. On the other side, *nothing*. Empty space and stark black rock were framed by the portal's edges. If this was moonbase, then moonbase was no more.

Everyone in the chamber was thrown violently to the floor. Their shouts and screams were cut short as the air was ripped from their lungs. The grappling mass of men and Blackjacks was slowly sliding across the smooth floor, drawn by the force of the escaping atmosphere toward the vacuum on the other side of the portal. Rogers was nearest to the portal; he had stood in front of his men when the screen had cycled. His feet were braced against the frame's edge, but flying debris was pummeling him. He couldn't hold on for long. With a last exhausted breath, he shouted, "Joaquin! Grab onto the others!"

It took the Blackjack a moment to register Rogers' comment. Grappling limbs were everywhere as the crew struck out for a purchase, a handhold, anything to hold them back from the portal's gaping mouth. Suddenly Joaquin saw what Rogers had meant. By holding onto the others, anchoring them, it would be possible to form a human chain reaching to the teleportal's command console. He grabbed the nearest body, McNab, and failing the breath to speak, he mimed the idea. Others

followed his example. Only Rogers was out of reach—
dangerously close to the portal's mouth and obviously
starving for air. His face and clothing were cut by the
impact of flying objects.

It was better for those on the chain. The air was less
turbulent there, the purchase more sure. By gasping, it
was possible to secure at least shallow, unsatisfying
gulps of air. But the situation was still desperate. And
the chain didn't quite reach. . . .

As the lightest present, Ruth disengaged herself and
Carberry filled the gap. Using the chain as a human
ladder, Ruth pulled herself along its length. As nearly
prone as possible to avoid the airborne rubble, she
made her way hand over hand to the portal housing and
pounded the closing sequence into the machine with her
fist. As suddenly as it had opened, the portal closed,
and the air was abruptly and incredibly still.

The crew lay collapsed a long moment, gasping for
breath. In the interior of the pyramid, rumblings were
heard as dislodged roofing and rock shifted to a halt.
Otherwise, the only sound, painful in everyone's ears,
was their own great gasping for breath.

When Ruth and Joaquin regained their feet, they
rushed to Rogers' prone body. Fortunately, he lay inside the portal. What would have occurred if his body
had been dangling halfway through when the screen was
closed made Ruth wince. As it was, Rogers had taken a
savage beating. He was deeply unconscious and severely
cut. At first, Ruth thought he was dead, but out of a
slack mouth his voice gritted a few words. They were in
Prl'lu.

The others were slowly recovering. Some were still
unconscious, or nearly so. Others with stronger consti-
tutions were lending a hand. McNab and Carberry were
supervising first aid and Rauber had already dispatched
someone to see if the tunnel was still clear and to secure
quick help. By the frown on his face, he clearly didn't
expect much quick assistance, though. The destructive
decompression must have affected everyone in the excavations. It would be a miracle if no one had been killed.

• • •

"Stig-mod zested, winia belador, bealo hycgendra, broga pram odrum . . ." Rogers flailed in his coma.

Two days after the accident, Rogers was still deep in some alien dream. Ruth watched over him constantly and Joaquin too was a frequent companion. During his stints of watching over Rogers, Joaquin translated for the others. Sometimes it was Jak't'rin who spoke through Rogers, sometimes Aquintir. Twice the man had stirred close enough to consciousness that the murmured words from his mouth were in English. Both times though they had meant nothing to Ruth or the others—they belonged to his former life, the world of the twentieth century.

Ruth bathed his wounds and kept him comfortable. The men, summoned from the fields and forests, stood around helplessly or played games of dice. The whole community, Blackjack as well as man, mourned and worried over Rogers' health. Ruth *knew* he was going to recover, or so she said. She reserved her worry for the teleportal project. Evidently they weren't going to get back to Earth via the Moon.

On the third day in the makeshift hospital, Ruth shouted for Joaquin. "He's coming around! Hurry, he's asking for you!"

When Joaquin reached the hut, Rogers was repeating a phrase over and over. *"Wearon yo-zeblad, eal zefaelsod, wearon . . ."*

Joaquin gave Ruth a sharp look. "Has he been saying this all the time?"

"For the last few minutes. Since he called for you."

"Exactly these words?"

Ruth was a little flustered. "As far as I can tell; why, what do they mean?"

"They're numbers. 0678' 423' 1414'. Just numbers; do you know what they mean?"

"I don't have an idea! Talk back to him, will you?" Ruth's voice was impatient. "Forget the numbers, try to get him to come out of it."

Joaquin spoke softly with an even accent. *"Eacne*

eardos, pa se ellerzast?'' In his sleep, Rogers seemed to hear. He stirred slightly and moaned. ''*Aflet lif-dazas, ond pas, ae nan zesceaft*!'' Joaquin spoke. ''Do you hear me Rogers? Do you understand?''

The figure on the bed drooped back as though exhausted and Ruth quickly checked his pulse. Joaquin kept repeating, ''*aflet lif-dazas*!''

Rogers repeated the words, but his voice was dull. Over and over Joaquin worked with him. At last, Rogers spoke the phrase with some spark, then repeated it in English. ''Come back. Come back?'' He opened his eyes and, unmoving, focused on Ruth and Joaquin. He looked at one, then the other, then hoisted himself onto his elbows and demanded of Joaquin, ''You got the numbers?''

''Yes.''

''Thank God.'' Rogers shifted his legs off the bunk and Ruth put out a restraining hand. ''No!'' Rogers said sharply. He pushed her hand aside and pulled on his boots. ''The moonbase is gone, but I know where to go—and we'd better get moving.''

''But where?'' Ruth asked.

''Well, it's obvious that we can't go back the way we came,'' Rogers said. ''Aquintir knew of a place, though . . .'' His voice trailed off. ''You got the coordinates?'' he asked suddenly. ''We've got to get to a spacecraft depot known as Ararat. And it's on the teleportal system!''

PART TWO

6.

"Damnation!"

The day was one of the sharp, cloudless, perfect days peculiar to southern California, but where Falstaff hunched it was cold and dark. Still, despite its discomforts, she had chosen her hiding place well. From this vantage point, high in the side of the tumbled ruin, she had a near-perfect view of her small world. Unfortunately, at the moment, a Prl'lu ship hung suspended over the valley, as it had these past four days, in clear view of her own small observation post. Anything that stirred in the valley would be in its view as well.

She cursed softly under her breath.

Things stood at an impasse all right. There was no immediate danger of discovery, but she really couldn't afford the waste of time. Somehow she had to get back on the road to Las Vegas, even if it meant taking a chance. All her short life had been spent learning how to avoid chance-taking, but it was that or find a way to decoy a Prl'lu warship. She picked up two pebbles, wiped them clean, and popped them into her mouth. They'd keep her from feeling thirsty while she thought it over.

She had a lot of thinking to do.

By the time the sun reached the ridge of the valley, she'd reached a decision. She couldn't waste any more time hanging around like this. She'd have to make something happen. Win or lose, her mission wasn't going to be much advanced unless she put some of her talents to work here and now. Since even with those talents she saw no way that she could escape across a barren valley under full view of an airborne warship, which was doubtless equipped with all manner of weapons, besides the searchlights that illuminated the valley all night, she'd have to make sure that the valley wasn't quite so barren when she made her break. A tall order, but she thought she'd found a way.

At one time or another, she'd had a great deal of survival training. It was a proper and never neglected part of an Aussie's education. Some children elected to take the full course—in offensive as well as survival arts. If they did well, and she'd done *very* well, the instructors took care to impress upon their charges the more arcane survival ploys. After all, a heavy investment had to be protected.

One thing she'd learned to look for and recognize in Pre-Collapse buildings was the remnants of heating and air conditioning systems. In many parts of the world, including gas-rich Australia and southern California, a very inflammable mixture of C_3H_8 and oxygen had been piped into buildings for these purposes. And very often, in spite of the intervening centuries, a significant amount of gas was sealed up and waiting in stray pockets, tanks, pipes, and other repositories, as explosive as ever. And free!

It had been cold and dreary these last few days, and one of the first things she'd done when she found herself trapped was discover a source of gas and tap into it. Because of that, she'd had hot food every night for dinner. She'd also noticed that the gas jet had been surprisingly strong. Evidently she'd tapped into a real reservoir of the stuff, sealed off for centuries. It was still under pressure.

And, she hoped, it would get her out of here.

It was going to be tricky, but a really big explosion should distract the warship long enough to give her a good chance at escape. And if a sizable fire got going, who was to separate her shadow from all the others? It was a good plan and she set to work on it.

The first thing to do was to plan for an explosion late at night, after the Moon set. It would take six or seven hours for the lower chambers of the ruin to fill up with the explosive gas. And she'd need a fuse of some sort. While she thought that over, Falstaff crawled back into the gloom of the ruin and made her way to its deeper recesses. Her makeshift tap into the gas system wouldn't handle all the gas she wanted to release. Methodically, she set about drilling holes in six or seven likely spots. She scattered them to be sure the lower sections of the building would fill up uniformly with the gas. If her plan was to work, the detonation had to be large!

The building lay on its side, surprisingly intact, but during the long years since its collapse, sand and drift had built up around it so that the lower part of its structure was almost subterranean. It made a perfect trap for the releasing gas. It was late evening by the time she'd opened up the system completely. The lower levels of the ruin were filling up nicely.

She was gasping for breath when she finished, and her head was swimming with a dull ache. That wouldn't do if she was going to make good her escape. She climbed back up to her observation post to get some fresh air and wait out the last hours before the Moon set.

From her niche she saw what she expected: the Prl'lu warship riding high over the valley, its searchlights directed at the ruin and at anything else that might be used as cover. She saw one of the lights suddenly directed up and flashed across the night sky. An answering beacon appeared high on the horizon only a few seconds later. Another waiting warship. Well out of her way, but she wondered why the heavy surveillance? She wasn't the only party the Prl'lu were lying in wait for. She smiled and wondered who else was lucky. Then she stretched out on her back, wriggled her shoulders to get comfortable, and took a nap.

Two hours later she was awake. She was good at that. Sniffing cautiously she climbed back through the ruined rooms, down to the level above the pooling gas. Even

here the smell was evident. Very soon the air close to the
floor here would become saturated with the fumes; the
gas would build up until the mixture became rich
enough to explode. That was what she wanted, and she
began to hunt for a good spot to put her fuse.

It was simple really, and foolproof. A hot little campfire in the bottom of a five-gallon tin canister. The fire
would burn and smolder away, protected from the
rising gas by the sides of the can. When the fumes
reached the top of the canister, they'd pour in like water
down a drain, ignite, and this half of the valley would
go up in a fireball.

The trouble was, there was no way to predict with any
accuracy just when that would happen. Some time in the
next forty-five minutes seemed about right, but she
didn't want to be anywhere nearby when it went up.
And yet, if she started out too soon, the warship would
get her before the explosion had a chance to work its
confusion.

She'd have to trust to luck.

She had already picked a spot to bail out from. It was
on the east side of the building and faced up the valley in
the direction she wanted to go. Unfortunately there was
no cover there, so her escape would have to be up over
the valley sides—no mean climb. The walls she'd have
to go over were made of buildings on the side of a major
thoroughfare that had collapsed into steep piles.

She counted down to the moment when she told herself it would be time to bug out. She gave herself four or
five minutes to make her break. Any more and the
danger of being caught by the Prl'lu would be too great.
She didn't think it would take them even a minute to
spot her once she broke away from the building. Still,
four minutes was the minimum she could allow if she
was going to be safely beyond the explosion.

She wanted to start, but steeled herself and held on.
Finally she took a good big breath and jumped. She
rolled down the slope, away from the building, picking
up speed as she went, but all too soon her momentum
died down and she was on her feet running. As soon as
she got up, she could feel the hot searchlight on her back

and though she managed to run out from under it, it started tracking her jerkily, now to this side, then the other, catching her on the swing.

The chase was on!

Five yards to the right, three to the left, she spun on her feet and tried to make her progress up the valley look as random as possible. "One. Two. Three!" she counted aloud. Once the explosion came, *then* she could break for the edge. Twelve feet and she dove to the ground in a roll. So far she seemed to have them outsmarted; the searchlight swept the ground but only caught her on brief tangents. Even that was too often. She could feel the cold sweat on her back.

Now! Now, now, now! Why didn't the damn building go! Couldn't keep up this broken-field running and very soon the Prl'lu would find the pattern in her lunging about. Also, she was already opposite the best spot to scale the wall; it wouldn't do to let it . . .

The ground lit up and she thought they'd caught her again, then the burning air threw her off her feet. The building had gone up!

The fireball was immense, and for a full minute, maybe more, the sky showered masonry, and dirt, and cutting shrapnel. She lay winded until a piece—could have been anything—scored her cheek. It wasn't deep and the blood felt cool and she raised herself on her elbow. The valley floor was a flickering, god-sent pattern of light and dark. She could see the ship seeming to waver in the shimmering heat; or no, could be the explosion knocked it a good one. She ground the sand out of her eyes, grabbed up her kit, and took off for the valley wall like a rabbit. She felt like she could run right up it. Made it halfway and started scrabbling for the edge, grabbing this and that, pulling her way over the top and rolling flat down the other side. She lay there, eyes closed, gasping for breath.

"Well done!" somebody said.

7.

God, it was late. The lamp was giving way to the morning. Rogers rubbed his forehead and bent back over the
table. A lot still to do, and worse. Damn; it was late and
bound to get later.

He rubbed his face again and tried to bear down. It
never ended. Accounts of lading, rosters of men, inven-
tories of weapons.

Sure, it did; but at the tag end of the night Rogers felt
very alone. Too long a life. Too many memories. Too
many people. Maybe he preferred it so late, when the
rest were off to bed.

God, no, he didn't mean that either; but sometimes it
seemed that they came and went. His mother, his dad,
his friends, and brother. College friends, war buddies.
Wilma.

There, that was a maudlin note. Scratch out another
line, fasten on the report, and try seriously not to let the
numbers swim. Anything rather than sleep.

Outside the birds were singing, tentatively at first and
then harsh and irritating. His head bowed again and he
folded his arms over his ears. He put his head down
heavily on the table, just for a minute, while he squinted
the grit from his eyes. Oh, surprising how they burned
ashut. Burned and felt thick, so dark.

The dream began just like it always did. It, or another
to take its place. A death, a funeral, a ceremony he
didn't understand.

But nearly did.

It was the waning days. An empire lost or already
finished. The days seemed long. That's how you could
tell it was winding down. Sarendon, she was the dead
one.

The body was hurt and curiously strained with the
disease. He wouldn't have recognized her, but maybe
that was the plastic veil. Doctoring was scarce these
days; none of them could afford to get ill. Still, it

toughened the race. A virtue made of necessity. She was to be burnt.

The weak deserved to die. That was it, the foundation of the new practices. So a woman died and it was proper to express contempt.

He loved her, had loved her, so he took part reluctantly. But it would look strange if he stood apart. So they filed past the swaddled corpse. And as they passed they didn't look, but each spit from the side of their mouth. His turn. He walked by like the others, followed the custom until he felt the spittle slice through the gaps in his teeth; then he hurried on. It couldn't matter to the dead, he thought, and then considered: What if it did?

It certainly didn't help the living.

The dream flashed along, the golden moments perverted themselves, the muscles in Rogers face twitched, the alien voice was guttural in his throat. Sharp and menacing. He screamed.

It shook him from sleep, and he panted before drawing his hands back across his face. It hurt that time, the acid still stung in his chest.

Rogers got up abruptly and went to find some breakfast. Some coffee. He wasn't sure, but he thought he'd just seen the Prl'oi Empire die.

8.

They didn't even give her a chance to ask. One on either side bundled her along down the slope, away from the fire, away from the airship. At least that was all right.

Falstaff thought there were only the two of them, but it was pretty dark to tell and this night at least wasn't desert-silent. A whole army could be trooping around and she'd never know. She was off her feet as often as she was on them. The two guides—make that *guards*—hustled her along so fast she was worried they'd all take a tumble, but they seemed to know where they were going. And what they were doing; they remained obstinately mute to her questions.

They reached the bottom of the gully and started picking a way along it. They were going roughly at a right angle to the first road, heading south. After ten or fifteen minutes, Falstaff was thoroughly winded by the treatment, but her companions seemed bothered not at all. She was angrily demanding to be let go, for the fifteenth time it felt like, when one stopped and planted his dirty hand over her mouth. The other ducked ahead and was very quickly out of sight.

She took her time for an opening; then, struggling in his arms, she leaned back and kicked him with her full weight on the shinbone. She twisted her foot as she did to make it a cutting blow. For a moment the man didn't budge at all; then, perfectly impassively, he struck out with his left foot and kicked her back. She was so surprised, she stood for it.

"Fun and games?" Guard Number One was back and he seemed amused. "All's clear, we'll head on out."

Guard Number Two took his hand off her mouth and carefully wiped it on his pants, then he reached down and rubbed his leg. "Not much fun, but she's pretty game," he said drily.

"Damn you!" she could hardly contain her anger, "just what do you think . . ."

"No more questions, or *answers*, before we get back to camp." Guard One spoke sharply. "Despite your bonfire, this country is pretty heavily patrolled by the Prl'lus. Understand?"

Reluctantly, Falstaff nodded *yes*. Of the two evils, these grimy-looking characters were definitely the lesser. Until she saw her chance, she had better play along.

Indian-file they made their way forward, squeezing tight at the head of the canyon to edge around an obstruction. Once through, they were in a small clearing and Falstaff saw her two guards for the first time. She also saw two tethered ponies, with packs. The two men fit somehow. They were rigged out in buckskins and wool-lined jackets. Everything about them could have been wrangled from the countryside.

They mounted quickly. Given a preference, Falstaff got up behind Guard Number One. She could still feel her ankle smart. They rode for over an hour, but it was hard to tell whether they'd made much distance. They had gotten through beyond the fringe of the ancient city. The heaps of rubble no longer described parallel and cross-hatching gullies; the land began to run to something other than scrub vegetation. In the distance, over her left shoulder, Falstaff could still see the glow of her "bonfire" and the winking lights of Prl'lu warships on the prowl.

It wasn't long before they neared their destination. Until now the conversational silence had been unbroken, but Guard One leaned back and warned her to keep silent "until we're right in camp. You'll know when." So saying, he looked around a moment in the dark and put both hands to his mouth and neighed. It was a very loud neigh, loud enough to startle the ponies, but it made a good signal. Twenty yards away it would be hard to tell it from the real thing, unless you were listening for it. And these hills must be full of wild ponies. She'd been hoping to trap one herself. Someone in the hills answered and she heard the echo rocking down the valley. Or was it an echo? It seemed that these people were very careful about visitors.

Their ponies started forward and before long Falstaff found herself in an artfully concealed camp. There must have been a hundred people there, but from beyond the lip of the gully you could see that no one was skulking in the dark—instead men and women were walking about openly, enjoying open fires in a community of pueblo houses. "Not ours," Guard One said in reply to her obvious astonishment. "We take what we can find, and make the best use of it we can. This country is riddled with old Indian dwellings. We move from one pueblo to another."

"So when do I get to see the boss?" She could be as hard and as slow as he was. Somehow she had an idea that this was a culture in which everyone pulled his or her weight.

"Right now!" A cheery voice broke the air and Falstaff turned in her seat to see a young woman, barely in her thirties, walk up and grab the other pony's halter. "You too?" she asked and took charge of the palomino Falstaff shared with Guard One. Following his example, she got off and together they followed the woman while she led the horses to their paddock. "I'm called Dane," the woman said. "Dane Empson; I'm mayor."

Falstaff introduced herself and gave a brief account of her experiences just up to being "befriended" by the two lookouts, whose names she learned were Kurt and John. She pointedly omitted any details about where she'd been and where she was going. If these were the kind of people who would want to know that, then they were just the kind of people who shouldn't know.

Dane didn't seem overly curious and she didn't seem too impressed either. This was obviously a community that lived by its wits and didn't have much liking for the Prl'lu either. If she wanted to make an impression, she'd have to do more than just escape from under a warship's nose.

Dane said seriously, "I've got to reach a decision about you. There've been plenty of Prl'lu spies and traitors, you know." Falstaff didn't know, but she got more nervous. "You say you were traveling up the coast and you don't say why and I don't care if you're lying or not. We've got a big thing brewing here. I'd hate to see it messed up."

Kurt, Guard One, spoke up, "Mayor, if you please?"

She did please. She tousled the hair at his neck and said, "I see you've made a conquest of my man. . . ."

"Well, I won't go that far," he grinned, "but for my money she's straight. Hightailed out of that fire like a rabbit—*and* it cost them a warship." That was the first time Falstaff had heard the airship had gone down. She was glad.

Dane nodded and said, "Well, she feels right to me, too. Falstaff, you're in as long as you want to be. I'll show you a place to bed down for the night."

There wasn't much more to tell. The morning broke clear and Falstaff, feeling slightly out of place, did her best to contribute to the camp routine. No one seemed to find it unusual that she was there, but no one seemed to be overly friendly, either. Whether they were waiting for further returns or what, Falstaff didn't know. She was wondering, though, if she'd be stopped if she just took off. The answer to that was short in coming. Dane sought her out.

"Falstaff, I didn't mention last night . . . Mention! We either keep mum or shout about it. We plan a raid on the biggest Prl'lu prison camp this side of the Sierras. We've been planning it for months and tonight's the night. We're going to break the humans out of the L.A. detention center—those who want to be broken out," she added darkly. "Karl and I have been discussing it. We can't let you leave just now—it's a chance we can't take. You've been through that area recently and we need your help. What do you say?"

What could she say? With the best intentions, this guerrilla band kept her captive, and she certainly didn't mind lending a hand in the fight against Prl'lu hegemony. "I'm up for anything!" She didn't feel quite so sprightly, and a nagging portion of her conscience reminded her that she was due very soon at a conference that certainly was more important than the odd raid on a Prl'lu installation.

But was it? Fighting was what this was all about!

She said yes. Their preparations were methodical but quick. Falstaff was given her own pony—they seemed resigned to the fact that they'd have to trust her a little if she was to be of any use to them.

The packs were already made up and they were simple enough, with explosives instead of bedrolls. Falstaff asked about the lack of dis weapons and Dane answered, "Well, they don't grow on trees, you know. Except for captured bombs, we haven't seen any of those for the past year. Nor since the Prl'lu takeover, anyhow."

"But how can we fight the Prl'lu without comparable weapons?" Falstaff asked.

"Karl will be carrying a dis pistol. I'll be carrying another," Dane said, "but weapons like those won't make the difference. Surprise and a good deal of confusion are what we want." Falstaff nodded uncertainly, but her gut gave a leap; that was just what she wanted to hear. *That* kind of thinking would win the war, not bullets or guns. That was what she'd been schooled in, and she began to look forward to tonight.

They didn't wait until dark. They wanted to reach L.A. and the prison camp well before the Moon went down, before it would be too dark to give the prisoners a helping heavenly hand. They would take it on themselves to make sure that, dark or not, the Prl'lu guards didn't follow the prisoners into the hills.

The ride was tedious and Falstaff had the unpleasant sensation of riding past much of the landscape she had already passed on foot. Not long after the gutted building, the band began to depend on her for direction. Karl kept an eye on her, she was interested to note, during the first few miles, but after that he treated her orders and deliberations as calmly as did the others. Of course, by then he was probably as lost as they were.

Falstaff, even with her compass, would have had a hard time making sense of her map and leading the way had it not been, ironically, for the Prl'lu warships, which brightly lit up sections of the sky. She asked about them.

"You mean besides the one you knocked out of the sky?" Karl said humorously. "I'm sorry to say, all that trouble you had was a mistake; they were out looking for us. Little matter of a raid on their power plant. Riled 'em up."

Dane spoke up a little sharply. "And it might have scotched this raid, Karl! Your scouts have no business overstepping their orders. I've asked you to keep their reins pulled in and I mean it! One more problem like that and your precious scouts will wish they hadn't." So saying, she wheeled her horse around and turned back to check the column.

"Is she always so tough?" Falstaff asked.

"Maybe so," Karl answered slowly. "It's hard to tell. Mostly she manages things without any problems to get steamed about."

"Well, I should think so. You know that little *problem* nearly got me killed."

"No," Karl smiled in the dark. "Not you, you're not the sort that gets killed."

They rode for a while in silence; then Falstaff said, "Don't you think it's time I was filled in on our ops plan?"

"Not much to tell. The camp's big. Laid out in the L.A. basin. Big, flat, level plain; the place must have taken a big one during the Collapse because there isn't a hill or a building standing. Perfect spot for a work camp. Place is guarded by dis walls. Walk into them and *zap*! You just aren't there. During the day the inmates are busy building the Prl'lu digs out under the sea. At night the place is sealed up like a walnut."

"Then how do we get in?"

"Well the generator plant is outside—probably so the guys inside can't get at it. That's the easy part. We're just going to take it over and wreck the place. After that we split up and everybody takes a group of the innies back to the meet-place."

"Meet-place?"

"The camp. It's only temporary, anyway. Just be sure you bring your group back by a roundabout method. Make sure no Prl'lu are on your tail. Wouldn't do to show them the way."

They cut short their conversation, since they were nearing the hills overlooking the basin. Dane joined them as they rode up the steep, dark canyons. The ride up wasn't so bad, but Falstaff knew the way back would be on foot. And just when she was getting used to her mount. There'd better be another one for her when she got back to camp, she resolved. She'd earned it. Her thoughts were broken when they crested the hill.

The sky was bright with the reflected light of the camp. The basin stood open and lit; the prison camp itself must have covered 50 acres of one-story buildings. The interior was laid out in concentric circles and paved, well-lit roads joined the buildings to each other. The activity on them seemed free and uninhibited. None of those looking on had seen anything like this since before the war. Falstaff, Dane, Karl and the rest were accustomed to living in the dark, in skulking hideouts lit with hooded lamps. How ironic, that all this "freedom" should be possible only in a Prl'lu prison camp, within the black empty bands of the encircling dis beams. There in the darkness outside was the real freedom, but Falstaff had a sinking feeling in her heart. Would the camp inmates realize this? Or would some prefer their bright servitude to Prl'lu masters?

Falstaff saw a white blockhouse outside the dis walls; the generator, she guessed.

"Well," Dane began, breaking the silence. "It's time we got moving. Karl, you pick out your boys and we'll get started on that beam. The rest of you, circle the camp and when the beam is down, go in, lead your groups out. No more than six for each of you! If you try and take out more, you won't make it. Of course any of the inmates who want to are free to head for the hills on their own. It'll be best if you simply mingle in the confusion, *appear* to know what you're doing, keep calm, and cut your group out that way. Don't let on that you have a destination in mind until you reach the hills." She paused. "Oh yes, *don't* go in until the beams are down and the lights are off! If you do, we won't be seeing you back at camp. Any questions?"

There was a low murmur but no questions; then Falstaff crowded her horse up to Dane's and said, "And me? I'm going with you to the generator?"

"You are not." Dane sounded amazed. "This isn't any time for glory hounds."

"But . . ."

"No *buts*," Dane said firmly. "You haven't fought with us before and there's no reason for you to come along now. In fact, there's every reason for you to skedaddle if you want to. You were all but forced to come along; we needed you this far, but your duties are done."

"I can help," Falstaff said indignantly.

"You can help by obeying orders. Now get moving."

"And if I bring a group back?"

"You'll be welcome; that's all. Like all the rest."
Dane sounded a little friendlier, though. "And I wish
you good luck." She wheeled her horse around to the
group preparing to take the generator building.

Falstaff found the trip down the hillside more difficult than the climb, even though her horse had the advantage of the light cast off by the camp. At first the
light worried her, but before long she realized that for
viewers inside the golden circle the glare must mask her
shadow on the hillside. That didn't set her mind at ease,
though; she only worried the more about a misstep, a
dislodged rock, and discovery.

It took her nearly forty minutes to get into place near
the base of the hill and directly in front of the lit en-
closure. During the final few minutes, she worried that
the blackout would catch her unprepared. Now she
worried that Dane and Karl and the rest had been surprised and caught, or worse, and that she was waiting
for friends and a signal that would never come.

It came.

Suddenly the basin was dark and Falstaff cursed herself for not guarding her eyes against the light. A fool's
mistake! It took her a couple of minutes to regain her
night vision, but, impatiently, she nudged the horse forward all the while, trusting to its night sense and instinct
to keep them both out of trouble. Meanwhile she
rubbed her eyes angrily.

Scattered shouting began to fill her ears and she
thought she detected a low rising moan that was difficult to place. It seemed almost a tangible thing, but as
she neared the compound she realized that it was the
buzzing hum of thousands of worried and confused
people. Hundreds of the more daring stood just inside
the dis beam fence, but none had tried to step through
yet. When she crossed the no-man's land with her horse,
a surprised shout went up—a low rumble that grew and
mounted from points all around the camp until it filled
the air.

Falstaff knew then that her companions had made it.

Men and women began running out into the former no-man's land. Some surrounded her horse as she made her way forward. Others—mostly loners, a few couples —took their chance and headed straight out for the dark and the hills. She saw others start across the zone and falter, and rush back toward the light. She hoped they were salvaging belongings or finding their kin before starting out, but she had her doubts.

No one tried to stop her on the way in. And so far there'd been no sign of Prl'lu, but then, the camp was huge and with the dis beam fence, the Prl'lu would have no reason to guard it in force. No, their armament would be mounted out in the hills, in the airships she'd already encountered. The thought prompted her to look to the stars. Yes! She was right. The ships were swinging back toward the basin. It was time to get a move on.

Inside the camp she quietly got off her horse, playing indifference to the crowd that surrounded her. They shouted questions, advice, and some, she was sorry to note, cursed her roundly for causing trouble. Those were the ones who would never leave, who were happy with their Prl'lu masters.

She found it surprisingly easy to blend in with the crowd. Once off the horse she gave it a sharp slap on the rump and it began to head home of its own accord. Only those standing closest to her could tell that she was the intruder; when she pushed past them she was as invisible as any of the thousands of others in the dark. She began to edge her way back to the rim, where the prisoners gathered in groups, nervously contemplating escape.

It was easy! She was almost astonished at herself. She simply walked up to a bunch of people, some of them carrying supplies; all of them stamping their feet and debating the wisest course; all she had to do was walk up and offer herself as guide.

When dawn broke, Falstaff ordered a halt. They'd been constantly on the move since the breakout and the ex-prisoners were unpracticed hikers. Even more important, the Prl'lu were sure to be on the prowl in force after last night, and it wouldn't do to travel in broad daylight. She chose a narrow ravine filled with heavy brush for their stopping place. None of them questioned her order. They were bushed and made no secret of it, flopping heavily to the ground and whining after a drink. She hadn't even told them her real role in this escape yet; she'd been saving that until exhaustion made them tractable. If they were looking to her to solve all their problems now, she could only imagine what they'd be like after they found out she was responsible for their safety.

She decided not to tell them.

She went about setting up a day's camp quickly and efficiently. As she did, she thought about them; all seven of them. Dane wouldn't be pleased she'd exceeded the quota, but a young boy, ten or eleven, had wandered up to them as they were rather noisily clambering up the canyons in the first flush of escape. He was alone and she had added him to the group. She was glad she had. He was the only one all night long to show any spunk. He was excited and eager and deadly serious about escape. She was reminded of herself at that age.

The rest were adults. Four men, two women, all between twenty and forty-five. She coaxed them along, but otherwise she had very little to say to them, and they had very little breath left for conversation. She decided it was just as well. If she'd been called upon to describe her life in the camp, she'd be in an embarrassing position.

The day passed slowly and pleasantly enough. Falstaff remained awake to keep watch while the others slept—all but Bret, the youngster, who was obviously too wound up to sleep. As she sat cross-legged in a spot overlooking the ravine, he stretched out in front of her and plied her with questions. His spirit never flagged as he asked questions about the forest, the hunting, what she planned to do about dinner, which way they should go, ad infinitum. She was touched by his enthusiasm and not a little relieved that he didn't question her role in the escape. She decided that she *had* to get them all back to the meet-place, if only so that Dane and Karl could take the boy in hand; he was made of the right stuff.

Falstaff waited until some time after sunset before she let the group set out again. The oldest and heaviest of the men complained about this; he felt chilled in the night air; but she was waiting until the sky darkened enough to let them see the searchlights of Prl'lu airships sweeping the countryside.

She took the lead, as she had the night before. Bret hastened at her side, making up by determination what he lacked in lankiness.

"How do you know which way to go?" he asked at one point. She showed him her compass and explained how it worked. He caught on quickly, but then he wanted to know how she knew which direction to head for in the first place.

"Well," she said, "we're heading east-northeast, because in that direction we're walking away from the ocean, and the Prl'lu are strongest here near the coast. The land changes inland; after we get over these foothills, we'll be going through real forest. Back there the Prl'lu don't have a chance to find us, not if we're careful. And that's where we might find some other humans, free humans."

"When will we get there?" he wanted to know.

"Another night's march, maybe. Or maybe tonight, just before sunup. Depends on how well our legs stand up. But when we get there, we'll be safe!" She said this last loudly enough for all of them to hear it. The thought of safety might encourage a little more exercise, and anyhow, it would prepare them all for some stiff hiking.

The night sped along and they made good time. Again most of her companions were too breathless to talk and Falstaff had time for some quiet reflection. She liked what she'd seen of Dane and Karl and all the guerrilla outfit. And she approved of the camp-break. It was well thought out and executed. If a hundred little bands were doing the same across America, they had a good fighting chance and her trip to the Las Vegas conference might indeed make a difference. She hoped so.

Occasionally she and Bret talked and again she was encouraged. The boy had some spunk and he hadn't been cowed by his internment. The adults seemed much more affected. They were docile and a little frightened. Not that they didn't have cause to be, but she would have respected them more if they'd made some effort to hide it.

She liked hiking at night. In the darkness, even minding scrub-brush and branches, it was possible to lose oneself in the mere physical act of walking. Her stride was effortless and rhythmic. She felt like she was floating along, immersed in the dark. She let her mind roam and catch up, if not on sleep, then on a little daydreaming. Another trick from the outback—the body insisted on dreaming, as much as on rest, to cleanse the mind. If she couldn't have the one, she could have the other.

The sound broke her concentration and alerted her with a start. A long sighing neigh; it could have come from any direction, could have been a wild horse, or a released stray, but she was sure it was not. The rest of the party hadn't noticed, not even Bret. They just kept plodding along, oblivious to anything except their own footfalls.

She checked the sky. It was near dawn. She'd either have to find a place to camp or trust to luck and good fortune that Karl or one of his minions was nearby and that the meeting spot wasn't far beyond. She decided to trust and when the light came up she didn't signal a halt. It was one of the women who spoke up this time, and Falstaff answered sharply that they couldn't stop until they found a less exposed spot. She was really waiting for a repeat of the neigh.

She'd about given up hope when it came again and was answered by another one, clearly from another direction. She halted the group, saying that they could take a brief rest, and prepared to go off and hunt up the source. As she was about to slip into the woods, Bret asked, "Can I come along? Please," he added. After a pause, Falstaff said it was all right. Not wanting to frighten the child, she made a game of it; they were finding water. The neigh repeated itself, once, twice, but then was silent and she had to trust to instinct to head in the right direction. She began to worry. If it was Karl, she would have expected him to come looking. With her gaggle of chuckleheads, any experienced woodsman within a mile should be able to tell they were coming. What could be wrong?

Bret was just asking, "Haven't we come awfully far?" when they happened onto Karl's group. It all became depressingly obvious. Two of the women were on stretchers and Karl was limping gamely along on an obviously painful and badly burned leg.

"Why hello," he said with a wry smile. He kept on walking. "You two alone?"

"No," Falstaff said, "the rest aren't far away." She motioned toward the stretchers. "They all right?"

"Will be if we can get them into camp. I make it about four miles, what about you?"

"Lost," she said sheepishly. "But I thought we were close. I'll bring mine over this way and we can at least relieve your stretcher-bearers for the last leg. I suppose the meet *is* secured?"

"Had a scout in there this morning. I'm surprised you didn't hear his signal."

"I guess we did," she answered, and then impatiently shifted her pack back onto her shoulders. "Be right back."

"Aren't you going to ask what happened?"

She smiled quickly. "We'll have time for that back at camp."

Falstaff turned into the woods, trailing Bret. As soon as they were safely out of sight of Karl and his group, Bret asked Falstaff who they were and what they'd been talking about. He had overheard enough to be puzzled by the meeting. She decided not to keep the boy in the dark any longer. When he got the full story on the way back to the others, his excitement was contained. He blurted the truth out as soon as they reached the resting place, but thankfully her charges were still too exhausted to care about how they'd been duped. When she told them that shelter and a hot meal waited four or five miles away, they showed some interest, though, and

when she told them about Karl's group and the two
injured women, they not only were attentive but insisted
on going to help right away. Falstaff began to think a
lot better of them.

It seemed like a homecoming, though only Falstaff
and Karl had ever visited the glen before and only Karl
could be said to be really coming home. Still, all the ex-
prisoners were made warmly welcome, given hot food,
encouraged, and generally made to feel important.

So far most of the groups had traveled in within a few
hours of each other. Not very strategic planning, Dane
told Falstaff, but you couldn't expect greenhorns to
spend too much time in the woods. Besides, they'd be
breaking camp in a day or so.

Bret was the only child who had taken the plunge, and
he was made much of. Dane took care, though, that he
wasn't mothered too much and insured that he got
treated like a new recruit. As soon as Falstaff saw this,
she relinquished her temporary and unofficial guardian-
ship. The boy was in good hands.

All in all, the raid had been a great success. Their
ranks were swelled many times over and the new
"recruits," as Karl called them, brought some useful
skills to the assembly. Not that all of them would stay,
but Dane thought most would. A bout of guerrilla warfare suited a man, or woman, who'd been in prison
awhile. She thought most would like to get a lick of their
own in.

They all did their best to convince Falstaff to stay.
She spent the night and two others, resting up, helping
out, and firming her friendship with Dane. Although
she couldn't say just why she had to leave, she was obviously sorry to go, and that made her leavetaking much
more of an event. When she finally did pack off, on a
fresh pinto horse generously provided from Karl's own
string, the whole camp came out to send her off. She
said a simple goodbye and left.

She headed north at first, in the direction Karl and
John had caught her going. It never was wise to show
anybody what you were after. A couple of hours and

she turned northeast again and set off in earnest.

She figured it might take a week or so, no more, to reach Vegas.

9.

"I am very disappointed," Shak't'kan said slowly. "I expected greater sensitivity on your part, Ascham, not to say a minimal degree of competence. That this prison breakout occurred at all is clearly due to the most gross negligence, but that you failed to see how it could be turned to our advantage, that is fatal in a Commandant. I'm relieving you of your command."

"As you order, my lord." Commandant Ascham bowed and began to leave the room. Shak't'kan sharply bade him to stay.

"For the moment though, you are most useful to me here. I'll decide what is to be done with you after you serve me this night. I assume you know that you have much to win and little to lose by serving me faithfully these few hours?"

"I do," the commandant said weakly.

"Then, do you have the dis fence back in operation?"

"Well, my lord . . ."

"Ascham!" Shak't'kan's tone was piercing. "No excuses. That's over and done with. You are a dead man unless you are of some help to me tonight. Now, are the dis fences back up?"

"No, my lord."

"Well, at least that's one thing settled. Did you kill or capture any of the saboteurs?"

"No."

"And have you made any effort to round up the escapees?"

"The hills are being combed, my lord." Ascham sounded relieved to have something to report. "By light we should have most of them. Indeed, we've already rounded up several hundred. They wandered out of the camp but never left the area. And as you know, sir, most of the prisoners didn't attempt to escape at all."

"Didn't take their chance, you mean."

"As you say, sir. Most of the humans are content with their lives here; or, if not content, at least they prefer the familiar life of the inmate to the unfamiliar life of the fugitive."

"I agree. Docility is our best ally. But," Shak't'kan's tone sharpened, "what can you tell me of the less docile ones, the humans who engineered the escape?"

"As yet, not much, sir. As you know, our airships were on patrol at the time of the attack. Very likely the humans they were looking for were the same gang that arranged the breakout. There were no guards posted inside the camp and the perimeter patrol was overwhelmed by the escaping prisoners. And not one of the technics posted to the generator station is living. There were some casualties, we think, on their side, but they must have carried away their wounded or dead with them."

"Not very good, Commandant," Shak't'kan's tone was dry, "but it will do for now. If you don't mind telling me, though, just what have you done?"

"Well sir, I intend to order . . ."

"Don't bother, I'll tell you what will be done! Have the camp perimeter patrolled until the fence is back in place—and when it goes up I don't want any strangers outside the perimeter, or in the path of the dis beam, do you understand? I want all available technics working on the generator station. *And* once we get it working I want another dis beam placed around that one. If you'd taken that simple precaution before, we'd have had none of this. Order out the patrols in the morning; tonight, I want them flying over the camp and keeping our remaining prisoners in line. I want a census and I want it fast and I want Holcomb and I want him here now!"

"Holcomb, sir?"

"Now."

It was actually several minutes before the human was brought in, though as ranking human in the prison camp, Holcomb's whereabouts were always monitored. For better or for worse, this was one human who had learned compromise the hard way. Either he pushed the humans into obeying their Prl'lu overlords or Shak't-'kan did it for him. And Shak't'kan had a fatal way of teaching by example. Besides, Holcomb was aware that his position had certain advantages.

"Well, my dear Holcomb," Shak't'kan greeted him, "I trust you've had an exciting night?"

"You might say so."

"And I hope you have been persuaded by events tonight that most of your humans are content in our charge?"

"I'm not sure what you mean." Holcomb sounded as if he did, though.

"Come, you know that even with the restraining fence down, only a small number of the humans chose to leave, and of those, most didn't wander beyond the valley."

"So I've been told."

"And you. Why didn't you leave?"

"That's a laugh. I know that I'm monitored. There was no chance that *I'd* get away. Anyhow, I have no life outside this camp and since you engineered me into that position I'm quite sure that these questions aren't genuine. What are you leading up to?" Holcomb had been pacing, but now he paused and leaned against the wall facing Shak't'kan. His face was strong and his eyes were direct. He treated the Prl'arek commander like an equal. He was the model of unbowed humanity. But a sensitive onlooker might have felt his stance was too comfortable, to sure. Holcomb had some of the air of a capable and valued executive, not a sworn enemy or even a studied competitor.

"You're right. I knew you'd be here—after all, I've made a home for you, haven't I? We've accomplished together what neither of us could have accomplished separately. You know that."

"All right. I'm a whore and you're a pimp. What kind of trick do you have up your sleeve this time?"

"A very good one, I think. We are making a minimal effort, just for show, to recapture the humans who escaped tonight. We're doing this because I want you to look good. The brave hero leading your charges out of the wilderness."

"What are you talking about?"

"Haven't I made myself clear? You are to escape with the rest—oh, a little belatedly, perhaps—but I will arrange for you to escape with all the trappings. I have a use for you on the outside."

"Don't be ridiculous." Holcomb sounded accusing. "You know that I'm compromised."

"You have wit enough to explain away your little indiscretions, I should think. After all, let's say I held a gun to your head?"

"It would be my duty to have my head blown off."

"Ah, but I threatened to kill off your people. You were acting in their behalf."

"A point. But even thousands can't be levied against the good of the race. No, if I'm to explain my actions, particularly the policing of malcontents and human renegades, I'm going to have to do better than that."

"But you will, Holcomb, you will. You are going to march into one of the human guerrilla camps a genuine hero, at the head of a column of escaping prisoners. You'll be able to do this because no one is going to stop you. There are several hundred escapees scattered about the hills to the east of the camp. You are going to round them up and lead them anyway. *They* will be your alibi. Not even the renegade commanders will choose to believe that the man who had led hundreds to freedom could possibly be a traitor."

"And how am I going to accomplish all this? More to the point, what will all this accomplish?"

"Holcomb," Shak't'kan sounded pleased, "you do stick to the point. And I have great things in store for you. How you handle the humans is your business.

What comes after is my business. I expect you to seek out and link yourself to the humans masterminding all this insurrection. You will sit in on their affairs, mislead them if you can, but, most important, I expect you to report to me. You are to be my spy. But have no qualms. We do not seek to destroy the renegades, but to turn them to my advantage. And yours."

"The advantage, my lord?" Holcomb sounded dry.

"The domination of a world! Be reasonable, Holcomb. The Prl'oi have won; only a few human stragglers deny that and what conceivable fantasy they speak from is beyond me. No, we have won; but I have a place for you and as many others as you can control in my plans. Humankind needn't die, but it must accept the inevitable. That is my position. If my son Sataspes wins power, you won't even have that. All humans, including you, will be exterminated once their usefulness is over. I don't have a kindly son," the Prl'arek lord added unnecessarily.

"I get your point," Holcomb said. "And I have no qualms. But I do have priorities. What assurances do I have of safety? And, don't forget my ultimate reward."

"You know that I can offer no assurances. Keep yourself healthy and I'll take care of you when this job is done. Do it well and I'll fulfill my plans for you, but the job itself is up to you. I trust that you are well capable of it."

"Thanks for the vote of confidence."

Shak't'kan nodded him out of the room. After Holcomb stepped out of the door the Prl'arek smiled and said to the empty room, "You're welcome."

Packing was easy. Military men never had much to pack anyway and prisoners of war even less. Holcomb was ready to go almost from the moment he left Shak't'kan's command room.

His bout with the Prl'lu security officer was something else again. He spent two hours rehearsing and memorizing drops and communications techniques. He didn't expect to have to use any of this, but the security officer, like any other specialist, had his stock in trade and he was going to be damned if anyone, even a lowly human spy, got by without going through the rigors. The only important piece of training Holcomb had, in his opinion, was instruction on how to replace the battery in his long-range compiece. For security's sake the unit was as small as possible, about the size of his buckle, and he had it fastened into the leather of his shoe. Not very comfortable to use, but secure enough.

He left quietly. As few humans as possible were to know that he was taking his exit in this belated and treasonous fashion. It didn't hurt to be careful, even though the remaining humans were themselves collaborators, if only because they'd also passed up their chance at a legitimate escape.

Two Prl'lu subalterns accompanied him into the hills. He wore his jump belt that far, but once he was well beyond the camp's perimeter, he unfastened its buckle and let the webbing float away into space. An escaping prisoner wouldn't be so well-equipped.

On the hillside, his Prl'lu companions handed him a map and compass. Then they told him that a large number of escaping prisoners were making their way northeast just on the other side of the ridge. That was all Holcomb needed. The Prl'lu took off back toward camp. Holcomb started the long trudge up over the ridge and toward the other humans.

He just hoped it was going to be as easy as Shak't'kan had said.

10.

The darkness was broken by gleaming crescents and sharp cutting edges of light. Rogers swung gently in space at the end of a long plastic tether, until he reached down and released it from his belt. The slight exertion sent him tumbling, but he corrected his drift with short squirts from a jet pistol held in his right hand. In his left, he held up a small, boxed gyroscope that he fervently hoped pointed the way home toward dinner.

His progress was unimpeded. He traveled miles of space in minutes. All around him darkened ships either caught the light from distant suns or were wrapped in shadows that made them nearly invisible. Still there was plenty to look at. Thousands of ships, all empty, except for the few Rogers and his men had commandeered; thousands of ships to be explored, plundered, and put to good use.

He felt pretty good. He and his Rangers were well on their way back to Earth, though this time Earth wasn't his for the taking. When he thought about his incredible luck, he had to shake his head and grin. It seemed nothing ever went too far wrong for Tony Rogers. The thought pleased him and he tried never to forget it for long. He felt that as long as he continued to believe in his own luck, luck would believe in him.

This time it had landed him and his men in the middle of the biggest military arsenal that he could imagine: thousands of decommissioned Prl'oi ships hanging in space as bright and shiny as the day they came off the assembly line. They might have been left there, unattended, fifty thousand years ago. Just another sign that *something* calamitous had happened to the galaxywide Prl'oi Empire before humans arrived on the scene. The problems on Earth were just the dying tremors; that thought, too, cheered Rogers. That and his own special knowledge of the Blackjack Prl'oi cut his next job down to manageable size. He and his men faced a formidable enemy back on Earth, but not an invincible host.

His suit radio crackled alive. "Tony, do you read me? Tony, come in."

He grinned again; that was Ruth calling him to dinner. "Yes, doctor?"

"You're late. Commissary's open!" He grinned wider still, and Ruth continued. "That green gunk again, you know, your *favorite*."

His smile collapsed. The Prl'oi grub they'd been eating was nutritious, Ruth had seen to that, but it tasted like axle grease. And the green stuff was the worst! Ruth seemed to think it was an important part of their diet, though, and kept putting it on the menu.

"Any luck?" she asked.

"Some," he said. "I found two more atmospheric cruisers and about a hundred nonstratospheric battleships. We've got everything we need to fight a war in space, and more. I'd feel better, though, if we could come up with more space-to-surface craft." He paused for a moment while he used the jet pistol to correct his altitude. His destination was the huge battle-station he and his men had adopted as their base. Rigged near its operable airlock was a plastic net the size of several football fields—that was his target. With any luck, and a delicate hand with the pistol, he'd be setting down within an easy grope of the airlock portal. "Okay; all set here. What were we about?"

"The ships, Tony, the ships."

"Oh yeah, well. It stands to reason that the s-to-s craft are out there somewhere. The old-time Prl'oi didn't restrict their activities to space. We have evidence enough of *that*. It's just a matter of finding them. . . . And, Ruth . . ."

"Yes?"

"It's awful big out here." He was about thirty yards away from the net and right on mark, thank god. Too late to correct now. He drew up into a ball and his leisurely tumbling motion sped up so that he was getting quite a somersault. He landed hard into the net and its flexible strands stretched to absorb the shock. In a minute he was crawling crabwise toward the portal.

"Coming in," he warned.

"I'll be there to meet you," Ruth answered.

"The big news of the day," Ruth reported, on the way to the commissary, "was that we were able to keep the teleportal open almost a full two hours!"

"So why the green dinner?" Rogers asked ruefully. "Why not fresh food?"

"Tony!" Ruth tried to look shocked. "And you the Marshall of all you survey. We thought we'd better move some heavy machinery first! Before the damned thing gave out again. And when it did, brother, you could hear young Carberry all up and down the station. He's ordered dinner shipped in so he can work straight through and try and get it opened up again this evening."

Rogers said tiredly, "But it was to be expected, I guess. Two hours is a record, isn't it?"

"Guess it is, at that."

"Anybody I should know about stuck on the other side?"

"No, for the most part all present and accounted for. But I'll tell you, Tony, this teleportal trouble is playing havoc with our schedules. *And* god forbid the thing crashes while anyone's enroute."

For a second, Rogers' mouth tightened, then he said, "I wouldn't let that possibility get around. Anyhow," he continued, "we have no reason to believe that teleportation isn't instantaneous. In which case, either you make the trip or you don't. Nobody gets caught halfway. So give me a break, will you, and stop all this speculation?" He sounded tired again as they turned the corner into the commissary, but he managed a smile or a nod to everyone interested, collected a tray and, with Ruth, parked himself next to Joaquin and Jackson. They were arguing amiably as usual, but stopped when Rogers sat down.

"Well," he said, "anything new to report, you two?"

Both spoke at once, but Jackson gave way and Joaquin started in. "We were discussing the training program. By now most of the likely pilot prospects, Blackjack and human, have had twelve hours instruction apiece and are as competent to run one of these things as anyone is. This morning before the portal shut down we all practiced atmospherics and landings on Blackjack. You're lucky to have our company this meal," he grinned. "We nearly got stuck on the other side."

Rogers snorted. "You mean nearly got stuck in the side of a mountain."

Jackson broke in. "No, the exercise went well, really

well. We won't have any trouble on that score."

"No problems with landings? No freeze-ups when the boys see something hard under them—like Earth? Nothing like that?" Rogers sounded pleased.

"Not a whiff," Jackson said. "The pilots are ready; any luck with the ships?"

"Not much. Still, tomorrow's another day. I have a hunch we just haven't hit the right quadrant yet. And when we do, there's going to be a hustle because that'll be the day *I'm* ready to head on to phase three!"

"Earth?"

"That's it. We've wasted enough time. To tell you the truth, I'm getting homesick."

Ruth sniffed and announced sotto voce, "Don't you believe it; he loves the attention here. . . ."

"And," Rogers continued hurriedly, "anyhow, I think the men are ready. It's just these damn technological foul-ups, and then the problem finding more of the s-to-s ships; and don't worry, I'm not forgetting the teleportal. By the way," he added, "anything new on the system breakdowns?"

Rogers was trying his best not to show how worried he was about this problem. Ever since he and the Rangers had teleported to the fleet, they'd been hounded by hundreds of inexplicable equipment breakdowns—not only the teleport, but power substations, airlocks, loading gear, navigational aids, the lot. Nothing serious taken individually, but taken together, the equipment mishaps posed a major threat.

After a pause, Ruth said, "No. Carberry's looking into it, as though he didn't already have enough to do. He hasn't turned anything up yet except what we already knew—that the breakdowns are randomized throughout the system and that none of them is very serious. That's the most peculiar part of it. There's been absolutely no equipment damage, not even singed wiring, just local system collapse."

"No opinions?"

"Some kind of fleet-wide circuit breaker tripping in when we least expect it," Ruth replied. "Remember, we may be able to fly these ships, but we didn't design them and we didn't build 'em. Frankly I'm surprised we're having as few problems as we are. It's just . . ."

Her voice trailed off and Rogers had to call her attention back to their conversation. "Just what?"

"Just that these breakdowns seem almost calculated to stall us here while doing little or no damage to the ships themselves. It's either coincidence or, well, maybe the Prl'oi did leave some kind of caretaker here. A caretaker in hiding."

There was a bit of a pause and then Rogers mumbled something the others hardly caught. Ruth shoved him in the ribs and he repeated himself: "Gremlins. You're talking about gremlins. . . ." His voice trailed off while he appeared to think it over. Finally Joaquin broke in and asked, "*What* is a gremlin?"

Rogers shook himself before answering, "Oh, a superstition pilots had in my time. Started in the Royal Air Force of the Great War. Gremlins are little invisible creatures who got into the workings of airplanes and caused no end of troubles. I wonder if we have them here?" So saying, he got up and shelved his tray absently. Then, leaving Ruth and his two captains, mouths agape at the table, he left the commissary.

Rogers was looking for Carberry. He traced his steps carefully. Only a twentieth of the battle-station had been adequately explored. You could get as lost here as you could on the surface of a planet. Lost worse. There were no sun or stars to point the way home.

When he found him, Carberry was, as usual, half-buried in a piece of machinery. Sometimes it seemed to Rogers that he could remember the boy's dangling sneakers a lot more vividly than he could place the face. He sighed and tried to catch the youngster's attention, "Ah-hem!"

The sneakers wriggled.

"Carberry?"

They definitely wriggled this time and Rogers had to grit his teeth and resist the urge to give the shoes a yank. After all, despite his eccentricities, Josiah Carberry was the closest thing to an engineering genius that they had.

"Carberry, it's Rogers. I have to talk with you." This time he could hear a muffled grunt from inside the machine and slowly, almost sinuously, the boy's body disentangled itself. When Carberry stood up, he had a sheepish grin on his face.

"Sorry, Marshall. Sometimes I get lost in my thoughts when I'm tinkering around in there. Anything I can do for you?" he added.

"Well," Rogers said and then stopped to think. What he wanted to suggest to the boy might sound a little strange. He decided there was no way out of that difficulty so he plunged ahead. "I've been discussing the breakdown problem with Dr. Harris and Captains Joaquin and Jackson. I gather that there is some kind of mystery about them."

This time it was the boy's turn to pause. "Mystery?" he repeated. "Oh, I don't know about that. The breakdowns are easy enough to fix. It's just that they're occurring all over the place and for no real reason that I can find."

"Isn't that a mystery?"

Carberry was slow to answer. "Well, yes, if you want to put it that way. There really isn't any explanation I can find. . . ." He chewed his lip awhile and then spoke up. "But, you have an idea, don't you, sir? That's why you've come down here." He looked at his own untouched tray. "During dinner."

"I do. But first I want to ask a few questions. For instance, aside from the fact that they shouldn't have happened, was there anything unusual about these mishaps?"

"No. I don't think so."

"Anything strange about the circumstances; you know—where or when they occurred, that sort of thing?"

"Maybe. The one thing I've noticed, at my cost," Carberry smiled ruefully, "most of these breakdowns are occurring at night. That is, except for the teleportal machinery, which breaks down all the time. But the rest of it, at night. Or in a pretty isolated spot. You know," he added, "the more ships we activate, the faster these accidents seem to occur. And I don't mean that we just have more equipment to go wrong. No; if I didn't know better, I'd say that the rate of breakdown increases every time we take another step closer to starting out of here."

"Thanks, that's all I wanted to know. Mind you now, eat your dinner!" Rogers nodded to Carberry and headed for the door.

Rogers' next visits might have seemed strange if someone was keeping track of him. He stopped off and spoke first with the old man whom Jackson had appointed Station Sanitation Officer. There wasn't much to the job really—just making sure that garbage got spaced as quickly as possible, but Rogers was well prepared to hear a few gripes on the subject. He found Private Edison forlornly scraping down an airlock.

"Just look at this, Marshall! I ask you! If I've told the men once, I've told them a hundred times to dessicate the trash before it gets chucked out of here. Cycle the airlock and the wet stuff turns to ice. And *I've* got to clean it out. Can't you . . ."

"Yes I can," Rogers broke in hurriedly. "I'll write the order tonight, but really I've come . . ."

"To inspect. Yes I know. Well, it's all ready for you, sir, if you'd care to take the tour."

"Well, really," Rogers began helplessly, "that's not actually what I came for tonight. To tell you the truth, I wanted to ask a few questions."

Edison dropped his scraper and took his time lighting up a cigarette. "Well, fire away," he said finally.

"You're in charge of sanitation for the whole fleet, is that right?"

"Garbage, Marshall; let's not dress it up. Yes, I'm in charge. As of today, that's eighty-three ships we've activated, though only a handul of those are troop carriers and those are the only ones I have much to do with."

"But you've been in charge of, er, garbage since we portaled here from Blackjack?"

"Sure thing."

"Well then, what I want to know is, have you noticed

anything strange about the garbage? Anything out of the way?''

"Out of the way, no; I couldn't say that." Edison rubbed his jaw. "No, 'cept there's always more than I'm looking for. Got any others?''

"Yeah. Except for the airlocks, what kind of venting do the ships have, and what happens to the liquid wastes?''

"Well you know, sir, this isn't a closed system. The Prl'oi who designed this ship expected to be able to use the teleportal for new supplies, that kind of thing. All the waste gets vented off. There must be several hundred vents to space in this ship.''

Rogers paused in thought. That seemed to cover it, but he had a feeling there was another question he should be asking. "That seems like an awful lot of potential leaks. Are there really that many?''

"No problem there, sir. Yeah, there are at least a few hundred vents, but they're blown clear with excess carbon monoxide; as I said, this is an open system. We don't recirculate the atmosphere. So there's no way oxygen can leak out of the system that way.''

"Well, what about the ventilation system? I realize that it doesn't quite come into your territory but . . .''

Edison sounded indignant, "Don't you believe it, sir. I may handle the garbage, but I'd better be up on the rest of this ship.''

"Well then?''

"We had an on-demand system. It's foolproof because it's nongenerative; no fussing around with algae messes to recondition the air, that kind of thing. When our available oxygen is used up, we just beam up another load of air with the teleportal. Cheap and efficient, and that's a fact. The Prl'oi must have done the same thing, because there's no sign of any air purification system on the station.''

"So we have no real idea of what goes in and out of the system.'' Rogers sounded glum. He'd had an idea he was onto something, a way to solve the little mystery he'd turned up, but the clue he'd been looking for had just been snatched away.

Almost, but not quite. Edison spoke up cheerfully.
"Sure we do. How do you think we know when the
station's oxygen level goes down? We'd be a headachy
lot if we waited until we were blue in the face. No, when
available oxygen is used up, a microcomputer detects
the excess carbon monoxide and dioxide surplus and orders up oxy replacement."

"And then?"

"And then," Edison sounded scornful, "the excess
gases are vented from the system."

"Does anyone keep a record of what goes in and out,
say over a twenty-four-hour period?"

"Yeah, we had to set up telltales to monitor efficiency. You want to know about discrepancies—I can
tell you just as soon as I check over the the tapes."

Now it was Rogers' turn to sound off, "Well get to it,
man. Get the lead out." Edison smiled calmly and
ambled out of the room. He'd take just long enough
obeying so that Rogers would be put in his place. When
Edison was out of eyesight, Rogers had to smile too; he
knew all about the perquisites of age and, as he was un-
deniably of advanced years himself, he kind of wished a
few of those perks would come his way. They never did
though, and so the 600-year-old man in a thirty-year-old
body could only smile.

Rogers left the room. As he walked down the hall, he
grabbed a crewman lounging outside of the dorm corridor and posted him to look out for Sanitation Chief
Edison. When Edison returned, he was to be sent down
to the supply office, Rogers said. He would meet him
there or later on the bridge.

The supply office was a cavernous warehouse buried
in the depths of the station. Rows of packaged food
filled its pallets. A lot of food was homegrown stuff carried in from Blackjack: preserved meats and vegetables,
canned fruits, smoked and dried cured meats. They all
filled the aisles, and even so were a meager portion com-
pared to the piles of containered nutritives the ancient
Prl'oi had left behind. Rows and rows of Rogers' de-
spised green gunk; more rows of pastes, loafs, and

syrups. The Prl'oi diet wasn't varied, but it provided all the vitamins and proteins essential to humans. Or so Ruth seemed to think. Privately, Rogers thought it tasted like K-rations, but he kept his opinion to himself; no one else in the twenty-fifth century had ever sampled the staple of World War I.

The supply-room officer was a young woman, Barbara Kent. Rogers knew her pretty well and liked what he'd seen. In any case, Kent was a breath of fresh air after dealing with the exasperating Edison.

After discussing what passed for the time of day in an artificial steel world that had no day, Rogers broached his question.

"Anything missing?"

Kent looked surprised. "What do you mean, 'Anything missing'; haven't you gotten my reports?" Rogers must have looked mystified because Kent hurried on, "Damn! I spend hours agonizing over these things and nobody passes them along. Yeah, since we hit the station we've been having a real pilferage problem and I can't understand why. Hell, everything's free! Why bother to steal?"

Rogers broke into a big grin. If anything could confirm his theory, this could.

"What's missing?" he asked.

"Smoked meats primarily, but several containers of activated charcoal and six or seven bags of lime have disappeared too. Hell, the stuff is only good for scouring out bathrooms, why should it be missing?"

"Do you have any idea when the thefts occurred?"

"All of them at night. And—this is what gets me— always when the room," Kent waved her arm to indicate the entire warehouse area, "is sealed off tighter than a bass drum."

"Any ideas?"

"Not a one. We've posted guards outside the door, even installed closed-circuit cameras." She pointed to two, mounted high on the walls.

Rogers had heard enough. He thanked Kent and left her shaking her head in puzzlement behind him.

● ● ●

His next stop was on the battle-station's bridge, where Ruth and Joaquin were running some trainees through their paces by simulating attack situations. Ruth greeted Rogers with a good deal of asperity. "Finally decided to drop in, eh? You know you promised to be here on time!"

Rogers looked sheepish. "Sorry. I had a sudden idea and had to follow it up. Forgot all about the practice."

"Forgot!" Ruth sounded angry, but when she caught the look in Rogers' eye some of the mettle left her voice. She willingly let herself be led away from the practice modules. Rogers beckoned for Joaquin to follow. When the three had found a quiet corner she said, "Now what's this all about?"

Rogers hedged, "That's a little hard to explain . . ." he caught Ruth's expression and hurried on, "but really you started it. When you suggested in the mess that all these breakdowns couldn't be sheer coincidence, I had a sudden thought."

"Your gremlins," Joaquin said.

"Yes. It came to me that *something* must be behind all these mishaps, so I applied the old Sherlock Holmes principle." Realizing that neither Ruth nor Joaquin had any idea who Sherlock Holmes was, he explained, "When you eliminate the impossible, whatever's left, however improbable, must be the truth. I've been doing a little investigating on my own and I'm convinced that there's some rationale behind the breakdowns. I think they're meant to keep us here in Ararat space and prevent us from teleporting the fleet back to Earth. And before you object," Rogers could see Ruth positively sputtering, "I don't think we are alone in this fleet."

His words hung for a moment in silence and then Ruth posed the obvious question, "If we're sharing the space station, don't you think we'd have caught on a good deal sooner?"

"I repeat, eliminate the impossible. Food and other stuffs are disappearing from a sealed warehouse. Impossible? Or isn't it obvious that at least one other person is on this ship beside us, a person who has access to a warehouse that humans or Prl'lus are unable to enter. Carberry has logged unexplained power drains from our reactor banks. Now this is a closed system; that power is going somewhere and if humans or Prl'lu aren't using it, someone or something is. And I don't believe our own men are robbing us or tapping the power. Why should they?''

Joaquin answered slowly, ''I agree. None of our men has cause to sabotage our work. Quite the contrary, we are all eager to get to Earth. But who or what do you suggest is at work here?''

''I expect to have a partial answer to that in a few moments,'' Rogers answered. ''I'm waiting for a report from Edison.''

''What does garbage have to do with all of this?'' Ruth asked.

''Just wait and see.''

Wait they did, until Rogers suggested they spend the time reviewing the practice session tapes. What he saw then pleased him, pleased them all. The Rangers were well fit to fight a space battle. Ensign Coltrera, for one, had a near perfect score. Out of seven simulated enemy ''blips,'' he had five dead-on hits and twice he'd cut his target in two. The other trainees had achieved only slightly less spectacular scores. The Rangers had shaped up nicely and most of them had already been awarded small, one-man fighters in consequence.

It was during a third set of exercises that Edison showed up on the bridge. He brought with him a pile of computer tapes and a set of developed films from the warehouse.

In front of the others, Edison spoke up to Rogers as jauntily as ever, ''Hope I found what you want, sir. Fact is, I *did* find something kind of interesting and if it's what you were driving at, I don't see as how you could have guessed. But like I said, the films are a bust.''

''Thank you, Mr. Edison,'' Rogers said drily. ''And what did you find so interesting?''

''Well, sir, you asked me to check into the venting system. Just how much oxy we're taking in, how much waste carbon dioxide and monoxide we're blowing out. . . ."

"I know. I asked you, remember?"

"As you say, sir; anyhow, that's the funny thing. We're taking plenty of oxy in. Tons of it a day, and that's a fact, but the amount of carbon dioxide we're venting out the other end wouldn't fill a balloon. Never seen anything like it."

"Wait," Ruth asked, "if we're not venting out carbon dioxide, how is the system determining when the oxygen level is getting low?"

"Funny thing you should ask that, Dr. Harris; I asked the same question myself until I was set straight. The computer telltales off the trace carbon monoxide elements. Evidently they're a more precise and important indicator of oxy levels."

Rogers broke in jubilantly, "But you mean to say that there's no explanation for the low levels of carbon dioxide given off?"

"That's right, sir. Defies common sense, and that's a fact."

Rogers dismissed the crewman and waited until he was out of earshot, then turned back to Ruth and Joaquin. "Well?" he asked.

"Well, what?" Ruth answered readily. "What are you suggesting? That someone's stealing our air?"

"No, of course not," Rogers began. He was more than a little put out by Ruth's skepticism, but Joaquin stepped in and made the connection.

"I think the Marshall means that whoever is stealing from us seems to require a carbon-dioxide-rich atmosphere. Is that right, Marshall?"

"You got it in one; I would add though that the missing carbon might indicate some kind of air conditioning or purification system."

"And fired lime is a good carbon dioxide generator," Ruth chipped in.

"Well, then," Rogers said. "You both see what I'm driving at. There's no proof, of course, but I'd bet our hidden guests are also behind those breakdowns—and

I'd bet they were here before we were. Any reactions?''

Ruth answered first. "We've come a long way to be stopped by gremlins. What do you propose we do about it?''

"Now *that*," Rogers said, "is a good question.''

That night the station was secured as usual: safety bulkheads up, nonessential crew tucked away in the dormitory areas where, no doubt, most of them would be shooting craps 'til near morning. For the moment, until four bells, the kitchen was empty and only a skeleton crew manned the bridge. The warehouse was locked up and as usual Carberry toiled away at his beloved machines. No one could understand how he got along on so little sleep, especially not Rogers, Ruth, and Joaquin, all three up past their own bedtimes and hidden in the sealed warehouse.

From his gloomy vantage-point inside a coffinlike crate, Rogers grimly chewed himself out for having the *worst* ideas in the known universe. The idea of cops and robbers still appealed to the child in this 600-year-old man, but the reality of his discomfort far outstripped Rogers' imagination. He hadn't felt rough lumber in his ribs since he was a boy in a treehouse.

Ruth hadn't even had *that* much practice, and she was gritting her teeth against the moment morning would liberate her. The only one of the unlucky trio to be serving his sentence composedly was Joaquin, who, as a Prl'lu, was also something of a martyr, and as a hunter was practiced in extended waits. He was more or less comfortably enveloped in a shapeless burlap bag.

The three formed a triangle around a tempting heap of charcoal canisters and sacks of lime. At least, Rogers hoped they would prove tempting; more than anything else he wanted some action, he wanted to prove his theory—and snag a gremlin if he could!

The station creaked like a ship of the sea during the long night. Rogers or one of the others started a dozen times at some barely heard sound that might be, just might be an intruder. It would have helped if they'd known what to look for, but the prescription they'd

come up with was awfully vague and very probably
wrong. After discussion they had settled on a small,
very small, carbon-dioxide-breathing creature, quite
capable of surviving in a normal atmosphere but more
comfortable in a slightly rich carbon dioxide mixture.
Otherwise, Ruth had pointed out, why the lime? The
creature was small, simply and obviously enough,
because no one had seen it, and a Battle-station, for all
its nooks and crannies, offered no obvious hiding places
for a large life-form. It was Rogers' theory that they
were dealing with a race originally put aboard the ships
as caretakers; he saw no reason to suppose that they
were of low intelligence. In fact, Carberry seemed sure
that it would take a highly intelligent and well-schooled
mind to dream up all the machine mishaps that the fleet
had been undergoing and still make them appear to be
simple accidents. *Gremlins* Rogers thought again.
Aerial poltergeists.

When it appeared, they hardly knew it. A soft tapping
came from somewhere in the farthest reaches of the
room. It meant nothing—even the clang of air in the
ventilators was louder—but the sound stuck, at least in
Ruth's mind. It was like the steam rising in a house, or
pipes cracking in the cold, or like very careful, very
methodical vermin beneath the floor.

Something was happening, though. A deliberately
muffled hammering in the bulkheads signified that.
Something fell to the floor, not from a height, but with
a loud enough metallic wrench to raise Rogers' and
Ruth's hair. Joaquin, of course, remained composed.

After that, nothing, nothing, noth . . . Ruth was
counting the silence out in her head; then the soft foot-
pads of more than one creature could be heard on the
steel floor.

Rogers gripped his "weapons." Over Ruth's protests,
he'd armed himself with nothing but a good strong club
and a grand piece of burlap sacking. As a child he'd
watched his grandfather trap muskrat with little else,
and he had a feeling, the same kind of itch his granddad
got in trapping weather, that that was all he'd need
tonight.

Anyhow, all the artillery in the world couldn't buy the confidence that that piece of sack gave him.

Ruth and Joaquin were the first to sight the creatures as they crept up to the bait.

Joaquin carefully prepared by clearing his mind for the hunt; he thought about ways and means, avenues of egress and escape, he studied his opponent and tried to anticipate.

Ruth was suddenly so full of other, confused, even rebellious thoughts, it made her dizzy.

She had felt her adrenaline, sapped by hours of waiting, suddenly surge to meet the unfamiliar. Her first feeling was a sort of fear, a cloying, resonating panic, which she could feel in her temples. It wasn't cowardice, just the jangling of nerves that makes your fingers seem too thick and your body all set to fumble when you call on it.

Their visitors pattered into view.

That was just it, the second feeling that stalled her so. It was absurd. What she'd expected she didn't know—but not this! They came almost silently; only their bare feet slapping against the steel deck could be heard. In ones and twos they dodged for cover, searching out shadows as they advanced on the bait. They wore belts about their middles, and functional harnesses hung with gear. They were handsome, Ruth thought, admiring their sleek fur, and they barely came up to her knee.

Suddenly conscious of their diminutive size and of the leaden heft of the pistol in her hand, Ruth was filled with a guilty knowledge of her own sometimes hurtful nature.

Woodenly she raised her pistol against the moment of Rogers' command, though she prayed it wouldn't come. Humans were full of hurt, and suddenly the thought embarrassed her.

Rogers' cue wasn't long in coming—the long, drawn-out whistle that was prearranged to mean "close and capture."

Seconds were lost while the three wrestled out of their hidy-holes.

The creatures were disciplined. When she realized

that, Ruth lost some of her finer feelings—she came out, pistol held steady.

And the creatures were rough. That was obvious in only a few moments. On command, they wheeled around and broke up into several fighting units. These set off across the steel flooring in a scuttling fast pace that eluded their pursuers.

By chance and ill-luck, Ruth was caught between a gremlin unit and cover. She hefted the pistol and released it. Short of killing the creatures, there was nothing she could do, and that seemed so pointless.

The phalanx began to split up, to run by on either side of her, and suddenly she felt something soft and warm strike the back of her neck. She could see gremlins lobbing something. It clung to her and she felt it turn hot on her skin. Not unpleasantly, but it ran and stuck and slowed her until, unbalanced, she fell to the floor.

And the fumes, they made it an effort, a very great effort. What to do, what to think? In a remote way she understood that she was going to die.

"Tony!" she cried weakly. "Tony." It took Rogers agonizing seconds to hear that feeble voice. Suddenly it looked like sixty or seventy of the furry gremlins were scurrying across the floor. More than enough, he thought, to bring a human down. And where was Ruth!

His eye caught a flurry of activity far across the warehouse. Too far, he thought, and then on impulse ran, ran as hard as he could—ran to Ruth's side and hoisted her up on top of a crate, where at least she was out of harm's reach. She was alive.

He cleared her mouth and nose of the sticky plastic, but that was all he had time for. A bellow from Joaquin pulled him away.

The gremlins had divided into a number of small companies. They were emphatically not retreating. Their battle strategy was well-suited to their size and evident capabilities. The tiny bands were lying in wait, lurking in the piles of crates and sacks. The dull red nightlight of the warehouse cast deep shadows, and for all Rogers knew there was a small army lurking in every one.

"Joaquin!" he called. "Take an end of this." He threw the Prl'lu a weighted end of his burlap bag. Rogers had to shout to make himself heard over the chittering voices of the gremlins. "If they charge us, kick for all you're worth! And *hold on* to your end of the bag. I'm going to net us a few!"

"Behind you, Tony!" Ruth shouted from her perch atop the crate.

Rogers rolled on his heels to face three packs of the creatures charging at his legs. As he turned several of them were already flinging the sticky globs at his face. He did his best to cover his eyes with his forearm and fended them off with the stick held in his other hand.

They were rushing him and sooner or later, he knew, one would get through. Not much of a problem, except that some were wielding sharp double-headed picks with oily, evil-looking points. He didn't doubt that one of those sunk into his calf would do plenty of harm.

He took his chance and looked up at Joaquin. The Prl'lu met his eye and with a swift one, two, three, they threw the net. It sailed, almost elegantly, through the air and settled with more precision than Rogers would have predicted on the heads and shoulders of a dozen or more of the attacking gremlins.

The rest seemed impressed. Most of them scattered across packing cases and stacked bundles in every direction. Only one healthy specimen lingered. The ambitious fellow had to be shaken from Rogers' boot, which he was doing his best to jab with the business end of his pick. Ruth, revived, hopped down and snagged him deftly.

"Tony! Watch your step!" she shouted suddenly. Rogers froze, foot in air, and saw that he was about to step on one of the little creatures, knocked flat and breathless on the steel decking. He took off his jacket and wrapped it around his arm, stooped down and lifted the furry animal to face level. "Watch it!" Joaquin warned, but Rogers had already caught the glint of the small pick swinging toward his face. He intercepted the weapon in midair and gently pulled it from the angry gremlin. The pick went into his pocket; the gremlin, he continued to hold at arm's length. Close up he could make out the creature's rough face. It was bare of hair. The black, wizened features were surprisingly human, a miniature of homo sapiens' physiognomy, like a marmoset's.

"Can you understand me?" Rogers said slowly, "Are you hurt?"

The gremlin said nothing, just waved its arms and legs feebly in Roger's grasp. It felt warm and alive and vulnerable and suddenly Rogers felt very concerned that the gremlin captives be treated decently. More than once in life he had felt very small himself.

"Joaquin," he ordered, "take a look around and make sure there aren't any wounded that've dragged themselves off into a corner or something." To Ruth, still extricating herself from the gremlin goo, he asked, "Would you go off and round up some help? And we'll want a stateroom, *completely* sealed off—air vents, everything! Do your best, will you?"

While Ruth was gone, he and Joaquin stood guard. For the moment they were silent; both knew there'd be a great deal to talk about in due course, but there was also a lot to ponder and assimilate. Tonight's events put a new perspective on a number of things.

Ruth returned with a more-than-ample supply of fresh-eyed, well-rested young security officers. They were full of questions, but Rogers' stony silence struck them mute. He ordered them to take every care against the little picks when they removed the gremlins one by one from the net, but added, "And I *don't* want any accidents—I hold you responsible for their safety as well as your own."

He watched the young Rangers at work and seemed lost in thought. Finally Ruth had to remind him of the creature still struggling in his hand. "It's been a long night."

"That it has," he answered. Rogers turned the gremlin over to a waiting officer and slapped Ruth and Joaquin on the backs. "We haven't done so badly, have we? A bit of mystery cleared up and we're another step closer to our goal. Not a bad night's work. I wonder why I feel so strange.''

Ruth and Joaquin exchanged a worried look. They'd seen Rogers like this before, when something from one of his alternate selves was ready to emerge. Didn't matter what; the transition was always painful to see.

''Tony, I think we can knock off for the night,'' Ruth said. ''Time you got some rest.''

He started to protest, but Joaquin stole his thunder. ''I'll see to it that everything's taken care of, Marshall. Not much to be done before morning anyhow.''

Rogers nodded dumbly and Ruth led him off to his cabin. Joaquin watched them for a long moment as they walked down the corridor. Finally he turned and hastened toward the bridge. A systems alert had to be posted, the night detail augmented, a great deal to be done. Joaquin didn't yet know what to make of the night's experiences, but he knew one thing; the three of them had started something that didn't necessarily end at lights out.

11.

After three days on the trail, Holcomb knew that Shak't'kan had underestimated the difficulties. Holcomb was striding along at the head of a column, a full hundred and fifty strong, give or take a few, for all the world like a general marching into an archaic battle. It was broad daylight and in the interest of speed he and his posted lieutenants made no effort to keep the column under cover. *He* knew how improbable their progress had been; he just hoped that the humans under his command were a great deal more credulous than any living, breathing being had a right to be, because if

Shak't'kan hadn't been manipulating the air search, they would have been located and corraled three days ago.

Still, people had a habit of believing what they liked —and everyone he'd encountered so far liked to think that native wit and steady spirit had guided them this far. No one wanted to feel like a dupe.

As to taking command, that had been a cinch. The escapees had been confused and scared when they hit the hills. Not one had contested his authority when he wandered across the ridge and began to gather the groups of three and four into a small and well-organized army bent on a special kind of retreat. At least, that's how he put it to them. They were a militia and he was their commander, at least until they made contact with the provisional guerrilla forces of North America. It satisfied everyone, bolstered their courage—why, it even sounded good in his ears.

He kept the ambitious ones busy scouting or hunting. He kept others on a twenty-four-hour watch for a Prl-lu attack he knew would never come.

In general, he felt he was doing remarkably well, but it was at the evening strategy sessions that his baggage of special knowledge became a hindrance. He was particularly worried about his plan to keep the column moving toward the northeast in the direction of the Sierra Nevada mountains. Prl-lu reports put that at the center of guerrilla activity in the American southwest. Unfortunately, most of his lieutenants, who were, naturally, unfamiliar with those reports, wanted to head south. Ironically enough, he was in the position of a man who had all the answers, but couldn't admit to it because he had them for all the wrong reasons.

It was not only infuriating but potentially incriminating.

"But why do you think we should head northeast?" The most vocal of all Holcomb's escapees was questioning him during the evening session. "At least to the south we're assured of an easy winter. Who knows, we may not contact a surviving guerrilla band before next year, and we'd better be prepared to fend for ourselves in the meantime."

This was precisely the kind of argument Holcomb didn't like, and he was characteristically terse. "Contingency plans for the southwest have always targeted the Sierra Nevadas as an easily defensible area. In any case, the coast is obviously too deep within Prl'lu hegemony. When I suggest we move east, I'm not speaking from ignorance!"

Obviously, his lieutenants weren't always comfortable with his ready answers. Still, the unit moved steadily and efficiently forward and sometimes he actually found himself feeling like the instrument of their deliverance.

Nothing stood in his way until they reached the Sierra Nevadas. The trip across the mountains was hard on Holcomb's men and women. Before they reached the foothills, they were whipped into an organized fighting unit, but none of them was prepared for the exertions they were undergoing. Sometimes it was difficult to spur them along, particularly as the likelihood of Prl'lu attack dwindled from the forefront of their worries. When the going got tough, Holcomb often thought of Marshall Rogers. Though he'd betrayed the Marshall's ideals, he still admired the man and took him as a model of leadership. But Holcomb knew he'd never be the leader of men that Rogers was.

It might have been different, he thought, if Rogers hadn't died on the Moon. Holcomb was the kind of man who needed another man to live up to. A living man. No sense following a corpse, he often told himself. That could only lead to a grave.

As time went on and the trip over the mountains proved even rougher than anticipated, Holcomb became uneasily aware that an influential coterie of his followers thought that that was precisely where he was leading them. They were well up the slope of Telescope Peak when an evening strategy session broke down into angry recriminations.

"This is getting us nowhere!" a black-bearded youngster named Chris Marlowe complained bitterly. "We've marched our boots into the ground pounding up these hills and we're farther than ever from meeting up with any other humans. What's more, I don't believe you have any idea what we'll find on the other side of these mountains!"

The unfortunate thing was that Holcomb knew very well what they'd find—uncompromising and dangerous desert, not quite a trackless waste. He'd been given adequate maps and in the desert the old roads stood up quite well over five hundred years, but there was no getting around the fact that he was leading them into some pretty unpleasant territory. They weren't going to like it, and he could hardly explain that the Prl'lu had told him that free humans were concentrating there.

Others of his command were chiming in with more complaints. It was cold at night in the mountains. The food was inadequate. Their pace was too fast. He couldn't tell the complainers that they were halfway there—that would indicate that he knew where they were going. By this time tomorrow, they'd be skirting the Mojave Desert, clinging to the foothills where a little water was still to be found. What he could tell them was that there was little or no choice.

He calmly turned a deaf ear to the others' complaints and began to draw with a stick in the soft dust of their campground. To the north his stick described a long line of mountains. Those were the Nevadas in earnest, not the little foothills they'd been negotiating. To the south he marked off an enormous basin. That was the Mojave. Nothing broke its surface, though in the narrow corridor between the two he carefully placed some pebbles to mark lakes and traced at least one river.

Before long, the others were peering over his shoulder and their talk had died down. Then he began to explain the map, building it up and adding to its detail as he went along. To their rear he put the Prl'lu prison camp in the Los Angeles basin, and over a wide semicircle of land surrounding it he cross-hatched the area Prl'lu search parties might be expected to hold sway. They had come that way, and it was obvious to everyone that there was no going back along that route.

The north, difficult. The south, impossible. Holcomb let the map sink in a bit and only then chose to speak.

"There's no doubt I got us all into this position. If I hadn't insisted, you might have gone south down into the Baja. The reason I chose this route is because I fought shy of the coast and even now I think with good reason. The Prl'lu are well-established in coastal waters. You know that. And we all know that they are weakest in the interior. In any case, we find ourselves here." He jabbed the makeshift map in the center of the corridor between the Mojave and the Sierra Nevadas. "We can't go back. I don't advise turning aside either north *or* south. Let me show you what lies ahead and then I'll tell you why I think we have to go that way." There were some angry murmurs. Not everyone liked Holcomb, even fewer liked his tone, but all knew that he was more knowledgeable about North American geography than the rest put together.

"Directly in front of us, over the shoulders of the Nevadas, lies a bad stretch called Death Valley. Where we'll cross it, it's comparatively narrow—thirty-odd miles—and we'd have to do it in two nights; that's no place to linger. Down the center of the valley you have a narrow river, the Amorosa, and with any luck it'll be wet. We'll camp there under whatever cover we can make while the sun is high. On the other side of the valley we hit open flatlands, desertlike, but there'll be some game if we look hard enough. That's on the Nevada side. Somewhere out there we know there'll be free humans—at least, before the war there were quite a few in that desert, and I don't suppose the Prl'lu will have driven them out. Those were tough types.

"We're going this way because there are very few Prl'lu in the interior. Once we're beyond the mountains and have established ourselves in the desert with a watering hole and some good hunting, *then* we'll be in shape to vote on the future. Not before!" Holcomb paused and looked around, testing the reaction to his plan. He decided to add, less sharply, "You don't have

much choice. It's got to be forward, whether you're
following my lead or not. I haven't done so badly so far
and I know where I'm heading, so I hope you'll give me
the benefit of the doubt and some support. It doesn't do
to let the others see that we're squabbling.''

Reluctantly, his lieutenants gave in. Not one had any
better ideas and certainly not one had the strength to im-
plement them if he had. As usual, Marlowe was the
hardest to convince; but once convinced, he was the
most able lieutenant. It was with a united front that
Holcomb and Marlowe and the rest led their people into
the desert the next day. Whatever difficulties they would
encounter there would be taken in turn and not made a
subject for censure. Holcomb's little army had developed discipline and it was all he could ask for.

The desert wasn't as bad as he'd feared. They watered
at Searles Lake before the crossing and several of the
men had fashioned huge skins for water, which they
fastened on their backs. They scarcely leaked at all, and
they proved a boon to Holcomb and the rest of the
group leaders. Very few of the ''ranks'' had learned as
yet to eke out a canteen properly. The moon was bright,
and they soon adjusted to moving single-file in the
darkness.

On their way through the valley, Marlowe, who
always had more energy than any of the rest, hastened
up and down the column, encouraging stragglers on
their way. Whenever he reached the top of the column
he'd stop and have a few words with Holcomb. They
weren't friends yet and they weren't enemies, just good
men with a temporary truce and a job to do. During one
of their conversations, Marlowe told Holcomb about
his life and the kind of work he wanted to do.

''I'm only twenty-three. I guess you knew that or
thought maybe I was even younger. I'm not, and I grew
this beard to prove it. I was a pilot during the war—it
didn't last long for me. I was shot down during my third
mission. On the coast, I was lucky not to ditch in the
sea. So I've got a lot of fight left.

''I don't know if I should mention it, but that's more

than I can say for most of these people. They've had the
stuff knocked out of them for sure." Marlowe saw
Holcomb was about to speak up and he hastened on,
"Oh; I don't mean they didn't have the guts to cut when
the gates were down. We've all got that far. But I don't
think most of them plan to do any more fighting.
They'll leave that to the ones who've never been
caught."

There was some truth to that, Holcomb thought, so
he remained silent. Marlowe continued, "People always
seem content with the status quo, I guess. I never do,
but then most of the people I run into are a good deal
older than me. I still want a little adventure, but I want
to feel I'm going about it responsibly, you know? I'm
not about to abandon these folks or anything. Which is
why I'm sticking with you, even though I think this
direction is for the birds."

Holcomb murmured something he hoped sounded
pleased.

"What I want to do when we get in touch with some
free humans is join up with some sort of guerrilla
gang," Marlowe went on. "I hear they're pretty open.
It's what you can do that counts. I think there's a lot I
can do."

"Undoubtedly." Holcomb's tone was flat. It was
hard to pretend enthusiasm since he *was* guilty of seeking to preserve the status quo, far more than any of his
followers knew. Life was ironic.

"Once we get through into Nevada, where then?"

That was something he could answer—at least
vaguely. "I think we should head southeast once we
pass beyond the north edge of the Spring Mountains.
That'll take us down toward the Colorado River, and I
think I recall that there's some sort of tributary along
the way. We may even be able to raft it." He didn't add
that Shak't'kan had indicated that the human guerrilla
bands were piling into that area, near the Muddy Mountains; that it was there he was expected to do his spying.

"Water then. At least that'll be a break. I hope we
can keep these types going that long, but I suppose if we
promise them a river they'll have a bit of incentive."

Marlowe slapped Holcomb on the back then and stood still. Pretty soon the column had drifted by him, and he was bringing up the rear. As the last man passed him, he thought to himself, *I hope we're doing the right thing*.

So did Holcomb. He had no idea whether this little venture would turn out the way his master Shak't'kan had predicted. It seemed to him that he'd run into a great deal of trouble, unpredicted trouble, already. Nothing to do but go ahead. If he didn't turn in the goods, Shak't'kan could betray him easily by broadcasting an account of the true state of affairs. That kind of thing was being done all the time—a page the Prl'arek had taken out of the human book called *Propaganda*. It worked quite well.

He expected to meet the human guerrilla groups outside of Las Vegas, if Prl'lu intelligence was to be trusted. These few resisting humans were sitting ducks —maybe he could make a deal for them. In any case, Shak't'kan seemed interested in the results of their meeting, so maybe they were all safe, at least until he reported.

At least.

At best he'd prove the savior of the human race, even if the race was doomed to slavery in the Prl'oi Empire. Better fed than dead.

Their second night in the valley saw the first casualty. A middle-aged woman lingered unconscious for a couple of hours, and died. There was nothing any of them could do for her. As Holcomb saw it, indeed as the rest of the group leaders saw it, there was no particular reason why she had to die. She just had.

Not all of the group saw it that way though.

"Bad luck," Marlowe said to Holcomb during one of his stints at the head of the column.

"Had to expect something like this."

"I suppose, but they . . ." Marlowe jerked his thumb over his shoulder to indicate the rest, "it makes all the difference to them. You're going to have to come through with *something* when we make camp or you're going to lose their confidence." His tone was flat; he didn't indicate whether his own confidence was at stake or not.

"Any idea what?"

"Oh, I don't know, food, rest, those free humans." It seemed to Holcomb that the emphasis was on the last.

"You think I can come up with a rescue party just like that?" His tone was scornful, but his look was questioning. He felt painfully anxious to find out what this youngster expected of him.

"Well, we've come a long way; maybe it's time we tried to signal up some help. I kind of doubt that any Prl'lu airships are patrolling this neighborhood," Marlowe said.

It was a good idea, and just might make the difference between civil mutiny and the kind of dull obedience he'd come to expect. Even if no one answered the call, and no harm done if they did, the mere exercise of signaling for other people might cheer his troupe up. Nothing to lose but a little dry brush.

"Good idea," he said. "Anything else?"

"Well, maybe we should be sending scouts ahead to plan out the easiest route?"

"Right again. Anything more?"

"Guess not," Marlowe said.

"Well then I'll add one. By tomorrow we'll be on the edge of the Shoshone River. I suggest we camp out there and make a real effort to contact other humans. If we have no luck, I think we should see if we can't fashion a couple of rafts and float as far south as possible. The Shoshone eventually empties into the Colorado, though we may have to portage a few places. All right by you?"

Marlowe was obviously embarrassed. Just as obviously, he wasn't about to show it. He said stiffly, "Whatever you say," and walked back down the column. Just as well, Holcomb thought. It was hard to hang around the righteous.

By next day the tensions had ebbed. It was Holcomb's private opinion that the river had carried most of their troubles away. Not one of the men and women under his command could resist dabbling in the shallows when they first got there. They washed the grime of the desert from their bodies, and the death, too. That night they were as excited as children, building a huge campfire. Most of them hoped it would attract help. Holcomb knew that a good smudge fire by day was far more likely to prove effective, but he let them have their fun. Tomorrow he'd have a few wet branches thrown over the embers.

That night, sitting around the blaze, the camp swapped stories about their life before the war and most volunteered their ambitions, colored very obviously by present circumstances. Marlowe was right; very few had fighting ambitions, but they were all patriots of a kind. Little reason to leave the prison camp otherwise. Holcomb contributed, too—wholesome, meaningless talk about human destiny and man's place in the order of things. Privately he believed none of it, but it kept the people feeling good and went a way toward dispelling suspicions. Some of these people might have some idea about his collaboration with the Prl'lu, he surmised.

The next morning the group set about building three rafts out of driftwood. The wood was difficult to find and he sent scouts up and down the riverbank looking for suitable pieces. A cordon of volunteers stood in the shallow river waiting to catch pieces set adrift by scouts upstream. Later on he'd send a crew downstream to help out there. There was no way they were going to build a proper raft, let alone three, but they could build a structure large enough for all to rest on as they kicked their way down the river. He wasn't sure all of them realized that yet, but he'd already polled a few good swimmers and he thought that the experiment might work.

It beat walking, anyway.

The day was uneventful but it was rather fun. Holcomb hadn't gotten to know all hundred escapees very well up till now, but he spent a good deal of time with them by the river. It made a difference in their attitude and in his, too. As pieces of piñon wood drifted down the sluggish current, his people jumped to catch them.

In the meanwhile, they waited to see if anything came of the brushfire.

Nothing the first day and nothing the second. By the third day Holcomb had decided they had to move on in the morning. The "rafts" were ready, and all the game in the neighborhood was exhausted. Besides, they were all sick of their diet and craved something meatier than scrub hare and gila-monster. Holcomb ordered them into the river that morning.

Privately he was surprised that no one had replied to their summons. According to Shak't'kan's intelligence, a good-sized band of resistance fighters was camped in this area.

The river was cold and several of his more timid following had to be half-coaxed, half-pushed into the water. Once in, they found places on the three adjoining floats, all kicking up a storm and supporting themselves on their elbows, over a hundred of them in a row. It looked like a convention of dog-paddlers, but Holcomb was content. They were safe and moving. Treading water was about all he expected from his charges anyway. When they came through and actually swam, he was not only surprised but pleased. All his lieutenants could swim, and they took turns paddling back and forth among the others, adding an encouraging word here and a supporting hand there. The rafts were no larger than absolutely necessary, and everyone was packed in shoulder to shoulder. It made for some hard feelings at first, but at least it kept the nonswimmers from worrying too much about drowning—they were too closely shoved in with their neighbors to fall off.

Holcomb decided to keep drifting through the lunch period. They were all waterlogged, but it didn't take much effort to float along in the midday sun. In fact, Holcomb thought wryly, it all felt more like an excursion than a desperate escape. He worried that his own complacency might be beginning to show. He hoped not; certainly he didn't want to give any of these people a reason *not* to worry. That would be fatal to his plans if not positively hazardous to his health.

He pondered questions like these for the rest of the afternoon. It did seem an idyllic day, at least. . . .

He shook his head abruptly, waking with a mouthful of water, and tried to grab some air. The river was suddenly a rough, rapid mess. Things had begun to get hectic.

They'd had no warning, or very little. Probably none of them would have recognized the signs if he'd noted them. You have to be a certain number of feet above the level to spot churning water up ahead. And white water blends in remarkably with the sky and the sun. They were gulping river before they noticed the white foam blown into their faces.

Holcomb tried to shout and almost drowned. The smart ones just held tight and let their bodies relax, limp in the water, trusting to the current to wash them through. The ones who stiffened up and fought the current didn't last so long.

By the time they drifted to shore, just before sunset, and all the survivors had been collected and accounted for, eight were dead. Whether their bodies could be found downstream . . . most of them were too tired to think on that. As weary as the rest, Holcomb ordered that camp be made for the night. Marlowe detailed men to gather wood and cut brush for shelter. The rest huddled around a small fire and shivered dismally.

Holcomb dropped off to sleep, thinking that for a commander with nothing to fear from the Prl'lu and advance knowledge of their route, he was doing very poorly indeed. Nine dead so far.

It was midnight when the sound of heavy footsteps in the gravel woke him from his sleep. He wondered vaguely where the night patrol was, then remembered guiltily that none had been posted. Everyone had been too worn out.

The footsteps were circling around the camp and there was a deliberation about them that Holcomb didn't like. He cautiously raised his head and spotted three intruders. He didn't dare twist around, but he was sure that there were more of them ringing the camp. It

was a couple of minutes before he was sure of it in the
dark, but he realized with a start of fear that the newcomers were humans, not Prl'lu, and with these he had
no businesslike agreement. If they were on the level, it
was a mighty strange way to greet the camp. And if they
weren't—well, not all humans were brothers under the
skin. He'd heard tell of guerrilla groups that had turned
outlaw. One thing he knew for sure; for the moment
power had passed out of his hands. It was up to the
strangers to declare themselves.

The decision shook the fright from him. Holcomb got
quietly to his feet and stood in the lingering firelight
facing the intruders. Their movement about the camp
stopped abruptly, but it was a long moment before
another move was made. Finally a tall, very slight figure
stepped forward into the light and approached him.
When the figure drew near, Holcomb tensed. Evidently
he'd been wrong; *she* was every inch a Prl'lu. Her face
was striking and utterly unique, its cheekbones drawing
the skin taut over the even features. It was a face that
Holcomb would never forget: the face of the Han Princess, Lu-An.

"Princess . . ." She stopped him with a quick motion
of her arm. He felt her hand take his elbow firmly, but
the pressure was somehow comforting. Silently, she led
Holcomb from the camp, and it was only when they
were out of the sleepers' hearing that she signaled a
stop.

"So, I see you have recognized me. Your face is
familiar, too; perhaps, you would refresh my memory. . . ." The princess stood impassively, waiting for
the answer, friend or foe. As far as Holcomb could
discern in the darkness, the two of them had left the
camp alone. He wondered at her courage, and spent a
moment composing himself before answering. "Princess, my name is Holcomb. You knew me once as Marshall Rogers' aide and subordinate officer." He was
about to continue, but he saw her mouth twitch at the
sound of the Marshall's name. He knew that at one time
they had been very close, that the princess had trusted

Rogers implicitly. He decided to keep his connection with the Marshall alive for her; it might be his one chance for her sympathy.

"When they hit the Houston gang, Rogers put me in charge of reorganizing the southwest forces. I was in at the Denver battle. Flew wing-guard on him. After the moonbase attempt, well, civilian authorities split up whatever organization we had left. The whole thing fell to pieces when Rogers was gone."

Lu-An said quietly, "I know."

"Well, if you were in on the last days, you saw it; we sure saw it all, a bloodbath and a stinking defeat. I was captured with most of my men, the ones still alive. Sent out to L.A. prison camp. Heard you were in the hills with a guerrilla band."

Lu-An didn't take the bait and after a moment Holcomb found himself telling her the rest of it, right up to the prison break. That's when he began to get nervous, but the princess went right on listening and soon he was telling her the rest of his story, as concocted by Shak't'kan, with a certain amount of satisfaction. He made much of their trip across the desert and of the river disaster, hoping to win her by their suffering. As far as he could tell though, Lu-An's features never varied; she was impassive, as only a Han princess could be.

When he'd finished there was a brief pause and then finally she spoke. "And why did you choose to come in this direction, Captain?"

Holcomb repeated all the reasons he'd given Marlowe. When he finished, the princess said simply, "I see," She stopped him before he could launch into further explanations. "Come. We'll get back to your camp now. It's nearly dawn and your people will be waking. It's well that you should be with them when they see my men." Together the two trudged back toward camp, quite silently, though Holcomb fairly brimmed with questions.

At the camp the escapees who were up were prodding the others awake. Strung around them stood a cordon of Lu-An's guards, most of them human, Holcomb was able to see. When Holcomb strode into the camp, he was painfully conscious that the others would be looking to him for guidance. He tried to look as large and confident as he could. After all, nothing had gone wrong *yet*.

When the rest of his people were awake, Lu-An mingled with them for a bit. Whispered rumors were traded among the little huddled groups. Before long everyone knew who she was and wondered what she wanted. When Lu-An finally beckoned Holcomb back to her side and stationed herself on a small hillock just inside camp, the silence was strained until she began to speak.

"As most of you know by now," the princess said in a low, calm pragmatic voice, "my name is Lu-An. I *am* a former princess of the Han Empire. But today I am a rebel, not unlike yourselves, although I have not so recently escaped from bondage. I have been leading this scouting party because we had word of your escape two days ago."

"Took you long enough!" someone shouted.

Lu-An answered, "It takes time in the desert. We are here now. In any case, we had to determine who you were and what you might want." The crowd began to murmur, and Lu-An raised her voice to drown it. "We had to do this because we represent the Provisional Government of North America, what's left of it, and you've wandered right into our backyard."

The murmur rose to a dull roar that died down slowly as Lu-An continued, "I'm satisfied that you belong with us. I think you'll like our setup. So pack up and let's get going!"

Someone in the crowd shouted, "So where we off to, Princess?"

Holcomb almost winced, but Lu-An was game. "Las Vegas, friend. What's left of North America is in Las Vegas! Thirty miles away!"

12.

Morning broke without incident, morning, at least as ship's time reckoned it.

It was early, at least two hours earlier than morning conference was usually scheduled. Department heads and ranking officers were shuffling into the conference room, most of them still rubbing the sleep from their eyes. Rogers was there, one of the first, and precious little sleep he'd had, but then most of them had spent a wakeful night.

The Rangers had been on alert since the early hours of the morning, when Rogers, Ruth, and Joaquin had turned up a hornets nest in the warehouse hangar.

Twenty-seven "gremlins" were caged in the specially prepared stateroom. So far their friends or family, if the species ran to either, hadn't turned up to claim them.

It was obviously a good time to hold a conference.

"Well," Rogers called the assembled meeting to order, "I'm sure that all of you have given some thought to last night's events." He looked around the table at the faces: Douglas, Joaquin, Ruth, McNab, Carberry, a few section heads, a dozen officers. He could tell the news hadn't set well with them. Their expressions, Joaquin's excepted, were pretty bleak. He almost felt guilty over his own growing sense of confidence.

"Cheer up! I think we can turn this to advantage."

"I don't think I understand, sir," McNab spoke up.

"Nothing to understand, just a feeling I have, but I can say this, we're a far sight better off today knowing the score than we were yesterday poking around in the dark." Rogers grinned at Ruth.

"How can we be better off when now we *know* we have an enemy aboard?" McNab sounded almost angry.

"Because now we know. One thing I've learned over the years is that once you've got all the facts straightened out on both sides of an issue you can usually work a deal. And that's what I propose. Now that we know we're not alone out here, I suggest we roll up our sleeves and do a little business—the old-fashioned kind where a bargain is a bargin and both sides come out ahead.''

He paused and let the others have a moment to digest this. Most of them had been brought up to shoot first and ask questions later, especially when confronted by the unknown. He could count on Ruth, as a scientist, to have an open mind, and in all his dealings with the humans Joaquin had never shown a sign of race hatred, but it might take the others some time to get used to the idea.

"You know," he continued after a while, "as far as I can make out, we don't have much of a grievance to press. We took over these ships without a thought about whoever or whatever might be camped out here. Who knows how much havoc we might have caused? Sure, we suffered through a deal of sabotage," he nodded at Carberry, "but no one's been killed. Until last night we don't know of a single attempt on a human or Blackjack life . . ."

Douglas interrupted. "But we didn't know these creatures were here!"

"True," Rogers answered. "But, as one of the little fellows might answer, 'What of it?' The point is we have no reason to believe they mean any kind of harm. All they seem to have been doing is trying to keep the fleet intact. What's to say they won't be eager to make a deal?"

"And what's to say they could be trusted?" McNab retorted. "Sure, they might make a deal, but they could be lying through their teeth, too."

"All I can say to that is that if enough of them lied to us, we'd get the truth, because the parts they don't invent would match one another, and the parts they did invent would not. I got that from a smart man who invented something we called the League of Nations, and it's good advice."

Finally, Ruth spoke up. "Well, I suggest we get it

over with. Let's go visit with our guests and see if we can communicate, much less come to an agreement.''

''Oh we can communicate all right,'' Rogers said, ''I haven't made myself clear. You see, I *know* what we're dealing with.'' His voice took on the peculiarly stilted timbre it had when he dredged up Aquintir and Jak't'rin from his subconscious. ''The Simbas are an ancient race, well-known to the Prl'arek who assembled this fleet. When the Prl'oi left, the Simbas were left behind as fleet caretakers. I don't know why. That was many thousands of years ago.''

Ruth broke the spell, ''They speak Prl'oi then?''

Rogers shook himself, ''I have no reason to suppose that they don't and I suggest that we go and start the jawing.'' He started to get up from the table.

From out of nowhere, the room rang to a voice raised in defiance and strong purpose, ''I would like to speak to the man called Rogers!''

It was a dramatic entrance, and, as such things go, Rogers thought it was extremely well done. High on the wall, the grating of the ventilation shaft was kicked out from within. It fell to the steel floor and rang clear as a bell in the suddenly silenced room. Standing in the dark opening, nearly filling it, was one of the little ''men'' of the night before, pick-axe hung rakishly over his shoulder.

''You see,'' the creature said, ''we have a great deal to discuss.'' He spoke the high Prl'arek tongue.

Rogers took his time in answering. He settled his weight back in his chair and leaned away from the table, making a show of relaxing. It was only when his eyes had held the intruder's for a long moment that he chose to speak.

''I see. Are you just dropping by or do you plan to stay?'' Under the flippancy, Rogers' tone was strong.

''I'll stay.''

''In that case, pull up a chair.''

''I will.''

Rogers nodded to Joaquin. The Prl'lu got up from his seat and lifted the Simba out of the vent in the bulkhead. The little "man" stolidly accepted the handling and did nothing to help or hinder the Prl'lu until he was deposited on the table. Once he found his footing, the Simba stepped back and quietly said, "Thank you."

Rogers made a mental note—it's no easy matter to retain your dignity when you're being slung about like an infant. The Simba pulled it off.

He walked up the gun-metal conference table like someone well accustomed to an audience. He couldn't have had a better one; the breathless silence followed him up the table. Up close and in the bright light, even officers involved in the midnight scuffle found reason to take a second look. The Simba's fur was a silvered brown and it grew short and sleek over his body. The face was pleasantly expressive under its wizened dark skin. Striding across the table, he reached almost to the shoulders of the seated officers, at least fifteen inches tall. The surprising angularity of his frame lent him a peculiarly human stance and gait. It turned him, in the eyes of the assembled officers, from an animal into a man. A man—at least as this special corps of Rangers now understood the term—an active, participating intelligence.

The Simba walked up and down the table before choosing a spot to sit. He was clearly satisfying his own curiosity and somehow that reversal filled the air with an extra degree of tension. Only Rogers seemed immune.

When the Simba found an empty space at the table opposite Rogers, he sat down abruptly and addressed the Marshall.

"Does it surprise you that I'm here?"

"Not particularly," Rogers said. "I have your people. I expected a response."

"But I take it that you are surprised to find us aboard this ship." The creature's features were unfamiliar, but Ruth, who was sitting closest, thought she could detect a tight smile on his face.

"Not at all," Rogers said. "We've known about your group for weeks. Just wanted to bring matters to a head last night."

"You lie." The words were flat. More than at any time she could recall, Rogers seemed evenly matched.

Rogers seemed to think so, too. Ruth thought he seemed to be enjoying himself.

"As you wish."

The Simba continued, "Nevertheless, it is time we reached an agreement, don't you think?"

"Why no," Rogers said slowly, "you see, we don't deal." This was more surprising yet, and Rogers took a long moment looking around the table, fixing everyone at it with a hard stare, ostensibly seeking their approval but actually, Ruth knew, warning them to sit tight. She felt the look linger over her and then pass.

The creature wasn't having any of this, though. "Of course you'll deal. The only question is when—now, or after lives have been lost. If you've known about us for weeks, you know we are positioned over the entire fleet, ready to strike. If, as I suspect, you only recently discovered our presence, well then I warn you, we are positioned over the entire fleet and are ready to strike." He was definitely smiling. "So we deal."

Wham! Rogers slapped the table so that everybody jumped. Only the Simba didn't flinch.

"O.K., we deal!" Rogers said. "We'll get down to brass tacks. What do you want, what do we want, that's the substance of it. Guests first."

"As you say, guests first." The Simba waited until his point was taken.

"All right," Rogers said, "we're the intruders here, but you can take it as a given that it won't be easy to force us out. We have reason to be here and reason to equip these ships and later we'll have a good reason to take most of them away. And none of our reasons happens to be negotiable."

"Fairly said." The little creature cross-legged on the table gave every appearance of being completely relaxed. "In turn, we have reason to stay, reason to fight, and reason to keep you from removing our ships. This is our home and none of our reasons is negotiable either."

"Impasse!"

"Impasse!" It seemed to Ruth that the two were grinning sourly at each other. She decided to jump in for better or worse and try to swing the tide.

"We have a number of your people. How many?" she asked McNab quickly. "Twenty-six. We give them up unconditionally." Out of the corner of her eye she saw Rogers straighten in his chair. "Unconditionally," she said firmly. "We don't need hostages to negotiate. Our strength is enough.

"Now I gather this fleet is home to you. I still don't know just who or what you are, but understand this: this fleet is all the home *we* have too, unless we can take part of it back to our system. We feel as strongly about it as you do.

"There are thousands of ships out here. I'm sure there's plenty of room for all. We can work that out. What we can't abide," and her voice, Rogers thought, was almost queenly, "is an enemy in our midst. Either we come to an understanding or we will have to fight!"

"Enemy or ally? That's what you offer as compromise." The Simba's voice was steely and there was something needle sharp in it that froze everyone at the table. The creature took a long slow look around the company, then let his gaze linger on Joaquin. "We cannot be allies with Prl'oi!" He spat the words out, then made an evident effort at self-control. He spoke directly to the Prl'lu, "Oh yes, don't be surprised. We remember your kind well."

He rose from his crouch and turned to face Rogers squarely. "At one time the Prl'oi Empire was everywhere. It was the strongest, most vicious force in the galaxy but, like most warlike peoples, the Prl'oi found that wasn't enough. They needed victims to prove their strength. And they found them. We have no idea how many races were killed off or enslaved before they got to us, but get to us they did. We served them for a time, as slaves, as caretakers of this fleet. That was thousands of years before the supply ships stopped coming, before only a few overseers remained to keep us on the leash.

Once we were sure they weren't returning, it was only a matter of hours before the last Prl'oi in this fleet was dead. Our kind has lived here alone in peace ever since. Until you came.'' He pointed at Joaquin. "With these!''

Here was a problem Rogers had hoped never to face again. *Damn these Prl'oi,* he thought wryly, *for making themselves so unpopular wherever they went.* It reminded him of the "only good Indian is a dead Indian'' maxim of his day. The way the Prl'oi had made enemies, it was a wonder that any were left to cause all the rumpus back on Earth.

Without much hope, he launched back into his by now very pat lecture on the differences between various kinds of strangers. He concluded by pointing out that he and his kind had a real and present grudge against the Prl'oi. "After all,'' he said, "our fight is going on now. It isn't a candidate for the history books.''

Rogers stood up, walked around the table to where Joaquin was sitting, and put his hands on the Prl'lu's shoulders. "If anyone has cause to pick a fight with this man,'' he said, "we do. Since we don't, and since he and the rest of the Blackjacks have agreed to fight *alongside us* in our battle to retake Earth, I suggest,'' he paused and turned to Ruth, "what am I suggesting?''

"That the Simbas don't want to mess with us?''

"That's it!'' He leaned over the table so that he was face to face with the Simba. "Look, you're so anxious to punish the Prl'lu, then let me and my Rangers get on with our chores. There are plenty of ships here; we'll take what we need and that's all. For that, you're more than welcome to come along.'' Finished, he squared his shoulders and walked to the door. His people got up from their chairs and filed out ahead of him. He lingered for a moment to say, "That's it. That's our deal. We'll be waiting for your answer.'' Then he turned on his heels and walked from the room.

In the corridor, safely out of earshot, Ruth turned to

Rogers. "Well?" she said.

"Well what?"

"Do you think he's convinced?"

"How do you know it's a *he*?" Rogers asked curiously.

"I can tell. Now how about it? Do we have a war on our hands or what?"

"Well," Rogers hedged, "I think it's a little soon to declare a cease-fire, but we can make the first concession and see where that gets us."

"What do you mean?"

"Like you said, we might as well release the prisoners. If it comes to war, our twenty-six gremlins aren't going to make much of a difference for either side anyhow. We'll keep faith *and* get the guard detail back to construction work."

"Speaking of work . . ."

"I was afraid you would."

". . . strategic formation exercises are scheduled for this morning. And after all, you were telling me only the other day about hotfogging?"

"Hotdogging," Rogers said wearily. "Okay, let's get it over with."

Rogers hung suspended in a fragile bubble perched on the battle-station's perimeter. This was the nexus of the station's navigational and military nerve systems. A thousand subsystems measured, analyzed, tested, sampled, deduced, summarized, and passed along in signs and symbols the information vital to the most trivial aspect of the station's home economy. Other machines in a rigid hierarchy measured, analyzed, tested, sampled, deduced, summarized, and passed along that imformation in their own right. By the time those signs and symbols reached Rogers in his transparent shell they had been compressed, folded, and packaged into something approaching the limits of human comprehension. With his hands delicately flicking from one pulsing light to another, eyes flicking over a field of screens, Rogers was able to extend his reach throughout the station and beyond to the clutch of splinters in space that represented his armada. His Rangers.

With his eyes darting in concentration and his hands floating effortlessly above the control board, Rogers was giving a demonstration in an ancient art, one learned in his youth—hotdogging.

"Dammit! Coltrera. Let's see some vigor!

"Colson, get the lead out!

"Paulding, Roger. Pay attention, dive, dive, dive!

"Form up there! Wing A: Dave Prescott, report!"

"Yessir!" Prescott's voice snapped into the space around Rogers' ears.

"Prescott. Ride your wing in a crescent. Trak'tim, you too. Wing 6: follow suit!"

He ran his grid like a board game: plotting, reacting, shifting his players. It took all his concentration and not a little sweat. So he was pleased when a green telltale warned him that his shift was nearly over.

With a practiced eye he examined his board—it wouldn't do to leave any outstanding problems for the next man in rotation. The switchover itself was difficult enough. When Rogers felt a slight change in air pressure, he knew his relief had entered the bubble, but he didn't look up from the grid. Instead he waited until he could hear someone hovering at his back and without breaking stride or voice contact with his Wings, he made sure that an entire cycle had been run and demonstrated, for his relief's benefit. Then and only then did he flip the countdown. "SEVEN, SIX, FIVE, FOUR . . ."

He prepared to shift over. "TWO, ONE, ONE, TWO . . ." He was out of the command pod and his relief was already fully absorbed. It was only then that he saw it was Douglas. Good, he thought; he could trust Douglas.

Outside the bubble a small delegation was waiting for him.

"Tony," Ruth said, "word came a half hour ago. They're convinced! Mouka—that's the top Simba—

wants to meet with you to iron out the details."

"Fine. You've set it up?"

"In your quarters at seven. I've told Joaquin and Carberry to join us."

"Us?" Rogers asked with innocence.

"Don't even think it. You made me sit through the tryouts; I'm certainly not going to miss the performance. Understand?"

"Got it." Rogers turned to his chief of staff. "Our fighters are ready. How about the rest of the fleet?"

"Ready to fly, Marshall."

"That's what I wanted to hear."

That evening in his stateroom, Rogers faced the Simba leader. "We've got a deal?" Rogers asked.

"We've got a deal," the Simba said. "One thing though: we fight under separate command."

Rogers was up like a shot. "No way!" he said. "Either you sign on as Rangers or you stay behind the firing lines. That's all there is to it."

Mouka was flanked by four of his fellows, who stood stiffly erect. "We're agreeing to cooperate, not signing on as allies," he said. His friends nodded agreement. "We're with you, but separate."

Rogers made a show of impatience. There was no way he was going to relinquish control. He tried to put that across. Evidently it worked.

"Of course," Mouka said, "under actual firing conditions, we'll do our best to cooperate."

It wasn't much, but it was a start.

"Actually," Rogers said, "I was thinking of using your men in an independent role."

The alien leader looked pleased. "What are you driving at?"

"Well," Rogers said, "I've been training my Rangers as an elite attack force. We've had comparatively little ground experience and absolutely no infiltration practice. It occurs to me," he said wryly, "that months of actual sabotage experience should count for something. We could use your Simbas as preliminary shock troops. 'Chute you guys in. Wait for disorder and, bang, we'll start the war. All the time you'll be behind the lines keeping out of sight and doing what you do best. Hell, your size will make it work. Are you with me?''

Mouka held a hasty conference with his men. ''We're with you,'' he said.

''But you have to train with us!'' McNab was saying. ''There's no point in launching a haphazard attack.''

''We're not included in the attack force,'' one of the Simbas protested.

''That's no excuse for ignorance,'' McNab said.

He got his way.

''When we hit ground, we go for the nearest soldier. If we're clear we bag our 'chute.''

''You hit the ground. When I say hit I mean *dig*! Get into the ground! Burrow! *Then* you take the enemy. If you screw around, you're dead. If you advertise you're dead. Above all, don't get caught!''

''Sarge, what happens if we're caught? I mean . . .''

''Hang on until help comes. When in doubt, kick.''

''Your mission is to sneak into the Prl'lu cities and cause whatever damage you can. If possible, make it look like an accident. But cause that damage! Go for the heart and escalate. Whatever happens, remember you're gremlins!''

''Tony,'' Mouka drew Rogers aside. ''I think we're ready.''

''I think you're right.''

''Have you set a date?''

''Thursday.''

''Can't wait.''

Rogers was perched in the balloon. All over the ship people waited for the transition. Four hundred space-to-surface fighter craft hung off the battle-station's bow. With a flick of a switch, he signaled his armada to take flight. It was an unlikely fleet, ships of every size, shape, and purpose, whatever Rogers could figure a use for. And of course, whatever he could find a pilot for. As it was, he was leaving hundreds, maybe even thousands of ships behind, packed in mothballs as they'd been these thousands of years. Still, that was only equipment. It made him feel fine that nobody—human, Blackjack, or Simba—had elected to remain behind. This was one of those special moments when he felt he could do no wrong.

The battle-station was building up speed. Now it led the rest of the fleet and all Rogers could see from his bubble was a sparkling expanse of space. There were no signposts out here, no points of reference, but Rogers could tell by his instruments that the station hung on the very edge of the teleportal field—a space warp huge enough to swallow cubic miles of ether and whatever else drifted into it. The mathematics of the thing were beyond reckoning, or at least that's what Carberry said. "Just enjoy it," he had added.

Rogers had a pretty good idea that Carberry under- stood rather more than he let on. Certainly when he had prepared a flight plan his calculations had more physics than reckoning in them. None of this would have been possible without the kid, the hot young prof with the eager hands. Rogers was grateful, and suitably im- pressed; the kid was now a major.

It wouldn't be long now. FIVE, FOUR, it was com- forting to give up to numbers, THREE, it was so trite it helped, and TWO, and so we're down to ONE, and Rogers held his breath while space flipped and ONE, TWO, where was THREE, and space simply opened, they were home.

PART THREE

13.

The Prl'oi ship hung in space, one of six strung out through the solar system. Waiting and watching. On its bridge a bored officer wheeled his chair slowly in a semicircle, checking in turn the dials and flashing scopes that would reveal anything unusual, any unaccountable presence in its huge sphere of surveillance.

For months nothing, not even a stray chunk of rock. On the limits of its farthest scrutiny, nothing. Out here, far from the warmth of the inner planets, the desolation was near complete. The officer sometimes stirred himself to curse the crummy luck that had placed him back of the beyond on a pointless errand. Not very often and never out loud. Shak't'kan's displeasure was to be feared always; besides, even cursing took too much effort.

Only five shared the ship with him; only two shared his monthly shift. The three others were frozen away in stasis. In nine more days they would be awoken and the new shift would begin. For a month they would take turns in this seat, eight hours on, sixteen off. The days never varied.

The circuit completed, he slowly prepared to swing his chair back. He'd never bothered to count how many circuits he made in a shift: five hundred, a thousand, more? But he'd made a bit of a game of it. The trick was to push off just hard enough so that the chair on its casters ran out of steam as he reached the far end of the board. So he rode all night back and forth. A childish game, but it passed the hours.

He braced his long legs against a gray metal bulkhead and counted down to the moment he'd push off. He liked the feeling of anticipation.

He was good at this; he could glance at the board and detect a minute change in any one of the dials without a second look as he rolled by, quickly at first and then slower as his momentum died down. It helped that the ship was kept at an efficient half-gravity.

This time as he rolled by he saw something wrong, something more than a minute change. Damn, he couldn't believe his eyes! Nothing like this, it couldn't be true, it had never been anticipated! Then he was scrambling awkwardly to get up out of the rolling chair. Under the half-gravity, it wasn't so easy. The seat was still moving quite swiftly on its casters and when he planted his feet on the steel floor, chair and officer suddenly took an undignified tumble.

It was a clumsy fall, stealing vital moments of control. He hit the steel deck hating fate, duty, and the rest, knowing he might already be a dead man.

Raising himself woozily from the floor, he peered at the board. What he saw made him feel ill, but he staggered to his feet and forced himself to hit the proper sequence of buttons. He slumped back to the floor and sat staring dully at the console until his shift relief came pounding into the cabin. It was already too late and not a shot had been fired.

On the screen, space was filled with a bright flashing mosaic of light. The glare filled the screen and he saw that his instruments had not lied, this was a visitation, a death.

The cloud of light bore down swiftly, hugely. Soon the screen as well as the instruments were delineating size and mass and number—an armada such as the officer had never dreamed. He and his fellow officers stood motionless, unnerved by the onrushing sight.

The ships were upon them, then all around. Hundreds of them, circling, flashing, finding their mark and toying with the victim. The officer shared a speechless last moment, watching his fellows prepare for death. He noticed with some satisfaction that neither had thought to look to the beacon. It was flashing warning red, activated when he'd punched the alarm, indicating that the lasered message was sent off. Whatever happened, Shak't'kan would soon have a report. And he alone had thought to perform his duty in the hour of death. It was some consolation.

No it wasn't.

Las Vegas.

Maybe it was a boomtown. Certainly it was beginning to show new signs of permanence. Even street signs had begun to show up in the part of the city the provisionals had marked out for their use.

The city was an oddity, in a way almost a reproach. Alone among the larger American cities it survived nearly intact, advertising an age when man was free to commit follies on the grandest scale.

Why it had survived was anybody's guess. Of no military value, it had missed out on the near total destruction visited on other, less fortunate cities, those that had participated more fully in the Third World War. Isolated, the aftermath of war had passed it by. Maybe the city survived because it was itself a folly, a last-chance saloon perpetuated in an uncaring desert. Those few who came here had nowhere else to go, and they looked out for the town. No water, no crops, no point. Five centuries in the perfect weather of the desert had preserved the empty city like a dessicated corpse.

Rogers had visited it once, in the days before Shak't'kan. He'd looked forward to it, had expected to feel right at home in this last remaining relic of the twentieth century. He'd been wrong, maybe even a little hurt. The city held no place for him, no nostalgia in either his past or present lives. He cut short his stay.

But now Las Vegas was home to the Provisional Government of North America. It was roomy, central, out of sight, and above all available.

Besides, the troops liked it.

•   •   •

Lu-An was walking across the compound at a brisk pace toward the auditorium in the Sands Hotel, or what was left of it, where they had made their administrative offices. Falstaff ran to catch up with her.

The heat in the summer sun was surprising. Falstaff was gasping by the time she reached the Han princess. "How is it?"

Lu-An flashed a smile, "Runner just came in. News from the East, from Colorado."

Falstaff took her arm and stopped her. "Bad news or good?"

"Bad." Her tone was short.

"The trustees?"

"Well, if we get a move on, we'll get the news first."

"Hope so." They started back toward the auditorium. "Look," Falstaff said, "the trustees don't matter if you aren't on our side. Are you ready to declare war or not?"

"Don't you think we need more time?"

"I do not!" She flushed. "And I don't think you do!"

Lu-An went on a few steps in silence, then she turned to the Aussie and smiled. "Good," she said. "Of course you're right. We're as ready as we'll ever be—but there's more to consider."

"Like what?"

"Like the fact that we have no communication, no network, no system! How can we attack? Isn't that what this conference has been deciding?"

"Well the conference has been deciding wrong, and the trustees are a scared bunch of turkeys. You must know that! Why, this is our only shot. When are things going to get better?"

"Holcomb says the Prl'oi are moving into the sea cities."

"And then we'll be better off? Do you know how to fight a city in the sea? Look, at worst we'll be forced back underground. We're already fugitives, so what? The point is, we ought to be fighting a war of attrition. *Then* if we get a break we could win."

Lu-An smiled cautiously. "Well you've got my vote,

and I hope we can convince the rest of the council, but you see what we're up against. What kind of break do you see us getting?''

"Oh, something we're working on back in Sydney."

"You've been holding out on me, my friend."

"Not really. Just waiting for a chance to put a private word in."

"Well, it will have to wait," Lu-An said, suddenly preoccupied. She was watching a small crowd collect before the Sands' entrance. "It seems news of our guest has got around. We'll talk afterward."

Inside the auditorium there was more than a small crowd. It seemed as though most of Las Vegas had assembled there. As Lu-An walked in the door, the crowd parted to admit her. She walked steadily toward its center, confident that there she would find the runner from Colorado.

She was right enough, though when she reached him she might have wished she was wrong. He was a tall man, tan and lean, and she knew him too well. He was a blow-hard and braggart. Worst of all, she suspected he was questionably committed to the cause. He was giving the crowd a mouthful and none of it good.

"Colorado looks bad, friends. Real bad. We need provisions and we know where to get them. Yes, we've been offered winter stakes by the Prl'oi. I'm not saying we'll take them. Not saying we shouldn't, but in Colorado most of us see no reason to keep up this war. We go our way, the Prl'lu go theirs . . .''

His reception wasn't exactly cordial, but he wasn't doing morale any good either. When Lu-An burst through the crowd, she turned in front of the runner and addressed everybody. "I'm sure Cord will have a lot more to say to you later, but the trustees and I really must ask him some questions first. So if you'll please . . .''

The audience started breaking up, though unhappy mutterings could be heard. Still, Lu-An had little or no opposition as she firmly led the runner to her private office. Falstaff stepped smartly behind.

When the door was closed behind them, Lu-An demanded, "What do you think you're doing!"

"Just telling it the way it is, Princess," Cord sneered.

"Your mouth may have gotten you into serious trouble," Lu-An warned.

Cord pulled himself up and carefully planted his feet on the floor. It was almost comic, Falstaff thought, the show he made of menace. "And what are you going to do about it, Princess?"

Lu-An walked behind her desk and sat down. She motioned to Falstaff to take a chair and then she fingered an intercom. She raised her voice to be heard clearly in its microphone, "Moore, please send in a couple of guards." She turned to Cord, "I'm putting you away," she said, "for the duration."

After Cord had been removed, protesting loudly, and the door firmly closed behind him, Lu-An relaxed behind the desk. "What do you think?"

"I think he's a fool."

"Granted, but what if what he says is true?"

"What of it? Shak't'kan's just trying to confuse us, split our people. Of course he can suborn Cord, Colorado, anybody he can reach—*until* the fighting starts. Once he shows his true colors, his credibility has had it. Nobody will dare deal with him then. And," Falstaff raised her voice to make the point, "it's in our power to tip his hand."

"True; we can start the operation any time we choose. But is it safe, are we ready? And, frankly, after Cord's little scene, I wonder just how much Shak't'kan already knows about our plans."

"Quite a bit, I'm sure, not that it does him any good. We plan on waging a guerrilla war; our forces are already dispersed and poised. It's not *what* we plan to do that he needs to know, it's where and when and since we haven't decided ourselves . . ."

"All right, all right. Tell me," Lu-An asked, "do you think we have any other less obvious traitors in camp?"

"Possibly, even probably. Shak't'kan certainly had more than ample opportunity to approach all the L.A.

escapees. Still, as I said, it hardly matters in this kind of war."

"Even so, I think I'll ask Holcomb to screen the escapees just in case."

"Fair enough, and now I'd like to tell you something that would make a difference if it did get out, a really serious difference. That's why I've waited so long to tell you."

"And why you were sent to the conference?" Lu-An's tone was shrewd.

"Precisely."

"Well, what's the news?"

"Something that might win the war for us."

"Don't be so mysterious, out with it."

"A pre-collapse submarine pen in Sydney Harbor."

Lu-An was speechless. Falstaff grinned happily.

After a few moments the princess quietly asked, "In working order?"

"Should be by now. They were close when I left."

"And the armaments?"

"Three Triton-class nuclear submarines. That won't mean anything to you, I guess; it didn't mean much to our people at the start, but take it from me that we've got some pretty intense firepower at our disposal."

"Shak't'kan's sea-cities . . ." Lu-An said, wonderingly.

"They'll be no problem."

"This will take some thinking."

"So think on it. Now I've got to be off. Running some troops through their paces this afternoon."

"Don't work 'em too hard."

Falstaff grinned, "I'll try and remember that."

Lu-An was laughing. "Holcomb, try to behave. We have work to do." It was late in the early desert evening.

Holcomb wasn't having any. He was bounding around the empty gambling floor, throwing showers of chips, emptying the boxes of coins in the cashier's pit and shouting hilariously, "You mean it? Submarines? My god, we could win this war!" He gave a loud warwhoop that filled the old casino and shook the dust from the hangings. "So we're set. We win!"

Lu-An said, "Not so fast, buster. A few things have got to be settled before we can even begin it properly."

Holcomb's enthusiasm wasn't that easily dashed though. "Sure, we're set. What's left to do? The troops are ready, Falstaff's seen to that; why I hear the people in Oregon knocked out an airship just last week. What's left to be done?"

"For one thing," Lu-An's voice was suddenly low and serious. "I want to talk to you about spying."

Startled, Holcomb stopped suddenly and sat down. He felt winded and bloodless.

Lu-An went on. "You've heard about that little scene with Cord this afternoon, haven't you?"

Rather dully, Holcomb said yes.

"Pay attention! Well, afterwards Falstaff and I decided that there was a good chance we had a spy in camp, probably one of the L.A. escapees. Got you so far?"

"Yes." The pit of his stomach felt black and bilious.

"I'd like you to give some thought to who it might be, screen the likely suspects, that sort of thing. All right by you?" Lu'An's tone said that the matter was done with, just another thing to be checked and rechecked before the great day.

Holcomb was having trouble finding his breath, but he summoned enough of it up to say, "Sure, no problem. Anything special you have to go on?"

"Nope, just a hunch, but see it through. Now what's say we go find Falstaff, throw a private party, and light up the joint!"

Holcomb let himself be persuaded.

It was nearly dawn. The desert sun, quick to set, early to rise, was already tingeing the desert. The frail blossoms of the cactus were shutting for the hot day and Holcomb was perched a few miles from the city on a low butte, nervously working a radio transmitter.

"L.A. Come in, L.A."

It took a few minutes, but he got through. He was impressed. Shak't'kan must have arranged to have his channel monitored around the clock.

"L.A. to friend. Come in."

Holcomb felt rushed and impatient. He gave that impression over the radio. "L.A. report is as follows. Provisional troops are ill-prepared, nervous, and generally unready for combat. Their officers know this only too well, since they are little better. Their plans are ill-organized at best, but they cling to the cut-and-run philosophy they've been using so far. They think they can hound you into a treaty. We've heard some word here that you've made an offer to the Coloradans and even the princess is encouraged. If you made some such offer now, I have a feeling most of them would jump at it. By winter you'll have them eating out of your hand."

A new voice interrupted the airwave. "Holcomb?"

He started. No one had any business using his name over the radio; he felt like smashing the thing, then he recognized the voice. "Shak't'kan!"

"That's right. I've heard your report, anything to add?"

"Nothing."

"That's good. I like brevity. But I have a few questions to ask. How many of the human troops do you think are in Las Vegas now?"

"Oh, most of them."

"But you don't think they're well prepared?"

"No." He tried to sound emphatic.

"Then," Shak't'kan's voice was slow and slimy, at least Holcomb thought so, "what's to keep me from taking care of the problem now?"

"Take care of it?"

"Never mind. I'm pleased by your report. Over."

"Shak't'kan? Shak't'kan, L.A. do you read me? Damn it!" He slammed down his radio and then, after a moment's consideration, found a bit of loose sandstone and carefully pounded his radio into gravel.

Then he started the long walk back to camp. He hated it; it gave him too much opportunity to think. He'd chosen up sides, once with Rogers, once with Shak't'kan, and now it was Lu-An. Just crazy. He was acting just crazy. And the worst of it was he'd thought he'd be able to quietly make up his indiscretions by turning in a bogus report.

He'd thought!

He needed to kick himself. God, it wasn't enough. He should throw himself over the butte. He hadn't quietly made up for anything! God, he'd heard it in Shak't-'kan's voice. There was no deal coming, no grace period. The Prl'arek thought all the troublemakers' eggs were in one basket. He was sending a mission to wipe out Las Vegas and everyone in it.

Including Lu-An.

And what could Holcomb do?

14.

"Do you think he's on the level?"

"Why not," Rogers answered grimly, "if I were him, I wouldn't go out of my way to report how badly we're doing down there."

The prisoner sat on the edge of a white hospital table. Ruth had just finished splinting and casting his leg.

"What about his ship? Any clues there?"

"Nothing much. Carberry still hasn't figured how to get the three Prl'lu out of stasis and the other two died when Douglas and his men boarded. No records, no nothing. Shak't'kan evidently doesn't run a decentralized command."

"What about Shak't'kan, any news there?"

Rogers laughed. "Well, I assume he's on his way. That ship was broadcasting a red alert that half the universe could have heard. I think we'd better be prepared for a helluva fight!"

As heir apparent, second in command, and chief rival for Shak't'kan's authority, Sataspes had been ap-

pointed to lead the defending space armada. His father
had made sure of it.

His fleet numbered the original patrol ships, minus
the one that had sounded the alert, eighteen other
cruisers with little enough firepower; he had just one
secret weapon of note, his flagship, the *Wrangr*.

And somewhere out there he planned to engage the
enemy.

Whoever they were.

Three days out, they'd had no luck finding, much less
engaging with, an enemy. Shak't'kan was being less
than understanding about the delay.

"Sataspes! I demand an explanation." His voice was
hard over the communicator.

"I have none, my lord."

"Have you sent out scouts?"

"No, my lord," Sataspes answered reluctantly.

"Why not!" Shak't'kan was roaring. "I specifically
ordered a reconnaissance first."

"My lord, considering the size of our fleet, I felt it
unwise to break formation. We have little enough
firepower as it stands."

"Sataspes, when you are First Lord of the Empire,
then you may think for yourself. Until then you will
obey my orders!"

"But, my lord . . ."

"Results, Sataspes. No '*buts*,' it's not like you."
Shak't'kan's voice was dry.

"No, my lord."

"Really, I question your intelligence. Find me our
adversary, Sataspes. And find out who they are. Tomorrow!"

The com piece suddenly buzzed static. Sataspes put it
down and turned to the watch officer. "I'll be in my
stateroom. Have Commander Teaspes report there."
He marched abruptly off the bridge.

Fifteen minutes later found him in a fine rage, pacing
his stateroom while Teaspes sat and gave him time to
vent his anger.

"My intelligence! He dares question my intelligence! And throws his position in my face, *my* face. Really, Teaspes, it is too much . . .

"He *orders* me to deploy our fleet. To what purpose should I deploy our fleet? If there's an enemy out here, I'll find it without diluting our forces."

"My lord," Teaspes interrupted, "do I gather you have another purpose?"

Sataspes looked up for the first time and caught Teaspes with a stone-hard stare. "Are you merely curious, Teaspes, or are you pumping me?"

"Anxious to do my duty. Only that, my lord."

"Your duty to whom? To me, or," Sataspes's voice was bitter, "to my father?"

"To you, my lord." Teaspes allowed himself a thin smile. "My fortunes are linked with yours, are they not?"

Sataspes stood still, appraising for a long moment his second in command. "They are," he said finally, "and they rise and fall as mine. Am I understood?"

"Perfectly, my lord."

"In that case, I do have a plan and you will figure in it. If not, then . . ." his words hung for a moment in the air, "you will find it better to remain in space. Clear enough?"

"Very clear, my lord."

"Well?"

"As you say, I will figure in it."

"Good. As you may have guessed, it has never been my intention to break up this fleet. I'm going to need it when we return to Earth, *all of it* in one fighting body. We will go through with these foolish maneuvers in search of some patrolship that probably mistook an asteroid for an attack force; then I will return to Earth as First Lord of the Empire. My Lord Shak't'kan has given me the sword of his undoing!"

The planet Saturn swung around the sun in its uninterrupted cycle, until now unvisited by the affairs of man.

Inclined to the plane of its orbit around the sun by 27

degrees, Rogers' flagship battle-station swung unseen
but seeing in the cover of Saturn's rings.

They were waiting. Waiting to see what Shak't'kan
would choose to throw their way. They didn't have to
wait long.

"The fools," Rogers repeated with the broadest grin
of his life, "the damn fools." He was studying the op-
center screen with the kind of glee he'd once reserved
for moving-picture shows. To no one's great enlightenment, he said, "It's Bunker Hill all over!"

"I take it that's good?" Ruth said.

"Better than good, it's classic. The redcoats march up
in formation, goose-stepping all the way to the cemetery
and the regulars, the minutemen—that's us—spring up
from behind every rock and blade of grass, ragtag and
barefoot, and we cut them down like so many logs."

"Meaning, I assume, that you've got a strategy in
mind?"

"Got it in one."

The screen showed Sataspes's fleet hanging in space
in a perfectly proportioned, compact cone. The *Wrangr*
was positioned at its apex, a sharp, angry point of light.

It made a formidable, gaudy, even breathtaking sight.
In comparison, the haphazard wing formation em-
ployed by Rogers was inelegant, chaotic and, he hoped,
unfair, sly and deadly. Not that Sataspes in his flagship
could have even an inkling that Rogers' armada was
deployed, as stellar distances go, right under his nose.
The attacking fleet was lying in wait, appearing like just
so much more debris in the rings of Saturn.

"Wings report!"

"Wing Able reports ready and sighting, Marshall!"

"Good, let me talk to them." Rogers was handed the
com piece, "McNab?"

"Got you, Marshall!"

"Good luck."

"Wing Beauregard?"

"All here, Marshall." Douglas's twang came through
loud and clear.

"Remember this is a hit-and-run operation; deliver

your packages and then hightail it out o' there.''

"Wing Charlie . . . Wing Dempsey . . . Exodus . . .''
The roll went on, and for each wing commander Rogers
had a word of luck, advice, or just friendship. He knew
that every man waiting for battle would be listening to
his words, many of them in single-man fighters, where
they would have little else to occupy their minds. Finally
he called down to the bubble, "We ready, Joaquin?''

"All set, Tony!''

Rogers turned to Ruth, "That's it then, we're ready
to roll.'' He scratched his head, and looked slightly
puzzled.

"What's the matter?'' Ruth sounded alarmed.

He smiled, "Just didn't want to forget anything.
O.K.,'' he snapped into the com, "let's go, Rangers!''

The ships flashed out of Saturn's rings, disengaging
themselves from the exuberant color into brilliant splinters of light. They swung in wide parabolic trajectories
toward the Prl'oi armada.

It took them only minutes to cross space and engage
the fleet. The Prl'oi ships had no time to react, no time
to go to alert. Rogers' Rangers were everywhere,
dashing here and there, diving on likely targets and just
as swiftly pounding past, out of reach.

The Prl'oi casualties in the first minutes of battle were
heavy, heavy enough to shatter the cone and leave most
of its ships isolated from their fellows. Dis beams and
laser cannons were in use on both sides. This kind of
fighting allowed for no survivors; when a ship was hit, it
patched itself as best it could or disintegrated in a perfect sphere of flame.

The laser cannon traced a web of light in the thinning
atmosphere of the exploded ships. Rogers' men soon
found that in the core of the cone the danger of being hit
by a rocketing piece of shrapnel was more real, and less
easily eluded, than the pursuing fireworks of a Prl'lu
gunnery officer.

Sataspes shouted into his com, "Regroup! Regroup

. . . What was that?'' The flagship rocked woodenly beneath his feet.

"Hit, my lord."

"Teaspes, damage report!"

The Prl'arek second officer looked strained and irritated, "Nothing we can't handle my lord, but what of the fleet?"

Sataspes looked to his tactical officer.

"The reports are coming in now, my lord, the patrol ships are gone!"

"And the cruisers?"

"Three at least have been hit."

"Order the fleet to regroup around the *Wrangr*! Nothing is to be allowed through."

"Yes, my lord."

"Marshall? Wing Farragut, Coltrera."

"Coltrera, come in."

"They're reforming, sir, what's left of them, around their flagship. It's going to be hard to get through." He sounded clipped and matter-of-fact. That pleased Rogers. The Rangers were handling themselves well.

"Casualties?"

"Light so far, thank god, but it's bound to get worse!"

"So what else is new? Carry on!"

"Wing Dempsey, come in, this is Rogers."

"Balfour here."

"Where are you guys? If you haven't noticed, the battle's this way."

"Marshall, we've cut out three cruisers and are in pursuit. Do you want us to turn back?" Balfour sounded reluctant.

"Putting up much of a fight?"

"I'll say! But we'll get them, if you like, Marshall."

"Go to it, but be sure you come back."

"Aye-aye."

Douglas threw his two-man fighter into a steep dive.

He wanted to penetrate the sphere forming around the Prl'oi flagship and put a few licks in down inside.

The Prl'oi cruisers were tight now around the flagship. It was going to be tough to get in, but he knew maneuverability was in his favor. That sphere of ships made it nearly impossible for the flagship to defend itself without chancing a stray hit on its fellows. For that matter, it couldn't dodge.

Or cut and run.

He swept down on the ship, saving his payload for the last minute. In this kind of fight it was hard to tell whether you were being fired on, unless you were actually hit. As he neared his target he began to think they hadn't seen him; he'd come up on their blind side. He prepared to take aim. "Steady, Matt," he called over his shoulder.

And they were cut open. A dis beam licked through space and flashed through the cabin, disintegrating everything in its way.

"Marshall, Marshall! We've lost Douglas!"

"Who's this?"

"Henley, sir."

"Henley, you're appointed wing commander, Beauregard."

"Yes, sir."

"We've got to crack that defensive sphere!" Rogers stood under the screen, gripping the edge of the console so that his fingers showed white. "Ruth, I'm moving the battle-station up. Tell Joaquin. Any new reports on casualties?"

"Twenty-eight ships, Tony."

"All right. I'm calling the fighters out, at least for a moment. Have them fly the fringes and make sure nothing gets away."

Ruth started working the com board while Rogers watched the lights on the big screen tally up what was left of the fight, for both sides. The Rangers looked good; he knew he should be encouraged, but the deaths hurt. He knew they'd hurt more when he had time to think about it.

"My lord, the battle-station is closing on us fast."

"And the other ships?"

"Retreated for the moment, sir, but hovering just outside our sphere."

Sataspes paced his bridge. Of his twenty-four ships, only six remained: the *Wrangr* and five cruisers; certainly not enough to stave off this incredible armada. And the cruisers were immobile. To move one, even for an instant, would crack his defensive sphere wide open and leave the *Wrangr* defenseless.

Defenseless in all respects save one—its nuclear armament. He could use that on the battle-station: It probably wouldn't knock it out of the sky, but it might give him a chance to get away—if he dared lift his sphere, which he didn't. His anger was turning to fear.

"Teaspes, your recommendations?"

"We go on fighting, my lord, until the end."

"Idiot! I need a way to get out of this."

"I understand my lord," Teaspes's voice was carefully blank, "but I don't think we can without sacrificing the fleet."

"*The fleet.* What fleet have we left? We must save the *Wrangr*."

"Five cruisers, my lord."

"What of them? Do you know a way?" Sataspes sounded confounded by events. Then he caught some straw in Teaspes's answer. "Tell me, how can I sacrifice the cruisers and save the *Wrangr*?" Sataspes was frightened and it showed. The note in his voice made Teaspes ill and he could see that the bad taste was shared by everyone on the bridge. This puling wreck was no fit commander!

When he replied his voice was cold. "I refuse to tell you, my lord."

"Refuse? I order you. I'll have you killed."

"As you wish, my lord."

Sataspes jerked a knife from his belt. "Tell me now!"

Teaspes turned his back and began to busy himself at the op board. He caught the knife between his shoulder blades and died almost instantly.

"Marshall?"

"Yes, Joaquin."

"We're in position and ready. What are your orders?"

"Let's lay down some fire and see if we can't crack the shell."

"How close do you want to get?"

"I want to see right down their throats."

Sataspes pulled the dead Prl'lu out of his seat with a hand lent the strength of panic. With the other, he roughly grabbed the young strat officer and forced him down in front of the op board.

"Yes, my lord."

"Arm the nuclear rockets!" The boy fingered the controls until a row of green lights shone brightly on his board.

"Draw coordinates on the approaching battle-station." The boy began to punch in the figures, then saw something he didn't like and checked them again. "But, my lord, two of our cruisers are also in that vector!"

Sataspes stood directly behind the boy, reached down, and grabbed him again by the throat. "Do *exactly* as I say!" The boy entered the coordinates.

"Now when I give the signal, I want you to fire in two bursts of three; the second burst should be timed precisely fifteen seconds after the first. Understood?"

"Yes, my lord."

"Precisely thirty seconds after that, I want you to make a course back to Earth, understood?"

"Yes, my lord."

If only his plan worked, it would leave three cruisers intact and able to delay pursuit. The other two cruisers, well, their sacrifice would buy him that tiny gap in the curtain he needed, that tiny instant he needed to loose rockets against the battle-station. It was a small enough sacrifice if it bought safety for the *Wrangr* and its crew.

Or so he thought when the firing began.

"Marshall, we're exchanging fire."
"Well, this is it, Ruth. Shall we go in for the kill?"
"Why not?" she said.

Sataspes's perimeter of cruisers was beginning to break up under Rogers' constant fire. The battle-station seemed perilously close. Sataspes ordered the rockets and when the boy seemed to pause, Sataspes slammed his hand down on the board a second too soon.

"Rogers, three missiles approaching!"
"Cut power! Hands alert!"
In his lap, it seemed to Rogers, the two Prl'oi cruisers suddenly exploded into immense fireballs. He watched them grow and take shape in the screen, like a pair of dumbbells, each growing larger until the bells merged into a single ball of flaming light. Before that could dissipate, something else ignited its center and it grew until Rogers knew its wash would engulf them.
"Hit the deck!" he tried to shout . . .
It hit him.

15.

"Are they gaining?"
"Perhaps a little."
Sataspes stood motionless on his bridge.

Rogers eased himself gingerly into a chair and decided against rubbing his shoulder—the motion would only make some other part of his body hurt. He was sitting in the commissary with Ruth and Joaquin and informally assessing the situation.

"I think we're in good shape," Ruth was saying, "much better than we have any right to expect. Most of us came through intact. Only thirty-four dead and well over a thousand of us left alive; we know the military situation back on Earth; we've fought our first battle, whipped Shak't'kan's space fleet, and survived a nuclear explosion, though," she winced, "I admit the last has left me feeling a little peaked."

Rogers was less sanguine. "Shak't'kan seems to have Earth firmly in hand. We'll need more than our pleasant faces to do as well there. And," he emphasized, "if that character in the flagship gets back before we do, it'll be just too bad. By now he must know a great deal about us."

"To what purpose, Tony?" Joaquin said. "We know from the prisoners that we've virtually finished their space fleet off; how can it help them to have the particulars on ours?"

"For that matter, how does it help us?" Tony replied sourly.

"A point. Still, we've just won a battle, let's not give up the ghost yet." Joaquin bestowed one of his infrequent smiles on the two humans. "There'll be time enough for that when we get to this Earth of yours."

Earth swam in the screen, blue and wet like a healthy pupil. Rogers didn't know why the image occurred to him—must be because his own were feeling decidedly raw. Even so, he could tell he had all the appropriate emotions at coming home; he knew because his stomach felt empty. He decided to fill it.

They called him from lunch when Sataspes's ship was sighted entering the atmosphere. It made a fine bright yellow splash as it entered the atmosphere with a little too much abandon, straightened out for awhile, and flew straight until it plummeted into Los Angeles harbor. By rights, Rogers reflected, that landing should have killed everyone aboard. He had a sneaking feeling that in this his proverbial luck wasn't going to hold.

Carberry was around somewhere, working an orbiting vector and practicing unholy mathematics on one of his female assistants. His crew had become rambunctious since the battle, Rogers thought.

Finally Rogers was told that they were in orbit. He gathered his inner group of officers and friends and took over the com controls himself. It was time to broadcast his first message to Earth; he wanted to make it good. He decided that no defense could equal the propaganda appeal of a good old-fashioned offensive rally, so he chose his words with a fine sense of the vernacular and a better memory; he took his text from Mr. Woodrow Wilson, humanitarian and once President of the United States of America.

> This may come as a shock to some of you—I hope it won't spoil your day—but this is Marshall Tony Rogers, come back to see what can be done to make Earth safe for the ultimate peace and liberation of all its peoples, human and Prl'lu both.
>
> If some among you are surprised that I declare this to be a war to end all war between all people, listen to me! Humankind is just one of the champions of rights due all of us. In this fight against Shak't'kan's tyranny, Prl'lu, and, yes, others, will join us in our struggle until those rights have been made as secure as the faith and freedom of all people can make them.
>
> Well, enough of intentions. My fleet, Rogers' Rangers, positioned just beyond Earth's atmosphere, has just closed with Shak't'kan's space force: we destroyed eighteen cruisers, five patrol vessels and, and, if I'm not mistaken, the Prl'lu flagship, just now wrecked in L.A. harbor.
>
> Shak't'kan, you have fair warning, keep out of our space, stay in your holes; we're here!
>
> Now I'd like to address the Provisional Government of North America, and for that matter, any patriot group within earshot.
>
> We *can* win this war. Up here we need to be filled in; you need our help. The Rangers *can* help.
>
> So hit them where it hurts!
>
> Cut and run if you have to!
>
> But please, help us do our part by doing your part. And most of all, report in. Our flagship will act as a

clearinghouse for all patriot activity around the globe.

Our object is, of course, to win the war. We shall be willing and glad to pay the full price of peace!

Sataspes was looking pretty bedraggled. He'd been hauled in right after the crash by a pair of husky guards, who had carefully guarded his identity all the way from the submerged wreck of the ill-fated *Wrangr*.

Taking a guess, it looked like his father didn't expect to make his miraculous escape public. And there could only be one reason for that.

All in all, Sataspes was in a bad temper.

When his father entered the room, Sataspes looked every way but up. Shak't'kan didn't care much about that, but he did care a great deal about several other things, including ineptitude, inefficiency, and moral incontinence. Evidently his son had been guilty of all three. In any case, he wasn't a gladdening sight.

"You realize that your stupidity is all over the airwaves?"

"No, my lord," Sataspes bowed humbly, "I didn't." What interested Shak't'kan was that he didn't deny the charge of stupidity.

"Well, what do you have to say for yourself?"

"We fought well, my lord, but were outnumbered."

"And mightn't you have prevented your misfortune by deploying scouts?"

The reply was reluctant. "Under the circumstances, yes."

"And you admit you disobeyed my orders?"

"Absolutely."

"Don't," Shak't'kan's tone was firm, "take this inquiry lightly. I have not, as you may have supposed, formed my opinion as yet. I await your maturity."

Sataspes was astonished, "My what?"

"That moment in which you finally decide to measure your sinecure against your too obvious ambitions."

"Go on!"

"No need to. I know all about it. All I want of you, understand, is obedience." Shak't'kan's tone was dry. "You must plot your treachery on your own time. I'm afraid much more pressing matters than the correction of a wayward son occupy my time. I should have you killed.''

Satespes drew himself up. "Do with me as you will!''

"Oh, I will, I will.'' Shak't'kan was unimpressed. He motioned to the guards and left his son in their capable hands.

Rogers, come in, Rogers. This is the Yellow Springs Expeditionary Force trying to raise Marshall Rogers!

We are under attack! We are under attack! Don't need your services as yet, but keep us in mind. Have just destroyed two Prl'lu airships and a generating plant. Keep us in mind! Rogers, come in. . . .

Marshall Rogers. Welcome back home! This is the Oregon Task Army, wishing you well. All Prl'lu in this area had better look out, that's all I can say! Actually none have come our way yet. Send us some, will you?

. . . in combat, repeat, are engaged in combat with Prl'lu force numbering three to four thousand, broken-field fighting, but the airships are killing us. Can you help Denver? Come in, please. In combat. . . .

"Damn it," Rogers said, "I wish there was more we could do. More *I* could do.''

"You've done enough, Tony,'' Ruth pleaded. "There's no reason to come unstrung because you can't be everywhere. Hell, sacrifice is what war's all about.''

Rogers pulled a long face, then smiled. "Wars are for a bunch of things, Ruth; they're never *about* anything. That's a distinction I think has some importance. Career officers and fools might find an art in war; all I find is purpose, and to tell you the truth I'm not big on purposes either. No war ends war for very long; war only ends lives. Still, I eat what they set before me.''

"Well, now that we're here, just what do you plan to do? You know, simply because you're back, people all over Earth will be taking heart, taking up the fight again. We've got our manpower; how do you plan to use it?''

"I've been thinking about it, believe me. I suppose it

would be a mistake to scatter our forces too much. That's my principal worry. No, I think we have to wait up here until we can sort the situation out; then we can figure where we'll get the most return for our efforts. You know, though, I hope we're finally called into North America. That's where I have my ear to the ground. Anyhow, I have a hunch that the fight'll be there."

Rogers paused and spent a time studying Earth in the screen. "Look, Ruth, you know as well as I do that there's going to be no easy solution. Sure, with luck we'll win this war, but after it's over, well, I hate to think of the problems. This planet needs one government to mop up and keep the place safe; after that industry has to be started, and commerce, and we've got the means now to explore the galaxy! That's going to come into it. In my time we had a theory that the only healthy society was an expanding society. Back then we were running out of space, but never again! Anyhow, I have an idea that you'd be pretty good running all this. After the war, we won't need a military government or any taint of the military. At least, that's the way I feel, and that's why I don't want to have anything to do with running the show once this is over." He grinned. "I'll find better things to do."

"Well, I can't doubt that. You always seem to come up with something, Tony." Ruth suddenly smiled. "Just remember, you aren't the only person around here in the market for fast times and a hard life. I mean it, Tony. I'll stick by you through thick and through thin. I even hope it'll be a bit thick."

Rogers looked at her seriously. "I'll remember that."

Ruth was embarrassed. "Better get back to work, I guess."

"I guess."

"Tony?"

"Yeah?"

"Things are going to work out, aren't they? I mean we're going to win this?"

"I hope so, Ruth. I really do."

•   •   •

Holcomb sat on the edge of his bunk, arms propped on his knees, face buried in his hands. From time to time he looked up and stared bleakly at the ancient concrete block walls and recently renewed paint of the old hotel room. He knew what he had to do; he just didn't know how to do it.

Funny, five hundred years ago a weekly supply of lives must have paraded through this room, lived it up awhile and then, unless Lady Luck had smiled on them, as it did so rarely in life, unless. . . .

He wondered how many had had to cover their faces, had had to blot out the memories, had been unable to. How many had slid open these glass doors, now purple with the desert sun, slid them open and greeted the dawn of a new day by sliding a leg across the rail. One leg and then slowly the other, taking some delight in its quiet, precise, lifelong workings. Two legs poised over the drop and then a sudden almost involuntary heave and that was that, the end of questions.

Possibly one or two. Probably most had only thought about it, as he was thinking about it. They hadn't the courage, or just possibly they had a reason to live. Did he have a reason to live?

It was a question worth pondering.

On the minus side he saw Shak't'kan's leering face, heard his last words in the communicator, sensed the airships flying this way to deliver death and more shame.

On the plus side, nothing, except that he couldn't do it, not without spending some more time with Lu-An. Spend it how? By rights, outlining what Shak't'kan was likely to do, what he knew. What he wanted, though, was to hold her body near his and feel that delicious, compact strength—then maybe he could die well. Or even live a while longer.

It was time, there was no more time, his blood pulsed with the sense of time running out and his solid strong face twitched with the thought. He put his hands down on his knees and hoisted himself up, stretched long and carefully, as though he were washing away his worries, and walked deliberately to the door.

Outside he navigated the halls with care and some
returning sense of wonder. The way he'd been brought
up—hell, the way any human had been brought up
in the twenty-fifth century—indoors meant maybe a
gathering hall and maybe even one or two small adjoining rooms. This antique warren, this *hotel* was enough
to give anyone nightmares.

Before long, he was outside Lu-An's suite and knocking for attention. It was barely sunrise, but he wasn't
worried about waking her. This was one woman who
was fascinated enough by the stuff of life that she didn't
allow herself to spend too much of it asleep.

"Come on in." The tone was brisk and very businesslike, but when he opened the door and turned into
the room, Lu-An's smile was fresh and brilliant. "Holcomb! I couldn't ask for a better breakfast companion." She pointed to the table set before her, loaded
with the hearty breakfast of a campaigner. "Have a
seat."

It was only after Holcomb approached the table and
stood reluctantly behind the chair that Lu-An noticed
something was wrong. She was up and around the table,
her face showing concern.

"Really, sit down." She took him by the shoulders
and trundled him into the chair, noting his pallor and
bloodshot eyes. She sat down beside him and held his
hand. "It can't be as bad as all that unless Shak't'kan
has landed, and I think I'd have heard about that!"
Realizing that he wasn't about to be cheered up, she
leveled her voice and asked, "Okay, what's the matter?
We might as well get it over. Now out with it."

Holcomb shivered slightly. She could feel it through
his arm. He began while staring blankly at the tabletop.
"Lu-An, there's no easy way of saying this. I spoke to
Shak't'kan last night."

●　　●　　●

This is the Los Angeles Free State, seeking support
from Admiral Rogers. Please come in. This is the Los
Angeles Free State seeking support from Admiral
Rogers. Please come in. This is the Los Angeles Free
State desperately seeking support from Admiral . . .

Thank god. Yes we read you, Rogers. We are a fifth-column brigade operating out of Los Angeles Prison Camp. We need weapons and help in order to convince the inmates to revolt. The situation is critical; twenty-thousand men, women, and children live here under Prl'lu tyranny. Please help.

"Well, that's it," Rogers said. "That's the one."

The miniature war council was convened in the ward-room. Rogers, Ruth, Joaquin, and Mouka were holding the hasty conference.

"What's your notion?" Joaquin asked.

"I don't mean to go overboard and commit all our Rangers at once," Rogers replied. "I think in this case ground forces are indicated. Not many, just enough to instigate some trouble and get the timid into the fight. It's not time to pull the stopper yet, but we can send in some cavalry; the trickiest, meanest little shock troops we can find." He looked to the Simba.

"We're all set," Mouka replied. "Matter of fact, if I'd had to keep stalling my boys any longer, we really would have had trouble. Just leave it to us." The creature stood on the table and rocked slightly on his feet as he made the declaration. He looked ready for anything.

"Well then get to it," Rogers ordered. "The stakes are high."

The two-man s-to-s fighters were easily able to carry sixteen Simbas if one of the full-size pilots relinquished his seat. It took only eleven trips to drop 178 parachuted Simbas over the Los Angeles Prison Camp. Rogers took the first flight in, "to get the lay of the land, so to speak." Truth was, he felt an itch to get out of his op center and see the enemy close up.

In this at least, he was disappointed. The trip went without a hitch and Mouka and his men hit dirt without a single Prl'lu being the wiser.

In the dark of the camp, the little creatures silently scattered. Teams of three had their instructions: keep out of sight in whatever nook or cranny offered and then, when the chance presented itself, gum up the works but good.

It was the kind of job they liked and Mouka knew his men were up to it. He was looking forward to the next several days.

Ducking for cover, they crossed the compound and headed for a perimeter sentry tower. On the fringes of the camp, Mouka estimated, they'd have a better chance at dirty dealing the Prl'lu.

Their progress was good. Even if some waking prisoner or alert guard had sighted them, chances were they'd be taken as simple varmints, or so Rogers had said. In the open spaces, Mouka and his men got down on all fours to reinforce the masquerade.

At the bottom of the tower, a hastily built tin-on-wood construction, he sniffed the air. There were Prl'lu about, and humans, too.

The tower was only twenty feet tall, but it was so far over Mouka's head that from where he crouched it was impossible to make out the sentry platform clearly. He had no doubt though that it was well-manned. His teammates were scuttling around the perimeter of the tower, looking for an entrance or, better yet, a convenient bolt-hole. While he waited, he became conscious of a slow, steady dripping. Curiously, he went in search of its source. Before long he found it, an antique air conditioner unit set in the wall. Moist air was collecting on its coils and dripping to the hard-packed earth. He sat and watched it a minute and then grinned to himself, swung his pick, and buried its point deep into the coils. When he pulled it out he could hear the hiss of Freon leaking into the night. Hardly a mortal blow for freedom, but somebody was going to have an uncomfortable evening. It all counted for something, he hoped.

A few minutes later he and his teammates evicted an angry badger from its den. They'd found their hole for the night.

"Come with me." Lu-An's tone was cold and brusque. Before Holcomb had a chance to move from his chair, she was already waiting impatiently at the door.

They walked silently through the corridors and Lu-An kept the pace so fast that Holcomb could only ask miserably of her back, "Where are we going?"

She didn't choose to answer.

"Sataspes, I'm giving you a chance to redeem yourself!"

Shak't'kan was sitting in his quarters, where his son stood between two large and impassive guards. "The troublemakers I've been hunting are assembled in the desert west of here. They call themselves the North American Provisional Government, the rebel Princess Lu-An and her human friends." His voice was uncharacteristically sarcastic, a sign, he knew, that he was at the edge of his temper. "My source tells me that for the moment they are gathered into one spot, *all* of our enemies. If we strike now, we'll no longer be troubled by hunting them separately in the hills. I've decided to send you."

In the days since his defeat and in the hours of enforced isolation under his father's guard, Sataspes had recovered much of his old, imperious nature. His voice no longer shook when Shak't'kan chose to interview him. Still he treated his father with the respect due his ruthlessness.

"Very well, my lord, I'll take command immediately," Sataspes replied. He waited for dismissal. It did not come.

"You are *not* going to lead *this* force," his father said flatly. "I've chosen Jawcove to command. You will act as his lieutenant."

Sataspes turned and stamped out of the room.

"Do we have any choice?" Falstaff asked.

Lu-An answered slowly, "I think so. If Holcomb's right, Shak't'kan plans to bring the fight into the city and get rid of us once and for all. Assuming he's under the impression that all our people are hunkered down in

Las Vegas at the moment—a piece of idiocy I wouldn't
credit if I were him, but Holcomb seems to feel
Shak't'kan's convinced—what else can he do? Why, it's
perfect!''

"I don't follow you," Falstaff replied. "You and I
may know that the bands are already disbursed, but as
you say, Shak't'kan almost certainly doesn't. That
means he'll put everything he's got into this battle. He'll
see to it that Las Vegas is torn apart, turned under, and
that will be that. We have to evacuate.''

"I don't see it that way. Sure, if we had a sizeable
force in the city we'd either have to clear out or put up a
pretty stiff defense, but as things stand we've got another option; we spread out and wait. Listen, the Prl'lu
will come in fighting, lob a few bombs, heat up a few
buildings, but then—then when nothing fires back at
them, they'll have to come down and find out why,''
Lu-An explained.

"Have you thought that they might just go on lobbing their bombs and heating up buildings?''

"Well, think of how it'll look to them. They'll know
that no sizeable force is crossing the desert. We couldn't
hide that from them, but they'll also realize that if we're
dug into this old city in any sizeable numbers we have no
recourse but to fight back in a big way, and even so,
we'd be fighting a losing battle. They'll know that too.
What they don't know is that there are few enough of us
so that we can spread out, dig in, and chance the first
volley without taking any big losses. They'll come down
to investigate. Maybe we're all dead? Maybe we were
never here? Maybe their spy has been lying to them?
They'll have to know for sure.''

"If he hasn't been lying to us," Falstaff said bitterly.

"I don't believe it. In fact, Holcomb may have given
us just the opportunity we need. They land, we come
out of the woodwork, and *wham*!''

"You make it sound too good to be true.''

"No. Just the break we needed.'' Lu-An smiled for
the first time that morning. "With Marshall Rogers
back, things have come to a boil. Anyhow, think of this;

now we can break our radio silence."

"And what about *Holcomb*?"

Lu-An paused a long while before answering. "I say we let him go to join the fight."

"After what he's done?" The Aussie sounded indignant.

"No. After what he's tried to do to correct it!"

Falstaff looked at her curiously. "Whatever you say, but I hope you know what you're doing."

"So do I."

Mouka waited for dark outside. He paced with five of his fellows in an old warren under the camp. They'd been fortunate, he thought. The place was riddled with bolt-holes and winding networks of tunnels, chambers, and straw-lined dens. Rabbits, gophers, prairie dogs, badgers—they'd all done their work here and it cut down on the work the Simbas had had to do.

And they'd done well. The camp was a shambles. The Prl'lu prison force was at its wit's end trying to repair and explain away a myriad of breakdowns, accidents, and misplaced articles. The humans were growing increasingly irritated, restive, and scornful of their inept captors. Something was about to break and Mouka was determined that tonight was the night.

When darkness fell, the six of them were quickly and silently out of the burrow and crossing the compound to the Prl'lu Internal Monitoring Center. They crossed a no-man's land to get there, running close to the ground on all fours. Overhead, a grid of lasers threatened any trespassers, but the Simbas slipped easily underneath.

They squeezed up against the center's cement wall, while Mouka scouted the perimeter of the building. All was clear. It was a hot night, and the guards had had the door of the blockhouse open to catch a stray breeze. With a low growl, Mouka signaled the others. Mouka at the lead, five of them shot into the blockhouse; the sixth pushed the door closed behind them.

There were eight Prl'lu in the room. In the first flash of the fight, with poisoned picks swinging over their heads, the Simbas cut that number down to four. The four who lived were those who had the wits to climb up on their desks.

They were screaming for help. One was fumbling madly at a transmitter. It didn't matter; he was too scared to get anything intelligible across anyway.

That was the one Mouka went for. Ducking a Prl'lu boot, he grappled his way onto the desk. That was all he needed; his pick sunk solidly into the guard's leg. The guard was dead before he hit the desk top. Already another was doing his best to stamp the Simba in turn.

A file cabinet went over and beneath it, the sickening sight of one of his fellows, crushed and pulped. Mouka was enraged. He clambered up on the dead guard's body, counting on his opponent's squeamishness not to step on him there.

He counted wrong. A heavy boot came smacking down. He rolled aside just in time. He could hear something rupture in the dead man's chest when the boot ground at the spot he'd just abandoned—rupture and cave in. The Prl'lu was thrown off balance. Mouka had his chance—he threw his pick and another Prl'lu was dead.

As he turned away, the last guard doubled over and died, a pick planted in his chest.

Silently the Simbas recovered their teammate's body and filed out the way they'd come.

All in all, Mouka felt good about the evening's work, exhilarated. After all, it was what they were here for. Back in the burrow he said to the others, "Things are going to crack wide open."

In the morning, when the guard's corpses were found, he was right.

Jawcove commanded the squad from the bridge of the airship *Ri*. Satatspes stood by his side. The ships hung in formation in the bright desert sky. One hundred eighty degrees of desert filled the screen, a hundred miles in any direction you chose to look. Empty.

Las Vegas was underneath, also empty—to all appearances.

Eleven craters smoked in the screen; buildings were reduced to rubble; where the beams had hit, sidewalks ran in slag.

The Tropicana was hit, the Sands, the Sahara, the Dunes, all rubble, smoke and crater.

And not a round had been fired in return, not a shot.

"Eleven airships, eleven bombs, they're blind if they can't find us." Jawcove was thinking aloud, but Sataspes chose to answer his thought.

"Blind, or gone, or dead."

"My lord Shak't'kan's information was reliable, I suppose?"

"Perfectly," Sataspes answered, "or so he believes."

"There's nothing to it then, we've got to land and find out for ourselves!"

"Falstaff here. Come in, command! Come in!"

"Got you, Falstaff." Lu-An's voice could be clearly heard over the radio.

"No casualties in this sector. How 'bout the rest of 'em?"

"Seven on the strip; two others. Do you think it's going to work?"

"It had better."

Jawcove took a full long look around his empty perimeter screens before ordering the descent. The ships had barely started down when Sataspes burst out, "No! It's a trick."

"How can it be?" The commander sounded flat and impatient, now that his mind was set. He was going about his duty in the only way he knew how: by the books and without an excess of imagination.

Sataspes knew the tone all too well; he'd only recently acquired an imagination himself. "Believe me, sir, to my cost I know. We shouldn't commit our whole fleet to one maneuver!" He sounded concerned, almost desperate, and the commander gave him a critical glance.

"That will be enough of that, Sataspes; we're going down."

•   •   •

"In position out by McCarren Field, Princess."

"Problems here, Princess, southwest sector. Smoke's drifting in on us pretty heavy. We're gonna have a good hard time breathing unless this scrap gets going fast. Permission to relocate?"

"*Denied*! Nobody moves until quarry is down. Repeat, nobody dare move until quarry is down. Understood?"

"Understood and out, Princess."

The airships gracefully fell on the city. At first it was hard for the hidden defenders to tell where they would set down, but as the ships lost altitude, it was clear that the central city was their mark, the area around the strip and the smoldering hotels. As soon as the craft were low enough to prevent line of sight, Lu-An ordered in the outlying guerrillas. They tumbled through the old city and the new ruins, eager to be in on the kill.

If this came off, it would be a great day for all of them.

Except Holcomb, Lu-An thought. Could he ever be healed? By her lights, he was repatriated already, but could he forgive himself?

The airships settled to ground.

"Commander, I request permission to lead the landing party." Sataspes's tone was formal. It wasn't that he wanted to go. He had a very good idea of what might be about to happen, but he realized that only a grand show would ever redeem his career.

"Permission granted."

Sataspes gathered six men and set out. It felt like that. A real expedition. He just hoped he'd get the traditional brass band on the return.

Lu-An, Falstaff, Holcomb, and several hundred others were there to greet the Prl'lu descending from the sky. The seven Prl'lu, Sataspes at the lead, disembarked—gingerly, Falstaff thought. They walked down the gun-metal ramps and fanned out in the road.

All around them the city was quiet; only desert noises

and the crackling of fires in the crater intruded. Behind piles of rubble, abandoned cars, storefronts, and on every perch, in every gully Lu-An's troops concentrated on breathing shallowly, quietly.

The Prl'lu scattered around the street, keeping up a line of talk that covered their nervousness, until Sataspes stopped them. He was as nervous as the rest, but he wanted to listen and listen hard!

The group traced a path down the rubble-strewn street, peering in windows, investigating alleys, circling the abandoned cars. Finally, even the defenders could hear the loud, harsh voice over Sataspes's com unit.

"What's the matter? Why haven't you reported?"

"Nothing's the matter, my lord, we're still investigating the road." Sataspes's voice was low. He was trying to be persuasive.

"You've gone far enough. I'm sending the men out."

"No!"

"Are you contradicting me!" Jawcove's voice was thin with anger.

"No sir! I mean, let us look around a bit more."

"There's nothing there. You've had your chance. Report to me instantly."

The troops started pouring out of the ships.

"Falstaff, come in? Falstaff?"

"Yes, command?"

"None of your people is to open fire until the enemy is well away from the ships and well scattered."

"Got you."

"Lu-An? Lu-An?"

"Come in." The Princess was tired. "Who is this?"

"Why, Holcomb, of course."

Lu-An's voice was suddenly restrained, "Yes?"

"I know you wanted us to hold back, but they came right through our front door. We've captured sixteen of them."

"What do you mean, captured?"

"I mean they walked in and we had to hold 'em or let 'em go. What do you think I meant?"

"Nothing. Sorry." She thought awhile. "Falstaff?"

"Yeah?"

"Are you ready to start the fight?"

"Sure we are."

"You've got the go-ahead!"

"Tony?" Ruth asked.

"Yeah?"

"How do you mean to handle this?"

"Wholeheartedly."

"Oh."

Tony and Ruth were traversing the atmosphere in a two-man s-to-s sliver fighter, well on their way toward Las Vegas. The rest of the airborne Rangers were at their heels.

"What do you think we'll find?"

"Don't know."

Lu-An's bulletin had been short and matter of fact. The headquarters of the Provisional Government of North America was under attack. Help wouldn't be turned away.

The gunfire was deafening. Sataspes led a group of men; their numbers kept increasing as stragglers reached his side. They had made an abortive effort to get back to the ships. That was proven to be impossible. Now Sataspes was beating a retreat into the desert.

"Terkan! Straighten out these troops!"

"Com, can you reach Jawcove?"

"Not a word, my lord. I think he's dead."

"Well, keep trying."

Falstaff's voice rose loud and clear over the communicator. "A bunch of them are trying to regain the ships! I'm going in ahead."

"No!"

Lu-An's order went unanswered. Falstaff was either dead or out of communicator range. There was action in that direction; at least, Lu-An could hear the fighting.

"Princess?" an aide prompted.

She had her own fighting to contend with.

• • •

It was a real fire fight. Falstaff leveled her dis pistol across her knee and took aim. The shot went true and her victim was split in half. His severed arteries spilled a happy red on the ruins.

"Come on, Dawson! Get your men up here!" she yelled.

They were beating their way in front of the ships before the Prl'lu had the wit to about-face.

"Two-face, Falstaff, two-face!"

She swung around instinctively, almost before the warning formed in Dawson's mouth, and burned two Prl'lu off the airships' ramps before they burned her.

Her troops were backing up toward the ships and Falstaff realized that at any moment more Prl'lu could come pouring out, burning her people from behind. It was a risk they'd have to take. The Prl'lu couldn't be allowed through.

"Marlowe!"

"Yes, Captain."

"How many of our men can you see?"

"Not many. You?"

Holcomb rapped his communicator against his thigh in worry and did some rapid thinking. Half the Prl'lu nation, it seemed, was bearing down in their direction, out of the city, toward McCarren Field, and he had no more than a patrol of men in sight. Even if the rest of the squadron hadn't bought it and would be ready and able to pop up just when he needed them, there was no telling if his men could handle this horde.

He could see Falstaff's people, far across the strip, slowly being beaten back to the ships. He hoped Falstaff would hold out, help contain them. In fact he knew that that was crucially important. If the Prl'lu got back to their ships, his side would have lost. Simple as that.

The question was, what could he do?

Suddenly he had an idea. The trick was to relieve some of the pressure building up in the street. Give the Prl'lu who wanted to *get away* from the line of fire a chance, just so long as they kept running away from the ships!

"Marlowe, we'll have to fan out and give the Prl'lu a chance to get through our lines. No more standing engagement—got it?"

"Hear ya, Captain!"

To his right and left the commandos simply vanished into the surrounding city. Las Vegas had taken a beating today—eleven Big Berthas and innumerable small hand fire—but this part of the city was relatively intact. He knew his men, knew them well. They had a chance against the Prl'lu ranks *if* they could find sufficient cover. And they had it, a narrow belt of it, before the desert: the scrubby, mean, back streets of the strip.

"Pick them off at will and don't be concerned if any get through to the desert. Just don't let them head back toward the ships. Any Prl'lu trying to retrace his steps has to be cut down! Pass it along."

"Already passed and ready, Cap."

"Marlowe?"

"Yes?"

"Good luck."

Holcomb led his wing into cover. He had a brief few seconds in which he could change his mind, but he didn't. Instead, he forced himself to pay attention to the matter at hand, like any other good soldier. When you were alone and in a sniping action, it was the details that counted.

He found himself on the second floor of a rickety old factory. When he rested his gun on the window sash, its rotten wood crumbled and a flurry of black ants were exposed. He wiped them away as best he could and settled down to wait.

Wait until the Prl'lu started filtering by. Not the first or even the tenth. Give them a chance to taste freedom, feel they had a chance at the desert. Wait, wait, ONE, TWO, carefully he squeezed the trigger.

"The Prl'lu craft have landed, sir."

"I can see that," Rogers replied. "Lieutenant, can you see anything special about those aircraft?"

"You mean beside the fact that they're Prl'lu, sir?"

"Yes! I mean that." Rogers groaned and Ruth patted him on the back.

"Well, there's a fight going on in front of them, sir."

Rogers sighed. "And what do you think they're fighting over?"

"The ships, sir?"

"The ships, right! Burn them!"

"Done, sir."

The Rangers swept over the strip, aiming their cannon at the offending ships. It was a great deal easier than exercises, so easy that Roger had to reprimand a pilot.

"Fischer?"

"Yes, sir?"

"What are you doing?"

"Shooting, sir."

"In the future, please shoot right-side up, will you?"

"Yes, sir."

Falstaff was backing toward the Prl'lu flagship *Ri*. She didn't know it was the flagship and she didn't know it was called the *Ri*, but she did know that the Prl'lu forces were determined to regain it. They were pressing the battle hard; she sighted and shot, sighted and shot, and allowed herself a few bursts in pure anger. Still they were coming.

Suddenly the sky blazed overhead. She ducked instinctively. Good that she had; a metallic stick of death fell from the skies and the airships at her back burst into flame.

"Dammit, hit the dirt!" she yelled.

The fight was fast and bitter then. The Prl'lu had nowhere to retreat. The defenders had nothing to lose. The battling forces roamed over the city like antique street gangs seeking new turf. It was a hard fight and people died on both sides, but once the Rangers put the Prl'lu airships out of business, there was really no contest. The Las Vegans were fighting on home ground and they went for points. The Prl'lus had no sense of strategy or logistics; they went for the quick kill and were killed in turn. All except Sataspes's squad, of course. They were doing more than a little damage. He, at least, had seen the wisdom of retreat.

"Split up and head for the sunset. We'll re-establish command procedure in the desert!" Sataspes ordered.

His troops were on the run. Jawcove and the rest, he supposed, were dead or captured. For his part, Sataspes had learnt the lesson of the *Wrangr* well—or half of it, at any rate. Survival came before gamesmanship.

There would be time enough for games when they'd reached safe ground, anyplace outside this unlucky city. Until then, his men beat a defensive retreat, bent low over their guns and backing out of the fire fight. When they were well on their way through the back alleys and smoldering ruins of the city and were out of sight of the pursuing forces, Sataspes gave the word and they turned on their heels and ran.

It was a better move than they knew. Lu-An's men couldn't believe their luck and spent needless hours cautiously advancing on nonexistent Prl'lu positions. By the time the humans had figured it out, it was far too late; Sataspes and forty others had fought their way to the desert and nothing could be done about it.

For that matter, there seemed to be little reason to bother.

Alone out in the desert, Sataspes huddled by a brush fire and waited for his men to arrive. In its flickering light, he conscientiously began stretching his legs; it was a long walk back to L.A.

The battle of Las Vegas was over.

16.

The Strip.

Once it had been the playground of the West, a place where the lights were always a little dim, bulbs glowing with mystery, romance, beguiling players to the tables, the bars, the slots, the back rooms, wide screens, crowded parties, empty stages, ugly weddings, cheap funerals, easy money, dead hopes, good times, bad times, open all the time. The Strip. The heart of the city.

The Strip had seen plenty, one time or another, plenty of death too. One time or another, when the blood soaked the sidewalks and the black desert flies peppered the congealing crimson, the neat men in white suits, professional, discreet, had spread the sawdust, swept and scrubbed the Strip until death vanished without a trace to taint the playground.

They didn't wear white anymore.

The day after a battle the dirty jobs fall to the winning side, and discreet, professional generals take their job very seriously.

Lu-An picked her way along the strip, supervising the mopping up.

There was a lot of it: dead to be sorted out and buried; fires to be extinguished; wounded to be cared for; prisoners fed, housed, and protected from harm. An ops center had to be put back together; there was a great deal to be talked over and decided. She remembered something that Rogers had repeated to her once, that nothing except a battle lost could be half so melancholy as a battle won. As ever, he'd known what he was talking about.

She was bone tired and more, stolidly anguished by the death and misery that as commander had become her stock in trade. Then too, she was hurt and still undecided about Holcomb, a man to whom she had given her trust and her affection. Holcomb had done well during the battle and even better before it by owning up. She felt no compunction about returning him to active command, even returning him to the Councils of the Provisionary Government, of which she was acting head, but she did not know if she could return him to the special place he had played in her own life.

Not, she reminded herself, that he'd ever accepted such a role. She had proffered it secretly and withdrawn it secretly. He might not even have suspected her feelings. Now she didn't even know whether she had had the right or the power to love and then choose not to love, in this silent fashion.

A runner came bounding over a hillock. Endless numbers of runners seemed to come over hills lately, or worse, over still-unburied bodies. They came with numbers and information and advice, and always with questions. More questions in a hundred yards down this strip than she'd ever had to answer in the ten days before the battle.

The runner was bouncing on his heels impatiently. Lu-An took pity on him—he was one of the young ones—and asked, "Well?"

"Captain Holcomb told me to report, Princess. It's Rogers. Out at McCarren Field. His fighters have landed."

"Right!" For the first time all afternoon, the princess sounded enthusiastic, "I'll get right out there!"

"Better hurry," the runner pressed on, "Captain Holcomb told me to tell you that Rogers was all for rushing into the city to congratulate you. The captain thought you'd rather meet the Marshall out there." The runner sounded a little awed. It wasn't every day that he had a chance to act as a go-between for such famous, even legendary, people. Even so, Lu-An thought she could detect something of Holcomb in the runner's choice of words, a hint that she should march out to the airstrip with her men, ready to be treated as an equal.

If that *was* what he meant, then Holcomb was giving her good advice, as usual. Certainly she didn't want to be discovered by Rogers amidst the death and squalor of the strip.

"Get off and tell Holcomb I'll be right along," she told the waiting runner. Then she did a little running herself, an easy campaigner's jog, until she reached Falstaff at the wreckage of the Prl'lu airships. The Aussie was sifting the ruins for anything that might hold a bit of useful information. When Lu-An got there, Falstaff was holding up a grubby tape to the sun.

"Got something," Falstaff said when Lu-An came running up.

"Have to wait." The princess was a little breathless. "You and I have an appointment over at McCarren with Marshall Rogers himself."

"That can't wait, can it?" the Aussie replied. She thrust the film into her shirt, wiped her hands on her trousers, and together the two women jogged back to the makeshift ops center for a brushup and reinforcements. It was clear to them all that this was going to be a historic meeting.

Rogers was leaning against the side of his sliver fighter. The silver ship was burnished blue, yellow, and black by the heat of atmospheric entry. In front of its rainbow colors, rakishly hoisting himself up by the elbows, Rogers, with his ruddy space-tan, made a fine and commanding, if momentarily indolent, figure. Holcomb's troops were ringed around him like disciples, listening to his laconic recitation of space adventures. Ruth and the Rangers, forty-seven s-to-s fighter crews, stood by and listened with amusement. Rogers was milking the tale for all it was worth and more. Anyhow, it was good to be back on terra firma again.

That was the way Lu-An and Falstaff found them; a somewhat sweaty and well-satisfied bunch of glory boys, pleased with themselves, pleased with life. She could see it herself, here on the edge of the desert; it was a glorious day.

Lu-An stood at the edge of the crowd and listened for a bit. It was good to see Rogers again, good just to hear his voice. He'd played an important part in her life and she was looking to him to help her find the best way to

live the rest of it. But it was important too that he see
how much she'd grown, discover for himself that she no
longer needed anything from him but friendship.

"... we would have had them too, but they shot their
own ships down to get at us ..."

There she chose to interrupt him. How much longer
Rogers' tale would have gone on, she didn't know; you
never could tell with Rogers. She rounded up her
"boys." They were all trained commandos and as per-
sonally loyal as they were proficient. They looked good,
and with them at her side she felt good; their loyalty
shone through.

The semicircle around Rogers parted and she walked
through at the head of her honor guard. Rogers broke
off his story when he saw her. A crooked smile greeted
her. "Lu-An, my princess ..."

"Hello, Tony."

"You did well this morning, I know."

"With your help, Marshall."

"Glad to have me back?" Rogers let his voice drop
just enough so that she'd know the question was in earnest. She was relieved, and felt just a little foolish. She
should have known Tony wasn't the type to blithely
assume that nothing had changed. More than ever, she
was glad he was back.

"Glad and more." She turned to indicate the troops
and the waiting Rangers. "But we'll have plenty of time
to come up to date on each other after we all get out of
the sun." She looked at them, all of them, standing on
the broken, steaming asphalt. It was getting on toward
late afternoon, but the sun was still high in the desert
and the men's faces looked seamed and tired, more than
they knew, by their day of battle. Another part of being
a commander, she thought, was being an efficient
mother. "Let's get our reunion indoors."

"Good idea." Rogers wanted to make this meeting as
easy as possible too. "For that matter, my men could
stand a chow-down if you have anything available."

Holcomb stepped in, "We do, sir, we do indeed, and
I've set it up in the Grady Bandstand—what's left of
the Grady Bandstand," he amended.

"You've always got it together, don't you Holcomb?" Rogers smiled happily. This was a day for it! Back on Earth, anything'd strike him glad. And it was good to see old friends.

The officers went back to the old air controllers' tower, where Holcomb had made a field post. Before they sat down to talk, Lu-An got her ops center on the line and instructed her officers in a number of small details. Before she got off the line, she handled a list of problems ranging from kitchen waste to sentry dispatches. She also took down particulars on a sheaf of radioed dispatches from guerrilla units out in the wild. To two of these, she ordered an immediate response.

By now her habit of command was purely instinctive, but Rogers was impressed. "I gather you're very much running the North American show," he said.

"There's not much to run," she said hurriedly, "because there's almost nothing I could do to help out another unit in trouble. Still, we try and keep tabs on every part of the country and we've sent trained commando personnel to anyone with spunk enough to ask."

"Quite a lot, I think. Don't you, Ruth?"

Ruth put her hand on Rogers' arm. "I don't think it's our place to praise, Tony."

"What'dya mean?" He was taken by surprise.

"I mean that Lu-An's in charge down here and instead of dropping out of the sky to tell her how well she's done her job, we should be asking her how to do ours."

Rogers was silent a moment; then shaking his head vigorously he said, "Damned if you aren't right! Lu-An, I'm ready and reporting for duty!"

The princess looked him full in the eye, trying to take his measure. Finally she broke a smile and said, "Enough of that, so long as you realize I've been hard at work. The question now is, where do we all go from here?"

"Well," Holcomb said, "if you don't mind, I have the answer to that."

When no one objected, he continued. "I've been

talking to your men, Rogers. You've been monitoring rebellions around the world and doing your best to encourage them without active participation. And by all reports, you've been very successful.

"I gather you've been waiting and looking for a situation that might really turn the tide in free man's favor. In other words, you're gunning for Shak't'kan, because without his authority the Prl'oi Empire would divide into a hundred separate scrapping city-states. It'd be comparatively easy to pick them off one by one. Am I right so far?"

Rogers nodded, impressed.

"Good. Well then, you think you've identified such a situation in L.A. and you sent some sort of attack force down to sabotage Prl'oi interests at the L.A. Prison Camp—another stab at getting those on the spot to take heart and take a part in this war. I don't know anything about these Simbas your men talk about, but I do know that camp. It's more than ready for revolt. Probably would've happened by now if I hadn't been such a chump, but Lu-An will tell you about that. The point is, you've isolated a chink in Shak't'kan's defenses. L.A. is the key to the southwest; but more than that, L.A. is crucial to Shak't'kan's plans for an impregnable under-sea empire. He has to be stopped before he completes his plans!"

They stared at him. None had suspected that Holcomb harbored so much anger, or that he had such a detailed and critical grasp of the situation. Lu-An was particularly taken aback; but, on reflection she was pleased. This was the kind of man she had always known Holcomb to be: proud, tough, and sharp. Very sharp.

"I have some more ideas on the subject," he continued, "if you care to hear them." There was still something missing in his voice, though, Lu-An thought. His look pleaded with Lu-An: *Give me this chance*, it said. She was all for it, but when would he realize that he had to forgive himself?

"L.A. is the key," he went on, "not only the prison camp, but the Prl'oi base under the sea. If we're going to do the job we've got to hit it from both sides. Do your airships have underwater capability?" he asked Rogers. "Shak't'kan's do."

"No."

"Then we have only one choice. The Aussie subs. Falstaff can fill you in about that. The L.A. seamount *has* to be taken from both sides! Believe me," he added. "If we pull this off, we'll have struck a blow that'll count. The war may drag on around the globe, but we'll have assured final victory."

Rogers looked at Lu-An inquiringly.

"Whatever Holcomb says goes for me too," she said. "He has a better knowledge and understanding of Shak't'kan than any of the rest of us, and he's a fine field commander."

"That I know," Rogers said. "Somehow, though," he looked at Holcomb closely, "I feel as though there's something else I should know."

"I . . ." Holcomb began, but Lu-An and Falstaff hurriedly shut him off.

"He's done a lot of undercover work," Falstaff cut in, "and there have been rumors. Unfounded rumors."

"Right," Lu-An was firm. "I've got to thank you Tony; you trained Holcomb well. He's the best man under my command."

There was nothing a soldier could do but blush. Holcomb blushed.

17.

Rogers was trying to fix himself a cup of tea in the wardroom of the *Wasp*, but he wasn't having much success. The sub would lurch fore and aft while he did his best to pour hot water into the mug. He'd brace himself against the next shock, take careful aim with the teapot, and the *Wasp* would suddenly do a quick Charleston on its keel. More scalding water, on the floor, on Rogers' coveralls, everywhere but in the cup.

"Darn it!" For that matter, he was definitely beginning to feel queasy. With a decisive crash, he abandoned cup and teapot to the galley stove, turned to take a chair at the officers' mess, and nearly knocked himself out on the overhead ballast bulwark.

"Darn it again, and to Betsy!"

"Why Tony, what's the matter?" Ruth's face was submerged in her own mug, but there was no mistaking her amusement.

"Nothing, nothing," he muttered as he slumped into his chair and promptly barked his knees under the low-slung steel table. "They call this a ship!" he said indignantly. "It's small enough to qualify for a homeowners' improvement loan. 'Save by Converting Your Attic Into Useful Space.'"

"Not everyone's 6'3", Tony. Most of us have found the *Wasp* to be quite comfortable."

"The Simbas would love it!" Rogers brushed the hair back from his eyes, "Well how about it? Ship's pool. I give even odds we're in Shak't'kan's backyard by two A.M. tomorrow."

"Fine," Ruth said. "I've got 3:15 pegged; Falstaff's going long at 5:30."

"What's Carberry got?"

"Not telling a soul. Says he knows for a certainty when we'll be there and its bad policy to take money from superiors."

"Hmphh! Somebody knows what's good for him. All right, peg me at 2:00 and you better hope I win."

Ruth tried to sound meek, "Aye-aye, sir!"

"See that you remember." Rogers got up carefully and went to find Carberry.

He found his chief engineer tending his charges in the reactor chamber. They were huge, sleek, steel things, capable of generating more power than the *Wasp* could ever use. Only a tiny portion of the engines showed at all; most of their apparatus was locked behind three feet of lead and concrete shielding in a section of the ship that could never be visited by its human crew. Not that they'd ever have occasion to visit there. The *Wasp*'s power plant had reached near perfection; the long-gone engineers of the twentieth century had designed into its engines a precision and efficiency that nuclear science had never surpassed, and crammed the whole thing into a package that would fit in the Navy's smallest offensive component, the attack sub.

"Carberry?" The young man was staring intently at a console, but when he looked up and saw Rogers, he tore himself reluctantly away. As always a little disheveled, he passed his hand through his hair in lieu of a more formal salute. "Skipper?"

"We're betting on our contact time down in the wardroom. I gather you've got a pretty good idea when we'll be approaching the Fieberling Guyot."

Carberry looked a little shamefaced. "Down to the minute, Skipper. It's a matter of propeller slippage. The deeper we're traveling the less turbulence, the more efficient our propeller becomes. Down here—and make no mistake about it, we're deep!—slippage approaches zero. All I have to do is figure the pitch of our propellers against the number of revs. See this figure here?" he pointed to a counter mounted near the main shaft, "that tells me how quickly we can go the 6871 miles between Sydney and L.A. with a little multiplication." He scratched his head. "Uh, got it, Skipper?"

Rogers managed to look amused. "Oh I think I can handle the essentials."

"Skipper?"

"Yeah."

"I didn't mean to keep back our contact time from you. It's going to be just about 2:00 tomorrow morning."

"Don't worry about that. Just so long as we're in position well before sunrise. That's when the shooting starts."

"Oh we will be, Skipper, we will be!"

"Good. And the two other subs?"

"Everything shipshape there as well."

"You know," Rogers leaned against the shielded bulwark, "I'm beginning to look forward to this fight. It'll be interesting to see what one of these things can do. A U.S. submarine!" He shook his head, "In my time, the U.S. and Britain were working to abolish the things. They were simply too dangerous. In the Great War the Germans sunk more then eight million tons of Allied shipping. It only cost them a couple hundred subs. We've really got something here. What I wouldn't give to know more about what happened after 1927. . . ." His voice trailed off and he spent a couple of minutes staring blankly into the gray metal floor plates. When he looked up again, Carberry's attention was already riveted back on the power console. He straightened up to leave the engine room and then remembered why he'd sought Carberry out.

"We'll have to surface for a few minutes tonight; have to check in with Lu-An and Holcomb, and maybe get a call through to Joaquin with the armada. Think you can arrange that?"

"Will do, Skipper."

Stooping through the bulkhead door, Rogers left the engine room. At his post Carberry was humming happily.

"How do you assess the situation?" Shak't'kan inquired stonily.

"I have no choice but to conclude that our fleet has been defeated, my lord," replied the officer.

Shak't'kan turned away to hide his worry. Worry was not one of the permissible emotions. "Are there any other possibilities at all?" he finally demanded.

"None that we haven't had to dismiss, my lord. The last report we had from Jawcove's flagship, the *Ri*, indicates that they had landed and were preparing to send out an exploratory attack force. Nothing since."

"I want an aerial reconnaissance immediately."

The officer hesitated and then gently reminded Shak't'kan, "We have no long-range cruisers to spare, my lord. To risk even one of the few we have left . . ."

"Then send a scout! But get me that reconnaissance

of Las Vegas. I'm holding you responsible to see that it's done and done properly."

"Yes, my lord." The frightened officer saluted and scurried off. Shak't'kan smiled grimly. At least this one, he thought, would do his job. And if he was scared enough, he probably wouldn't give too much thought to the implications of the defeat in Las Vegas. That was one of Shak't'kan's principal headaches—how to prevent these sudden and inexplicable reversals from filtering down to the troops. No one but he must know how devastating the tide of war had become: the crushing defeat of Sataspes's forces in space, the crash of the *Wrangr*, Rogers' incredible return with an armada of ships, and that armada's virtual control of the air, the flareups and guerrilla actions that had his people pinned in their cities and crying for support—support that he just couldn't afford to give them. And now another defeat, another setback, when the destruction of Las Vegas might have been the greatest feat of the war. . . .

Why had that fool landed?

And Sataspes. It would be too bad to lose him. The youth was hot and impatient, sometimes foolish, but he would have been shaped in time, turned into a useful asset. Was he dead, too?

With a sigh of exasperation, he turned back to the dailies from Commandant Yoxter detailing the situation at the L.A. internment camp. His frown deepened. The sabotage, if anything, was getting worse. And Yoxter, it seemed, hadn't come any closer to unearthing the culprits—or, crucially, taking action on the incredible massacre of the guards. Something had to be done about it.

He thumbed the com controls until a screen lit up in the wall of the chamber. Yoxter wavered into view, head bowed studiously over a pile of paperwork. It was enough to make Shak't'kan laugh, and he did. That a warrior race should harbor such bureaucrats!

The commandant was startled by the bellowing laugh and he craned his neck foolishly to discover its source. His face flushed when he recognized Shak't'kan in the screen.

"My lord!"

"Obviously," Shak't'kan said drily. "Any new developments on the massacre?"

"No, my lord."

Shak't'kan's face was grim. "Why haven't you taken any steps?"

"We haven't been able to detect the saboteurs, my lord. They seem almost supernatural, the way they come and go, not a trace. . . ." His voice broke down and for a long minute Shak't'kan stared grimly at the commandant. Then, evidently having reached a decision, he began to speak coldly. "I require you to do this. At night, without warning, round up two hundred humans apparently at random. Take them from their quarters. Do this while they sleep, but make sure, quite sure, that no human sleeps through the demonstration. Make sure that three-quarters of those you pick are women and children; I want to save as many of the workers as possible. Take them into the compound and kill them."

"My lord . . ."

"Kill them slowly. And put a good light on them. We want a satisfied audience."

"Well, I'm off."

"Take care, Holcomb." Lu-An sounded concerned.

"No doubt about that," he said. "But, Lu-An?"

"Yes."

"I'll never be able to take care of myself the way you've taken care of me. I appreciate it; I really do."

"Don't be silly!"

"Not silly, just grateful."

Lu-An smiled back. "Get on with you."

"Wish me luck. If we win, I'll call it the Battle of L.A., after you!"

"And if you lose, we'll call you a dunderhead."

"Fair enough. So long." He turned smartly and stepped up on a waiting flitter. In a few seconds it was gone.

Lu-An shook herself and walked slowly back to the ops center.

•   •   •

"Just strafing runs, mind you. I don't want any of our fighters to land unless I give the order," Joaquin concluded.

"What targets do you have in mind, sir?" The aide was shuffling markers on a map. Joaquin was circling the table and taking in the changing field with a practiced eye.

"We'll concentrate on North America, but don't answer any call for help further west than the Mississippi. Let's try and give Shak't'kan the idea that all our forces are now committed on the East coast."

"Do you think he'll buy that, sir?"

"He might. Anyway, he'll be so busy in the East that chances are he won't be looking for our airfleet in the Pacific."

"He can't miss them after sunup, not if they're anywhere near enough to do some good."

"They won't be hiding after sunup! Okay, who's next on our list for help?"

"The Great Lakes area."

"So. Send in some flyers."

"Yes, sir!"

"Ruth?"

"Yes?"

"What do you think? Lu-An and Holcomb."

"You know, Tony, you're a romantic?"

"Well?"

"I'm glad."

"So am I."

"My lord?"

"Yes."

"There's no doubt about it. Our forces were scattered and defeated in Las Vegas."

"The ships?"

"Destroyed."

"Sataspes?"

"No sign."

"Not a word of this is to be revealed."

"No, my lord."

• • •

The *Wasp* silently nosed up from the deeps. Her bow control planes were canted radically. It was Rogers' notion to make this quick. A quick surface, radio contact, and then an even quicker dive back to join the *Ondine* and the *Admiral Small* in the inky waters one-hundred fifty fathoms under.

"Fathoms eight, Skipper; five, four . . ."

"Raise the periscope, Carberry. Let's take a look before we commit ourselves."

"Up periscope, sir. It's awfully dark up there."

"Anything in sight?"

Carberry slowly scanned a full circle around the periscope silo. "Nothing that I can make out. Seas are running fairly high, though."

"We'll surface and take a gander." Rogers turned to a group of four waiting Rangers. "And I'll expect you to inflate that balloon and get the antenna up before I can say Jack Robinson. Understand?"

"Yes sir!"

With a wrench, the *Wasp* raised its bow up out of the Pacific straight into the air, then sank back like a playful whale. The crash as it slapped the water shook the whole ship.

"On the surface, Skipper!" The crew suddenly got very busy undogging hatches, checking trim, and then Rogers' ears popped as pressure was equalized and the sub was opened to the night air.

The radio crew were the first to hit topside. By the time Rogers and Ruth emerged into the chill ocean wind, the balloon was already half-inflated and whipping like a captured bird on deck. The air was full of the sound of running water, water pouring and leaching from every surface, trickling and dripping until it was rejoined with the sea. The waves cracked the *Wasp* hard, raking the ship from the starboard bow to the stern. The vibration of the propeller was lost in the uneasy gait of the ocean.

Finally the balloon was hard inflated and the crew slowly paid out the antenna until it stretched forty feet long and a good twenty or thirty feet above the waves, whipped so tight by the wind that Rogers could hear the hawser wire singing. The man cleating its dog-end looked up at Rogers and said, "All set, sir. Should be able to raise Las Vegas now."

Rogers climbed the conning tower with Ruth close on his heels. From that height, the sub seemed to weave perilously in the sea, but Rogers was enjoying himself. He found it refreshing to breathe uncanned air and shout into the wind.

"I'm ready," he telegraphed down to the radio room. After a second of hesitation, his speaker buzzed with static and he grabbed up the microphone, "Lu-An, this is Rogers. Come in, Lu-An!"

It was all going according to plan. The station in Las Vegas was on immediately. "Hold on Marshall, while I get the princess."

Rogers waited only a moment and then Lu-An's high, clear voice sounded over the speaker. "Tony, I'm glad to hear from you."

They hadn't bothered with a code. Rogers figured that if he couldn't outtalk any prying ears, he was too old to be doing this anyway. "And me you. Anything to report?"

"Holcomb has arrived at his destination and all his friends are ready and waiting to party."

"Good, anything else?"

"Well, news of our victory here has been making the rounds. Sparks here says that Shak has been hearing it from his people right and left—seems that every even mildly patriotic group in North America and Europe has finally heeded your call to arms. Having a little fun at Shak's expense. You started something all right."

Rogers sounded smug. "All it took was a good example."

"Which my people provided." Lu-An clearly wasn't having any of that. "This is your shot, Tony, don't muff it."

"I won't," he replied.

"Anything on your end?"

"We'll make our showing as discussed so long as Holcomb's on schedule. Its important that we're synchronized," Tony summed up.

"No problems that I know of."

"Then over and out, twenty-two skiddoo."

"Whatever that means. Until the big moment."

The speaker stuttered into raucous static. Rogers shut the circuit and turned to Ruth. "Looks like we're in business. If nothing goes wrong, Holcomb will be leading his guerrillas and the Rangers out of the L.A. hills at sunrise. At the same time we'll stage our attack on the undersea end . . ."

"Shouldn't we check with Joaquin?" Ruth asked. "Just for form?"

"I don't know about form, but he'd better have some air support handy. Anyhow, we should be raising him now . . ."

The radio sputtered to life. "Rogers, this is Joaquin. Can you hear me?"

"That I can."

"We're all set up here for the party. Is it still on?"

"Still on; anything else in your schedule?"

"We've been visiting troubled friends here and there. Nothing we can't handle."

"Keep up the good work."

"My pleasure, friend. Over and out."

"Out." Rogers motioned to his men, who were already poised and ready to lower the balloon. Carefully Ruth and Rogers made their way back to the hatch and down below. They were still blinking in the strong light when they heard the call, "all-secure," and Carberry ordered the *Wasp* back below the surface.

●　　●　　●

Provisional Government . . . Come in Government. Princess, are you there?

Reading you, Princess. Have some good stuff to report. A few scuffles outside the Prl'oi domed city as usual, but this time irregulars crawled out of the woodwork and pitched in. We had a full-scale battle on our hands. And we beat the pants off them. Still can't quite figure out how, but every man, woman, and child in this area was in on it. Niagara signing out.

Las Vegas. Could use some more help here. We've got

them on the run, but frankly don't know what to do with them. Eighteen thousand of them. Need advice urgently! Please advise. Johnstown, PA, signing off.

Need help desperately. Have stirred up hornets' nest. Need air and ground support, backup services, immediately. Please come in. Painted Springs. Please come in!

Lu-An paced the floor nervously. "I don't care. I don't care about Painted Springs or Johnstown! Can't you tell me anything more about Holcomb?"

"He hasn't reported in yet, Princess."

"No news from L.A. at all?"

"So far a complete radio blackout from that direction." Marlowe took Lu-An by the shoulders and forced her to meet his eye. "There's nothing to worry about. Holcomb is undoubtedly still in the hills with the Rangers. Believe me, once this thing breaks, we'll be hearing all about it. There won't be any point in maintaining radio silence then."

"I suppose you're right," she said. "I just can't bear not being on the scene myself."

"Well, as Rogers said, somebody has to run the show —and you're the one elected."

"Still," she said reluctantly, "this watching and waiting is just no good."

"Well, only another couple of hours to sunrise."

"All right." She flashed a hesitant smile. "Let's see if we can't tackle a few of these other problems while we're waiting. About Painted Springs—do we have anybody in that area?"

"A squad of commandos under Captain Mallouk's umbrella command."

"Fine, I'd like them flown in. I'll speak to Joaquin. What about Johnstown?"

"We don't have anyone within reach, not a squad, not a soul."

Lu-An turned a few circles around the floor while she thought about it. "They don't have the manpower to watch them, right? How about letting the Prl'lu go free."

"Go?"

"Sure. There's nothing we can do with them and there's nothing they can do in the woods. Give it a chance; they may like it!

"And now, about the kitchen detail. . . ."

"We should be sighting the Guyot shortly." Carberry threw the reassurance back over his shoulder; his eyes were on the sonar board. "Look for a flashing peak. Once we're in close, we'll be able to sight the city through the periscope's infra-red sequence."

The sonar unit scratched steadily on, its every idiosyncrasy already a byword among the crew. They'd heard and commented on every possible combination of sounds, but none of them had heard anything like the happy pinging that resounded early that A.M. A flaring light swept one quadrant of the board.

"That's it! That's got to be it. I do believe we're approaching the city!" Ruth sounded excited.

"You sound surprised," Rogers teased, "punch-drunk."

"If I do," Ruth responded, "you're the immediate cause. I'll be glad to be out of this after a week locked up with you."

"I'm afraid, my dear, you're putting the cart before the horse. Out of here we'll be nowhere but in the drink."

"If you two would give me a chance at the 'scope. . . ." Carberry reached for the periscope, brushing them aside.

In the far distance, Carberry could make out a dull red glimmer. As they approached, it began to mass into shapes and areas. They'd definitely found their mark. "Silent running!" he ordered.

"Beat you to it," Ruth said.

Rogers took the mike to the torpedo room. "Arm torpedo tubes."

"Arming, sir."

Rogers ran the obligatory roll. "*Wasp*!"

"Battle-stations manned, sir."

"*Ondine*?"

"Ready."

"*Admiral Small*?"

"All set."

"In that case and if we're all shipshape, we wait, gentlemen. We wait until sunrise!"

The three ships hung in the dark sea, already within strike range of their target.

18.

Holcomb was prowling the hills over L.A., just as Falstaff had months before. This time though, more than a raiding party waited for the signal to descend into the valley; several thousand trained and experienced commando fighters were lying in wait, including a good number of Lu-An's guerrillas, two hundred of Rogers' Rangers, and independent fighting units including Dane's people.

They were waiting for sunrise, the appointed hour to attack.

Holcomb visited several squads in turn, coordinating their plans. News of the victory in Las Vegas had spread far and wide and even those fighters who stubbornly remained autonomous of Lu-An's provisionals were impressed enough to acknowledge Holcomb's leadership.

He was crossing the hard scrabble canyons to the north, taking it slow to conserve his energy for the battle ahead. For that matter the hills were very dark, very old and mysterious and he could feel the weight of the darkness at his back—a brooding sort of pressure compounded of the land and the unseen presence of thousands of waiting men and women. He could sense them in the heat, Rogers' Rangers and Lu-An's provisionals, and not a few of those he'd led out of L.A. such a short time ago. It was possible to hear their shallow breathing in the dark, feel their rustling presence all around, settled thick in the darkest gullies and arroyos—all waiting eagerly, the pressure of their waiting building nervously toward sunrise.

The prison camp was laid out in sleeping regularity, square in the valley below. The shimmering desert heat gave its few burning lights an appearance of liveliness and motion that Holcomb knew was an illusion. Holcomb knew the rigors of prison camp life well, and even they didn't include an inefficient predawn roll call. There was simply nothing for a human work force to do in the half-light, and the Prl'lu were nothing but efficient. So there would be no early clangor and bustle to disturb the plan.

Not for the first time, Holcomb worried that the courier had failed to get through to those inside. In the interests of security, only the one courier had been sent in to forewarn the rebels there—the Los Angeles Free State, as they called themselves—warn them and the Simbas.

It wasn't good to enter battle with a clouded mind, particularly a worried one, and Holcomb decided to rest up with his men. He picked a spot on the hillside with a good view of the Camp and settled himself comfortably—it was going to be a wait yet.

There's an art to waiting and an art to getting comfortable that soldiers have practiced through the ages. They've had to; wars are rarely fought near hotels and all too often the working soldier is called upon to scorn the impedimentia of pack and bedroll. Holcomb found a bit of loose shale and scooped out a shallow ditch in the hillside, and there he wriggled himself until the loosened soil conformed to his body. Twice he stopped to pull out bits of stone, but soon he was settled and he began to clear his mind by staring into space and naming the stars. For that matter, it was a useful way of tracking time.

The sun wasn't due to rise for another hour, but Holcomb began to be conscious of a pale illumination of the sky. He sat up on the hillside, among so many recumbent shapes that had become disturbingly visible

in the lifted darkness, and took a good look around.
The camp was starting into life and that just didn't
make sense. Avenues and streets of lighting were being
flipped on at some central switchboard in big patches
and sections of illumination. Something was up.

Others on the hillside were stirring now, and below,
the Camp was full of unusual activity. It was too far to
see the movements of individuals, but masses of people
were clearly moving about from barracks to barracks
and then congregating in the central compound.
Holcomb could feel a sour burning in his chest; this had
a very nasty look to it.

Slowly he got up and started ordering his men to find
cover. His people were scattered all over the hills, all
around the Camp. Most of them would have to fend for
themselves if something had gone wrong. He just hoped
they'd move fast enough. For the moment, he concentrated on hastening all those within earshot into the
deepest part of the gully, while only he waited outside to
see what he could see.

He perched precariously behind a rock for five minutes, then ten. He waited and watched and tried to make
up his mind. What could be going on?

Soon the muzzle flash answered his question, and the
desert air carried the subdued moan of frightened
people. Then he knew what had happened and what
he'd have to do.

The Prl'lu didn't bother to rap on the barracks doors.
In some cases, they didn't even bother to turn on the
lights, just barged into the darkened sleeping quarters
and made their selection by feel and fright. This one
squealed, it was a child, take it. That one was soft, a
human woman, take her. They were handed out the
door and marched in line. Only then, sometimes, did the
lights go on and in the confusion did mothers know
they'd lost their children, or husbands find they'd lost
their wives. They were taken and marched before a
following crowd into the great compound, the center of
the camp. By then the lights were going on and everyone
was rubbing at bleary eyes and straining to see.

The Prl'arek commandant strutted then, paced in front of the crowd, before the assembled hostages. The ranks were drawn and no human could know precisely why, but they all felt a touch of certainty, something like déjà vu. Not one of them doubted that there was to be killing done this night.

A man saw his daughter across the chasm, across the line that Commandant Yoxter drew. And joining Yoxter, armed and ready, in a line reaching across the compound, were a hundred of his kind, armed and tall, casting shadows in the arcing lights. The man could see his daughter, in pajamas, small and thrust in front of the silent crowd; but from where he stood, also in the front, both crowds looked thick and cold with confusion.

Something was about to happen, somebody was to die, and the lines were drawn, but he had no way of telling on which side. *Please*, he thought, *turn your guns here. Away from my daughter, who has begun to cry.*

Yoxter turned and paced both crowds as though to judge their size. He didn't speak; he knew his silence would increase their fear. He studied and waited; he appeared to judge, but the decision was already made. With a deliberately inconsequent wave of his hand, the order was given, the guards gripped their weapons tightly, and a number of people were killed—two hundred, to be exact.

The father was not one of them.

The muzzle flash lingered in his eyes. The heavens were bright with it. L.A. was recorded on his iris forever.

Holcomb crawled up the arroyo until he was positioned just right. From his pack he pulled a pair of night binoculars and tried to use them, but the flash of weapons still haunted his eyes. It didn't matter anyhow. By pre-arrangement and careful planning, he was forbidden to begin the attack until sunrise. His push was timed to coincide with Rogers' raid on the undersea city and Joaquin's aerial attack. If he jumped the gun, he risked everything. If he didn't . . . Well, it was certain that more people would be killed. He tried again to focus with the binoculars. Now he could make out a mêlée of running, fighting bodies.

It was clear the battle had already begun.

He shrugged and, for a quick moment, in what was left of the darkness, smiled ruefully to himself. He'd let these people down once; he wasn't going to do so again.

He raised his voice in a shout that echoed through the basin, "We're gonna do it now, boys! Go to it!"

In the camp, the parents were the first to break ranks. They died in slow motion.

The father of the little girl made it farther than most, but then most had not actually seen their children smothered in flames. When he fell, his clothing and flesh wrapped in fire, he'd managed to stagger within a few feet of the commandant. In a way, he was responsible for Yoxter's death. The frightened bureaucrat ran from the stench and flame, ran past the cordon of armed warriors that might have surrounded and sheltered him. It was the second wave of wives and husbands, sisters, and relatives and friends that took him down, a fragile corpse, before they scattered and drew back to the barracks and sheds that afforded a little shelter, some defense against the retaliation that was sure to come.

Holcomb's shouting was a bit of bravado that he hoped would bolster the men's courage. It didn't do much toward prompting a confrontation.

His men were flanked in tactically decisive points around the prison camp's outskirts. That obstacle posed Holcomb his greatest worry. The success of the battle, he well knew, depended on taking out the dis beam generating stations that defended the camp. Since Dane's attack earlier that year, there had been two dis beam stations, both annexed to presumably well-tenanted barracks, and both equipped with their own little dis beam defense perimeters, courtesy of Shak't'kan's foresight.

There was only one way around it that Holcomb could see—artillery fire from the hills. One lucky hit and the obstacle would go down at once. Not as good as a flight of heavy cruisers complete with an airborne arsenal, but still, the nearest thing in a pinch.

They'd come prepared with three mortar and a somewhat unreliable bazooka. That was all; the provisionals' strength was in numbers, not in weaponry.

Holcomb took a squad into the valley, scrabbling down the lower reaches of the arroyo to make his way to one of the outlying generator stations. Lieutenant Derek Shute was his gunnery officer; the rest of his men were plain, dedicated fighters. They planned to wait until the mortars had forced a breach, and then. . . . Well, then things could get interesting.

If the mortars didn't work, it was up to the men on the spot. That was why Holcomb chose to go with this particular squad. He wanted to be on the scene if the hill artillery was no go. Shute carried the bazooka along as insurance. It was a tricky shot—a lob up and over the dis field and down into the station compound.

Holcomb hoped it wouldn't come to that.

The camp was still lit up bright as day, and the wash of its light bathed the valley basin. That made things difficult. The guerrillas approached the station compound on hands and knees, using every bit of natural cover they could find. At a safe distance, they lay down in the loose soil, crossed their arms protectively over their heads, and waited for the mortar fire.

It wasn't much of a wait.

All along, Mouka had been prepared for a reprisal of some sort. In fact, he had counted on Yoxter to supply the trigger that would throw the camp into full-scale revolt. Not a very pleasant game, perhaps; but then, Simbas fought dirty. So he and his men had waged a silent war against the Prl'lu masters and the human prisoners alike, doing their best to raise tempers on both sides. If anything, Mouka had been puzzled by the commandant's equanimity in the face of the Simba's irritating and pernicious vandalism. Evidently something more was needed to push the situation over the edge and so Mouka had planned an atrocity—the calculated murder of the Prl'lu guards.

His planning had paid off tonight at the cost of a good many lives, but the Simba leader was grimly satisfied. The Battle of Los Angeles had finally begun.

It was curious, but when the Simbas emerged from their hiding places, their crevices and badger warrens, storehouses and closets, to take part in the battle they'd engineered, neither human or Prl'lu seemed to question the tiny warriors. It was as though they'd been expecting the gremlins all along.

Perhaps both races had their minor demons.

The keening sigh of the mortar shell soaring overhead, the dull crack of concussion, the soft heavy blanket of settling dust, for Holcomb's squad this was the war. For interminable minutes they lay stretched in a field of fire while the mortar bracketed its objective. To the south, across the basin, another mortar shared in the deadly work. Holcomb counted the shots impatiently. One, a hundred yards short, another cast too far to the west, one lost in the dis fence—a sound that fell to nothing.

They were getting nowhere fast.

Holcomb was thinking quickly, assessing the situation and rethinking the problem. There was nothing for it, he decided, "Shute, you'll have to give a try. Lob a few and see what happens. And," he forced a raffish grin, "Do it the hell away from here—we don't want to be on the receiving end when you start drawing fire!"

"Whatever you say, Cap." In the flashes of mortar fire, Shute's face was pale, but he managed a quick smile. Then he was gone into the darkness.

It was a bad kind of fighting, Holcomb thought, when you were obliged to send men off by themselves, possibly to die.

He spent the next few minutes crouched next to his communications sergeant. The man huddled over a portable com unit, straining to hold the signal while Holcomb spoke urgently into the mike.

". . . you've got to do better than that!" He paused while someone on the other end made an excuse of some kind. "No way!" he shouted, "We're on line down here, do you understand? Shute's trying with the bazooka now, so concentrate your fire on Station B, but don't fail me, right? We'll handle A; you take care of B."

After that there was nothing to do but wait. As someone, Rogers probably, had told him long ago, war was nothing but hurry up and wait. Now Holcomb was discovering what that meant.

Suddenly there was a welcome explosion in the middle distance. The camp lights flickered just a moment as power shifted to Auxiliary Station A. It was a start and Holcomb allowed himself a deep breath of satisfaction, but his pleasure was short-lived. Suddenly there was a screaming in his ears and it seemed as though the sky was falling in. The screaming was genuine, he realized that all too soon. It was real, and piercing. Its note mixed the shrill whine of artillery with a throbbing human note. When Holcomb turned to the sergeant to get his reaction, he saw the man's hollow mouth fill with the scream and his tongue flap mindlessly in his face. The Prl'lu had opened fire.

Suddenly the raucous note of the com joined the din. Holcomb reached across the screaming man and thumbed the receiver. He heard snatches of a voice trying to report.

". . . think we got . . . guess you know, Prl'lu have opened fire from Station A, can't tell . . . if that's all right? Repeat, seek confirmation, is Station B destroyed . . ."

Holcomb wrestled the com pack over the injured man. The sergeant was writhing in the dust, but Holcomb didn't have time to stop and check his wound. He yelled into the mike, trying hard to make himself heard, "Confirm, B destroyed. B destroyed. Concentrate fire on A and Prl'lu battery. Do you read?"

He waited impatiently for a confirm and got nothing. He shouted back into the mike, "Do you read? Holcomb here, do you read!"

The com buzzed again. By now Holcomb was fed up, with life, with death and responsibility, and fed up with microphones. He gripped it tightly and shouted, "Well!"

It was Lu-An. "Is that you, Holcomb? I'm being patched in. Things going well?"

He shook his head, suddenly exhausted. "Not as well as they might be."

Lu-An's tone changed immediately to one of concern, "What's up?"

"You're not going to like it. I've jumped the gun. We've been shelling the stations for the last twenty minutes; we're catching some of it back now."

When Lu-An said nothing, Holcomb continued, "They were killing people down there. The damn fight had already started. I couldn't just leave them to. . . ." He tried not to sound defensive, but wasn't sure he had succeeded.

Lu-An merely said, "Too bad," and after a pause added, "Is there anything you want me to do?"

"I suppose not. Can't warn Rogers, can you?"

"Not a chance."

"Then there's nothing."

"In that case, best of luck."

"Thanks." Lu-An had signed off and Holcomb turned back to the sound of fighting. Even so, he felt wonderfully refreshed. Whether Lu-An approved or not, he'd done what he had to do. It was enough.

After a good deal of bullying on the part of the rebellion-minded underground of the camp, all the milling prisoners had been organized into a makeshift combat organization. Not so makeshift as to be actually embarrassing—a good deal of quiet thought had already been given to the ways and means of conducting a revolutionary war with unschooled and unpracticed soldiers of both sexes. For better or worse, the contingency plans were in effect.

Against armed and organized Prl'lu, the human counteroffensive was necessarily catch as catch can. The main thing was to keep out of sight. If something interesting presented itself, a group of two or three took a calculated risk. In this way, before long, one out of fourteen humans bore a power weapon of some sort. For the rest, well, staves and kitchen knives had been taken into combat before. At least at this point no human was so foolish as to believe there was a middle ground. It was fight or be killed.

The human revolt should have been doomed before it began. There has never been a successful prison uprising —only limited strikes with limited and conditional success. Under normal circumstances, the one necessary requirement of any guerrilla function is space, unlimited, incalculable space to roam and hide in. A prison compound, however large, lacks hiding places. No, the Prl'lu must have felt confident enough about the ultimate outcome. . . .

But this was no ordinary revolt. The humans could thank the Simbas for that. As Rogers had anticipated, they were the perfect cut-and-run fighters. Here now, then gone, and more than one Prl'lu died that night with a pick in his back. They turned the prison into a nightmare world of sudden blood and quick death. That was all to the good, as far as the humans were concerned. The shifting fortunes of war began to swing in their favor.

Shute knelt in the thin scrub and grimly waited for his bazooka to cool. The smell of cordite hung in the air and he was painfully conscious that every time he fired, the muzzle-flash gave his position away. Nothing for it though, but to keep trying. Station A had to be breached.

If only he could get closer—but that *would* be dangerous. This business of lobbing the bazooka shell with accuracy was an act of desperation anyway. The weapon just wasn't designed with marksmanship in mind.

He decided to move up cautiously—see if he couldn't get a better angle. Anyhow, he was itching to be away. As soon as the bazooka muzzle cooled, he took a grip on it and began to shuffle carefully upfield.

The mortar fire seemed to be dying down again, at least from the human side. In any case, it hadn't been having much effect, not since the lucky hit on Station A. Shute guessed it was up to him.

So far the return fire had been haphazard; with no real targets to try for, the Prl'lu had been peppering the general neighborhood, shotgunning for a prize. Fortunately for Holcomb's men, the station Prl'lu found their defensive shield as great a hindrance to effective gunnery as Lt. Shute did. Still, the lieutenant wasn't surprised when the field he'd just moved from suddenly erupted in fire. He knew he made a conspicuous target.

He found himself a sheltered spot behind a clump of pigweed and began to adjust the weapon. He couldn't sight it properly—he had to cant from the vertical and hope for a predictable trajectory. As he'd been taught, he visualized the rocket's parabolic flight as a rough triangle, so far up, so far down. It took a certain instinct to be good at this kind of thing, not everyone could do it.

The lieutenant trusted that he could.

He braced the tube against a patch of yielding earth and squeezed the grip. A blue-white flame burst the air and he snapped his fingers from the bazooka's barrel. Their tips were suddenly blistered.

With any luck . . .

The rocket mounted the sky, invisible and silent. It hung a teetering second before it took the descent, falling, as anything might, softly toward the earth in an uninterrupted and splendid arc like a toy. It found the Prl-lu compound and gently nosed into the dust.

The force of the explosion knocked Shute flat and sent him tumbling across broken ground.

Fun, he thought and then passed out; but his smile showed that in the years to come, this would be one of the good times. And *that* was enough.

"We're in!"

Holcomb's men were throwing themselves pell-mell in

a glorious footrace of victory toward the suddenly darkened camp. The nimblest had already reached the perimeter. They were in!

"No!" Holcomb stood straight up, head thrown back, and bellowed the order. He kept shouting until the cry was taken up and passed along until all his men had stopped in the night. They were breathing hard from the exertion. His voice steady and firm, Holcomb made himself heard over their rasping breath.

"It could be a trick. I'm going in ahead. Cover me at a hundred yards, and don't do anything impetuous, no matter what."

He started walking toward the Camp. Already his men were swarming through the shattered station searching for survivors; but others, most of them, were dogging his heels, falling back when he stopped.

His legs plodded on in a shambling gate. He could safely ignore them. It was his arms; he didn't quite know what to do with his arms, should they swing at his sides or be held stiff? As a compromise, he searched his pockets, adjusted his belt, kept them busy. The hard part was the face. If death was on its way, he wanted to greet it with a smile on his lips and a song in his heart, or some such fooldang PR, but for the life of him he couldn't manage it. He felt grim about death—especially his own.

He paused when he prepared to enter the no-man's land, where only a few minutes ago the dis fence threatened all trespass. After a moment, he shrugged his shoulders and strolled nonchalantly ahead, conscious of the men on his heels.

Halfway across the former barrier his men caught up with him, a wildly cheering, raucous mob. Holcomb felt good, but he wasn't about to let it show; over their shouts and war whoops he made himself heard.

"Lets try *not* to make this a pigeon shoot, fellas. You just hold on while I give it a try."

He walked on ahead, though still some of his men seemed reluctant to linger behind.

In the seemingly empty camp he made for the first

building, a darkened barracks. Nobody appeared as he approached the door. Just to make sure he poked his head inside.

Empty.

He walked on to the next, and the next.

All empty.

With a brief wave of the hand he signaled his following troops to come ahead. All around the Camp's perimeter the signal was passed—approach, but slowly. The guerrillas fanned out and followed silently, taking what cover they could. But Holcomb's steady purpose was infectious. The men willingly advanced with weapons leveled and nerves pitched high.

And Holcomb kept on walking.

The compound was dark and empty of life, but it held plenty of death, and after a while Holcomb became aware that it harbored a macabre kind of illumination too. Torn and smoldering bodies littered the parade-ground. In the last thick darkness just before the dawn, Holcomb picked his way between the women and children caught in death. There were men too, but the women and small children were horrible to see. Here and there a glowing ember cast an eery light, clinging for life in a man's chest or in his clothing.

After that it hurt to go ahead. *Too late*, he thought. *Much too late*. And his men followed silently, picked out in the suddenly glorious morning.

He reached the far end of the compound and considered turning back, but he couldn't face all the dead again quite so soon.

Holcomb waited for his lieutenants to reach his side. When they did, faces drawn, he ordered tonelessly, "Please take care of it, gentlemen, I'm going to have a look around." He nodded toward the far reaches of the camp.

His path took an aimless bent once he was out of sight of his men. He wandered where the streets led him, the gravel beginning to glint under California's morning sun. The clapboard barracks, erected by humans under Prl'lu domination, took on a happy new-day look compounded of the sun and the freshening breeze and maybe even a mild nostalgia. Holcomb had lived here once.

They found him, sitting quietly in a silent office— once it had been his own.

He didn't notice them arriving and at first couldn't find a face to go with the voice, which asked in the empty room, "Are you all right?"

"Of course," he answered dully, "yes, of course," he repeated.

"Down here," the voice said drily.

He looked and found Mouka, pick thrown over his left shoulder and legs braced against a large world.

"You the Simba?" Holcomb asked.

"One of them."

"A survivor?"

"That's right," the gremlin answered. "A Simba and a survivor. I'm called Mouka."

"Call me Holcomb," the human said politely. "Are there others of you—survivors I mean?"

"I should say so!" This time it was the Simba's turn to be astonished. "We don't kill so easy as all that."

Holcomb's voice was slow, almost angry, "I meant people from the camp. Humans."

"Of course! Didn't I just tell you?" The Mouka was indignant that anyone should doubt the success of his campaign. "Most of them, as a matter of fact. And now you can tell me who you are."

"I come from Marshall Rogers . . ."

"Why didn't you say so?" the Simba roared. "Well you can tell him that we've mopped up here and . . ."

It was Holcomb's turn. "He's not available now. I have orders that you're to report," for the first time his face brightened, "to me."

"Well, well. I see you've got it all planned out." The little being paced the length of the office hut. From the entrance, his small guard took up an excited chatter.

"That puts things in a different light."

"I don't see why it should," Holcomb said defensively.

"Oh, it's not you, friend." Mouka examined the human closely. Whatever he saw there must have been to his liking because he continued, "In fact, you're all to the good."

"I'm glad you think so." Holcomb said with some irony.

"Don't take offense. What I meant is that you're on the spot. I've been holding things up here until we got some word of the outside world. Why, with your men, we can finish this."

"Didn't the courier get through?"

"Courier? No, we haven't heard from a courier . . ."

"Well then, what is it you want from me?"

"Why, lead us, of course." The Simba was surprised.

"Lead you where?"

"The rest of the way, of course, to press the battle. Why, they're on the run, we can't stop now."

"The battle?"

"In the tunnels of course. We've pushed them back into their tunnels, and before long we'll have chased them down their tunnels into the sea!"

At that moment the sky screamed with the sound of aircraft. Joaquin's armada had arrived—right on schedule.

19.

The city clung to the edge of the cliff, perched above an abyss that reached into the shadowy depths of the Pacific Ocean. Like an ancient, inaccessible fortress hanging from some warring king's mountaintop, Shak't'kan's city commanded absolutely in its realm. Its lighted domes radiated dimly north, south, east, and west, below and above, and wherever its rays penetrated through the dense medium of the sea, Shak't'kan's authority was sure and violent.

Seen from a distance, the city was a pretty thing, a delicate filigree of lights sketching a spot of jewelry on the Guyot side. The sea water muted and softened the effect so that the glaring yellows and reds of the city shone magically in the middle distance. Up close, though, the city revealed its functional simplicity, a handsome but utilitarian network of capillary tunnels and tiny domes.

It was Shak't'kan's crowning achievement, this underwater city, but it was time he abandoned it.

"Skipper, I think you should get in on this." Sparks stuck his head into the wardroom, trailing wires. He was listening intently, an earphone clapped rakishly against the side of his head. Rogers looked up from a desultory game of checkers with Ruth and, seeing Sparks' expression, he immediately hastened over. Silently the radioman handed him an earset.

The sounds were coming from outside the sub, roughly in the direction of Shak't'kan's underwater city. Rogers couldn't distinguish much, just rumblings and sharp staccato reports filtering through the dense water. At this depth, with the immense compression of the sea, you could be sure that the sounds you heard from outside the sub were loud indeed.

"Any chance that ruckus is coming from one of our boats?"

Sparks looked thoughtful, "No, I don't think so. Captains McNab and Falstaff have orders to lay back. They're well out of sight, anyhow. No, I think we're getting something from the city."

Rogers turned to Carberry, "Come get an earful."

Carberry shambled across the wardroom and crowded into the tiny radio room. He grabbed the trailing end of Rogers' headset and cocked his head to listen.

The sounds, muffled as they were, suggested heavy machinery in motion. There was something distinctly purposeful about them and, Carberry felt, something menacing.

"I don't like it."

"I don't either," Rogers said, "I don't like it at all."

Sparks remained mute.

"What time is it?" Rogers asked.

"Another half-hour before sunrise."

"I don't suppose this kind of caterwauling goes on every morning," Rogers said dubiously. "I think we've got a problem, gentlemen. Shak't'kan may have something up his sleeve."

"I think you can bet on that," Carberry said. "The question is, what do we do about it?"

Rogers grinned. "I'll think of something." He clapped Sparks on the back. "Keep your ear out. And don't be afraid to holler!" He disentangled himself and headed back to the checkerboard, where Ruth was beating him sideways.

Shak't'kan waited impatiently while supplies were boarded onto his flagship, enough food and fuel to supply him for many days. The way things were turning out, there was no telling when or where he'd light again.

He stood by the port, ready to embark. Anxious messengers and minor officials waited on him, delivering reports of the battle still raging in the tunnels linking L.A. to the underwater city. They were a constant nuisance and he dealt with them shortly. They scurried away with his sometimes capricious demands.

He'd continue to command from his flagship once he'd established himself at a safe distance. It made no difference; he well knew that the underwater city was doomed.

"My lord . . ."

Shak't'kan looked up and saw the last stevedore leaving the ship. Imperiously, he brushed past the clerk and stiffly marched up the gangway. This time everyone else was to be left behind. It was best to travel light. He took his place on the bridge and beckoned to his captain to begin lock procedure. The harried officer began the eleven-step countdown:

"ONE: power to life support sub-assemblies . . . TWO: power mechanical sub-assemblies . . . THREE:

. . . electronics . . . chemical functions . . ."

Shak't'kan relaxed; for the length of the countdown he was cut off from the incessant bad news.

". . . SIX: ballast functioning . . . SEVEN: forward rockets armed . . ."

The seamount would have to fight its own battles. And if they couldn't manage . . .

Obedience, Dependence, and Fervor weren't always enough.

". . . TEN: crew in place . . . ELEVEN: lock released!"

The ship shuddered under the sudden pounding pressure of thousands of tons of sea water filling the lock. In his acceleration chair, Shak't'kan had a choice between holding on or covering his ears against the noise; he chose to hold on for all he was worth. The wrenching din was replaced by an ominous creaking of the boat's superstructure as the craft settled into submersible mode. Suddenly he winced against the pain of acceleration; with a jerk the city was behind them. Ahead, the open sea.

Rogers tried to visualize his little fleet hanging in the dark sea. It was deceptively difficult. The subs shifted in every current, registered every whim of the Pacific, but Rogers knew that the men and women he'd entrusted them to were doing their level best to keep them on course, ready and waiting for the big moment. It looked like it was finally here.

In a way, the image of his boats adrift in a black sea suited his mood—he felt very much in the dark. No prior experience in battle, on either land or in space, had prepared him for the constrictions of submarine warfare. It was the sort of thing he knew he'd look back on and favor as a challenge. If he lived to look back.

The sounds of lading continued on Sparks' earphones. As as precaution, Rogers ordered his fleet nearer the city. He had no way of contacting Lu-An or Holcomb for late-breaking news; he just hoped their plans hadn't gone awry.

Just then Carberry reported from the periscope

station. "Something up, Skipper. Better have a look-see."

His voice sounded tinny and featureless over the sub's intercom system, but Rogers knew that Carberry didn't take alarm without cause. With a spring in his step, Rogers made his way through the corridors, compartments, and bulkheads that divided the *Wasp* into a maze of specialized sections. They were on full alert now and everytime he passed through a watertight door in a bulkhead, he had to stop to undog it, then screw it shut from the other side. It all took time, but closing doors was the cardinal rule of submarine life, more important even than getting the commander to the bridge on time.

He paused a second as he passed through the aft torpedo compartment. Eight hefty metal tubes gleamed with a coat of new paint. There was a special smell to this room too, a smell of fine machinist's oil and damp kapok insulation. It was an encouraging smell, and Rogers carried his newfound optimism with him into the periscope station and up to the raised platform of the 'scope silo.

Carberry was there, eyes glued to the periscope's rubber eyepiece. He was using his body to swing the heavy shaft in a slow scan of the underwater city. "I think this is it, Skipper. They're opening the main lock. Looks like somebody's about to skip."

"Give me a chance, will you?"

Carberry stepped aside and Rogers focused on the lock. "You're right. I wonder who and why?"

"Do you think they've gotten some word that we're coming?"

"I shouldn't think so, not unless Holcomb started without us. How long is it to sunrise?"

"A few more minutes."

"Hold on . . ." Rogers gripped the scope handles until his knuckles whitened. "I think I can make something out. They're coming out. It's a big cruiser, the biggest!" He thought rapidly. "I don't want to let this one go. Get on the sonar phone and order McNab and Falstaff to close. We're not going to wait anymore; let's go in now!"

•　•　•

If there was any question that the city knew they were coming before, there was none now. With all three subs in full throttle, there could be no hiding. The vibration of their engines communicated itself through the ocean water for miles.

The first to take notice evidently was Shak't'kan's flagship. It broke course and nosed down, headed for the deeps off the edge of the Guyot, where it had a chance to lose itself near the ocean's creviced bottom.

Then Sparks showed up from the com room. "Hear it again, Skipper! Lot of random noise. At a guess, they're recycling the lock."

Rogers got on the sonarphone with the *Ondine* and the *Admiral Small*.

"Falstaff! This is Rogers, are you reading me?"

"Loud and clear, Skipper."

"Keep me posted, but you've got a free hand. That goes for you too, McNab."

"And you, Skipper?"

"I'm with you. Good luck."

As the *Wasp* nosed for the depths, the Prl'lu city groaned with the sound of locks cycling, groaned, and spewed out a deadly spawn of miniature torpedo boats.

It was going to be quite a fight.

McNab and Falstaff kept their respective boats well separated during the attack. That made sense; it divided the enemy's forces and provided a better shot at the city. To give them their best shot, Rogers dived straight for the onrushing torpedo boats. If it was at all possible, he'd keep them occupied while the others went in for the kill.

The bow planes were bent to their greatest possible angle and the *Wasp* was diving precipitously. Unfortunately, such extreme measures were taken at the cost of maneuverability. To compensate partially, Rogers ordered the emergency propulsion motor outboard. It caused some drag, but with short bursts of the motor at a slight tangent to the *Wasp*'s main propeller, Rogers would be able to effect greater control—not that that was going to win this fight.

The torpedo boats were moving on him fast. Too fast for the infra-red 'scope to track and calculate. It relied on such tiny variations in relative areas of heat that its computers couldn't cope with a quickly moving body. From here on in, Rogers would have to rely on the sonar.

The pinging was growing fast and incessant as the wolf-pack neared. "Short-scale pinging," Rogers ordered. "This is going to be hand to hand."

The enemy boats were close now, and on the short-scale screen they resolved themselves into separate entities at last. For the first time Rogers could count them. Eight, eleven, make that fourteen. Fourteen against three. They were hard odds.

It seemed to Rogers that his only chance was to catch them doubled up. A hard fact of submarine combat was that there was no small-arms engagement. You fought with torpedos and that was all. No such thing as small-arms fire below the surface. Since torpedos were a limited commodity, Rogers had to try for multiple contact with every "fish." Suddenly he felt like the tailor who'd finished nine with one blow—except Rogers was still waiting for his turn at bat.

Well, the only way to have any success at this game was to shoot from the hip before the Prl-lu boats had a chance to scatter. Rogers ordered his first volley now.

"Torpedo room! Tubes one, three, five, and seven. Ready!"

"Ready, sir!"

Rogers was tracking the massed boats on the sonar screen, calculating the complex vector mechanics more by intuition than anything else. The enemy had already split up into four distinct groups. There was every likelihood that they would disperse even further apart as they closed distance with Rogers' subs. It was all a matter of directing a torpedo to a point directly in the center of one of those groups, primed to fire after a clocked interval, just when it would be able to do the maximum amount of harm. It was a complex problem indeed.

"Torpedo room. Fire!"

The first burst of fish spat out of the tubes and Rogers and the crew could feel the boat give an appreciable jerk. Ruth, at Rogers' side, manning the sonar controls, caught herself on his arm.

Before the fish had met their target, Rogers was already giving orders: "Port sailplane to one-six degrees. Three-quarter speed! Rearm expended tubes. Are two, four, six, and eight primed?"

"Primed, sir."

"Fine. Keep them at readiness." At the moment Rogers' biggest worry was to move the *Wasp* well out of the way of any return fire and still keep the boat nose-on to the blast of its own torpedos. At this depth, the concussion of the torpedos' explosion, caught broadside, could shake the *Wasp* apart as surely as enemy fire.

"Starboard sailplane six degrees. Full speed!" The *Wasp* skewed around in the ocean in a dramatic arc. Under normal circumstances, both sailplanes were invariably moved together, or shifted out of sync for minute course corrections; Rogers' drastic maneuvering was dangerous and unprecedented, but it served the purpose, and the sub swung around into the groove.

The explosion seemed to come in several distinct intervals as the concussive waves passed the boat. The shock of it gripped the *Wasp* and shook the sub like a toy. If it had caught the boat broadside, Rogers felt sure, it would have ripped . . .

The second wave pounded past the boat. The water's turbulence made the sonar unworkable. Ruth, bracing herself against the screen, could get nothing but a violent din of pinging and a static fog of light. They had no way to tell whether their torpedos had gone true, or what was coming their way.

Even the sonarphone was affected. Over the speaker in the control room, a staccato burst of sound and then Falstaff's voice in broken bursts.

". . . chased by pack . . . gonna take a shot at the city and shoot past . . . can't make out McNab anywhere . . .

cruiser diving . . . trench . . .''

Sirens drowned the speaker out. Damage control was in effect. Rogers called for speed. He was taking the ship in toward the calmer waters at the explosion's core. There the turbulence should have passed.

"Beginning to get a reading on the screen, Tony." Ruth raised her voice to make herself heard over the sirens. Carberry was trying to get the engine room on the com and with all the power being expended, one way or another, the *Wasp* was becoming very hot indeed.

"What've you got?"

"It was a hit, Tony! Six of 'em!"

"The rest?"

Ruth sounded worried. "Scattered, I'm afraid."

"Well, we knew it wouldn't be a turkey shoot." Rogers managed a grin. "Don't worry too . . ."

His words were cut off. A few hundred fathoms from the *Wasp*, the sea erupted into a boiling cauldron of steam and white water. The enemy had found its range and was firing back.

"Okay," Rogers shouted into the com so that the whole crew could hear, "We're going in to lay one on the city!"

McNab was in trouble and knew it. The *Ondine* was being dogged by two of the torpedo boats just above the Guyot plateau. The hell of it was that there was nothing he could do about it. His aft tubes were empty; he'd already expended them on an attempt on the city. A foolish expenditure, he now saw. He'd fired too early. His fish had disappeared into the depths below the Guyot, gone so deep he hadn't even heard the blast.

And if he turned to fight, the enemy would be upon him before he could position the bow tubes. For that matter, with the *Ondine*'s comparative bulk, this was one race he was bound to lose anyhow. The torpedo boats were already gaining.

They were about to pass over the city, spread out on the edge of the plateau below. The *Ondine* had a clear shot. A shame, McNab thought, that they couldn't take it.

Why not? he suddenly thought.

If the *Ondine* fired at close enough range as it passed over the city, and then put on everything it had to escape the blast, the concussion might, just might, catch the two dogging Prl'lu craft just as they passed over the point of impact. That'd settle them for sure, and it wouldn't do the city any good, either.

McNab made up his mind to it. It was a long shot, and if they couldn't get clear in time . . . But then, they really didn't have much choice.

"Ready," he called down to the torpedo room. "Ready and fire!" The fish were off.

The *Ondine* shook with the expulsive power locked in its tubes and then McNab felt the tremor in the steel plating as his engines really poured it on and the propeller shaft reached for the rpms, reached past their ancient designers' specifications until the whole boat pounded with the revolving shaft. They were making good speed, they were passing the city by, any moment might be too soon, and McNab had already braced himself against the impact.

When it came, he didn't feel a thing. The *Ondine* was too close. It imploded immediately.

The city was already a shambles when Rogers dived on it. McNab's torpedos had shattered an entire quadrant and, once breached, the exploding force of the ocean—forcing itself down tunnels, supposedly watertight bulkheads, into every crevice, shaking the rock itself—had done the rest. And Falstaff's salvo had by good fortune destroyed the lock and the underwater port facilities. Rogers' diving attack was more a matter of getting his licks in than anything else. As Ruth remarked in a shaking voice as they skimmed over the city's outskirts on their approach, "This place has *really* had it!"

It had indeed.

Falstaff reported in. "Orders, Skipper?"

"How are you fixed?"

"Well enough. McNab bought it?"

Rogers didn't answer for a moment and then said, "Yeah. We could see it from here. He was being chased, tried to lead two of 'em into a trap, got caught in it himself."

"Did he get 'em?"

"He got them," Rogers' voice lifted, "and a sizeable portion of the city. He did damn well."

"Do you clear any more bogies?"

"None here. You?"

"One or two. What say you give them to me?" Falstaff sounded ready for the game.

Rogers thought a minute. "You've got 'em. I've got business down below." He looked at Ruth. "I think we should go after the one that got away."

"The cruiser?"

"The cruiser."

Ruth smiled and said, "You've got my vote."

"Now, who said this was a democracy?" Rogers growled, and sent the *Wasp* plummeting into the depths. As it passed the city, they could see sections of it imploding in a furious white froth. For the crew of the *Wasp* it was a lucky sight.

Before they got out of range, Falstaff called in, "To the *Wasp;* Good Hunting!"

It was a fine day for it, Rogers thought.

Shak't'kan had heard the battle from a distance and over the sonarphone had received more than one plea for guidance from the beleaguered city he'd left behind, but once he'd sighted the three dark shapes of Rogers' subs, he'd already resolved to let the city fend for itself. No, the smart thing, the efficient thing, was to look after himself, to fight another day.

It was Rogers he was running from. In his heart Shak't'kan knew it was Rogers. The man had the uncanny ability to be everywhere he shouldn't; and worse, no matter what Shak't'kan threw at him, he always came up for more. Shak't'kan couldn't understand it. The man's luck and tenacity seemed—well—more than human. He didn't fit at all into the Prl'arek's model of humanity, and yet, there he was!

Well, he'd dive his ship into the ocean floor, if he had to, to be away from him. Once he was out of range, he'd head for some quiet place to recoup his losses, maybe . . .

They headed for the ocean's depths.

"It's getting pretty deep, isn't it," Ruth commented.

"Deep enough," Rogers agreed. "Still, anywhere he can go, we should be able to follow."

"How can you be so sure?"

"Our hull is built to take the pressure. It's specialized, designed for that and nothing else. His cruiser can fly, go into space, who knows what else. But I don't see how a vessel designed to withstand both a vacuum and the ocean's considerable pressure can withstand either as efficiently as a vessel designed for one specific purpose." Rogers' words were confident, but Ruth knew him well enough to detect the slight worry in his voice.

The control room was silent then, except for the slow steady pinging of the sonar tracking Shak't'kan's descent. The whole crew felt the tension of the hunt and they stayed glued to their posts.

Suddenly the tempo of the pinging quickened and Rogers broke into a smile. "What did I tell you! He's leveled off. Now we've got him for sure!"

He called down to the engine room, "Manage any more speed, Carberry?"

"A little, Skipper."

"Well, now's the time to lay it on." The sub surged ahead.

Steadily the distance between the two craft decreased. The race was on and Shak't'kan was clearly losing it. He must have known that too, because his vessel suddenly stopped near the ocean floor to meet Rogers' head-on in combat.

Ruth's sonar suddenly started whining with sound. "Bottom, Tony! If we don't get him now he can stick close to that and get away!"

"We'll have to shoot it out then," Rogers replied. He

almost sounded as though he looked forward to it. "A kind of duel, and this is the O.K. Corral!" Nobody knew what he meant.

"All right, torpedo room, are you armed for a fight?"

"Yes, sir!"

"Carberry, let's take it in."

The two vessels slowly squared off one against the other. It was crazy, Rogers knew. This wasn't the way subs fought, but he could feel a wild logic in it, a feeling that this was an important act. He just hoped the contents of the cruiser were worth the risk.

"Tony!" Ruth cried out. A torpedo had been launched at them.

In return, he ordered a salvo fired; once it was out of the tubes, he ordered an evasive maneuver. The Prl'lu had been quicker on the draw, he realized. He hoped it wouldn't cost him the fight or his life.

The alien torpedo exploded. Close, too close, but the *Wasp* made it through.

He waited to see his own volley close. One, two, three, four, five, six . . .

A portion of their undersea world exploded again. Rogers felt sick; he'd clearly missed. . . .

But he hadn't reckoned on the concussive echo effect. His torpedos exploded harmlessly, well away from Shak't'kan's flagship, but instead of billowing out in a hollow sphere, the concussive force of the explosion pounded along the ocean floor, a storm of violent force, which picked up Shak't'kan's ship and flung it to the ocean floor.

Even from a distance, Sparks could hear the distinctive crack as the boat struck and broke its back.

The boat was disabled, not destroyed. Rogers followed it to the surface. There was no where else for Shak't'kan to go, and all Rogers had to do was rise slowly alongside.

The two vessels broke the surface only a few hundred feet apart. The striking blue water of the Pacific poured, gleaming, from their decks. Rogers was first up the hatch trunk and on the conning tower. It was a beautiful, warm, sunny Pacific day, and the ocean swell was gentle. With a start Rogers realized it still lacked a couple of hours to noon.

In two tries, a member of the crew managed to snag the Prl'lu craft with a grappling hook fired from a modified Very pistol. With the help of the heavy deck winch, the crew succeeded in drawing the two craft together. Now came the ticklish part.

So far there hadn't been a stir from the opposite boat. It was possible that its inhabitants were injured, or they might be lying low. There was nothing for it but to take a look. With Ruth and Carberry on his heels, Rogers boarded at once.

"Be careful," Ruth instructed everyone.

Rogers laughed. "You should take some of that advice yourself." He gave a sigh of satisfaction as he succeeded in undogging the hatch lock. "Well, we're in for it now."

"Lead on, leader!" said Carberry and, with a quick gulp of air Rogers disappeared down the tube.

In a moment his voice shouted up, "All fine so far. Come on and join me."

Carberry stepped down first, then Ruth. They found themselves in a dimly lighted corridor. "Emergency power," Carberry commented. Ruth nodded.

Rogers had disappeared and the two looked around a little bewilderedly. Which way to go? Suddenly, though, Ruth caught Tony's voice down a corridor connecting to the control room. Carberry shrugged his shoulders expressively and the two went to find the source.

When they caught up with it, they found Rogers standing in the center of the control room floor, deep in conversation with a shadowy figure slumped in a pilot's chair. In another chair sat a dead man. His neck was broken.

When he saw them, Rogers smiled gravely and said, "I'd like you to meet my two companions: Dr. Ruth Harris, of whom you may have heard, and the young man is Josiah Carberry, very likely a doctor himself one of these days."

The shadowy figure made an effort, evidently very painful, to sit up. It spoke in a deep, cultured voice, obviously a voice honed on command. "My pleasure. Of course I have heard of Dr. Harris. Many times."

Rogers said to the two newcomers, "And I'd like *you* to meet Lord Shak't'kan." He was at pains to keep any note of victory from his voice, and on the whole, he was successful.

Ruth was too astonished to speak at first. Carberry filled the gap by bowing stiffly and saying, "I'm honored, my lord."

The Prl'arek continued, "I am pleased to meet you before I expire." His voice was noticeably weakening. "Rogers, of course, I have always wished to meet, but under slightly different circumstances." He looked intently at the human. His fine, dark eyes almost seemed to soften. "You might have been one of us."

"Well, as to that, in a way I am," Rogers said a little uncomfortably.

"So?"

In answer, Rogers closed his eyes and threw his head back in an attitude of concentration. After a pause, his voice subtly changed, he began, "Aldrum nepdon. . . ." In the language of the One and Great Race he made his explanation. When he finished the little group stood silently until Shak't'kan spoke.

"So that was the way of it . . ." he sounded almost wondering. "Ah, what I wouldn't have given to have shared in your knowledge of the history of my race. I envy you, human."

"But," Rogers said, "you can share . . ."

"Don't be foolish." The Prl-arek gestured to his broken body. "I live, but barely. Only my spirit has kept me from succumbing the way my servant did. I have no time."

"There is a way." Rogers spoke in English, but his tone was flavored with the cadence of the alien tongue. "If you'll submit."

The Prl'arek looked him long and carefully in the eye and nodded, once, briefly. The motion evidently caused him great pain and he winced.

Ruth and Carberry stood silently by.

Rogers approached the chair and cupped the alien's massive head in his hands, then he closed his eyes and concentrated again, softly chanting, it seemed to Ruth, an alien song. After a few minutes Shak't'kan began to murmur in unison and the lines of pain in his face faded away. Deeply etched seams underwent a metamorphosis and his face seemed to mold and flow as though more than one personality shaped and fed his features. With a low note the song wound to a close and Rogers dropped his hands. Shak't'kan's head lolled no longer but sat firmly on his shoulders, erect and intelligent. His bearing had changed too. He sat powerfully in his chair, every inch a lord. Without a word he stood up and walked to Rogers' side. They looked well together, two strong giants of the Earth.

"And now," Rogers voice carried the note of satisfaction he'd so carefully avoided before, "Ruth, Carberry, I'd like you to meet My Lord Shak't'kan once again."

They must have looked bewildered, because Rogers laughed. His laugh was free and unfettered for the first time in a long while, and his grey eyes were clear and calm. The hints of alien thought that had darted there for so long were gone at last.

"Don't you see?" he asked. "Shak't'kan is our newest ally, or perhaps I should say, Shak't'kan, and also now Aquintir and Jak't'rin!"

"You mindswapped!" Ruth murmured aloud. "You gave them back . . ."

The Prl'arek's voice rumbled after, and to Ruth's ears there was a familiar note in it, too, "My friend has returned us what was ours, *and*, I'm afraid, passed on more than a little bit of Tony Rogers."

He broke into a wide, friendly grin.

Notes Toward A Morphology of the Prl'oi Races

by

Dr. Ruth Harris

The general confusion surrounding the history and biology of the so-called Prl'oi races has proved a stumbling block to better understanding and exchange between human and Prl'oi. In fact, I have no hesitation in saying that this lack of understanding has prompted the most heinous crimes in man's history; crimes, I wish to remind my reader, against both sides in what has too often been described as an historic struggle.

There is no biological imperative which sets Prl'oi and human at each other's throats! That is the lesson of modern history. It is, as well, the lesson of clear common sense and scientific reasoning. It is because I believe wholeheartedly in the true and necessary companionship of two great races that I submit these notes. At some later time I hope to expand them into a full-fledged treatise, but for the moment I have a pressing engagement to join Anthony Rogers on his Third Extraterrestrial Expedition. It is one of the goals of that expedition to further our inquiries into the extent and fall of the onetime vast Prl'oi Empire beyond the stars.

History records no suspicion that Earth harbored another, perhaps inimicable race until well after the Collapse and the diaspora from the Chinese mainland.

Anthony Rogers confirms our belief that a Pre-Collapse world had no notion that Prol'oi colonies hibernated in stasis creches located in every corner of the

globe. If they had, he notes with characteristic confidence, "we would have taken care of the problem and
no *buts* about it!"

Our best theorizing holds that the Prl'oi race came to
Earth long before recorded history. Otherwise, their
arrival could scarcely have gone unnoticed. It is my
belief that they could have arrived no earlier than the
Pleistocene Period. Rogers has also provided some
insight into this problem and concurs that the Prl'oi
settlement could only have occurred prior to man's
ascendancy on this planet.

Mankind's first confrontation with the Prl'oi took
place no earlier than the last quarter of the twentieth
century, most probably between calendar years 1980
and the year 2000.

This is a dark period in our history. Few reliable
records survive from the years after 1980 until the
lengthy Collapse Period had ended and the world
emerged again from its Dark Ages.

By deduction we may conclude that during our suspect time-frame 1980–2000, something—a devastating
nuclear war, climatic changes, earthquakes, a hundred
catalysts have been posited—triggered the Prl'oi stasis
creches in beleaguered China.

These were evidently worker creches—at least we
know that only Prl'lu emerged, and no more than a
handful of these. Lost in an alien world, without their
hereditary masters, the Prl'arek, these foundlings, did
their best to preserve a way of life that at best was impractical under the circumstances.[1]

Impractical though it was, the technologically superior Prl'lu, aided by the general chaos of the Collapse

---

[1] At this point I'll review what must be the most confusing aspect
of Prl'oi philogeny for most humans. The Prl'oi can be divided up
into three specialized subspecies: the Prl'lu, the Prl'arek, and the
Prl'an. There is just one base stock, an unspecialized embryo form,
from which members of each subspecies are raised and conditioned by
diet and training. In general Prl'lu are warriors and technicians;
Prl'arek are the leaders and scientists, Prl'an are the lowest rung on
the ladder, the ignoble servants.

Period, conscripted humans to serve as their less-than-willing slaves. Lack of manpower, or I may more accurately say, womanpower, hindered them in other ways as well. To this end, the Prl'lu bred with Chinese mainland humans and eventually a mongrel race, the Han, resulted.

This was the race that held Earth in thrall for some four hundred years until Rogers came to liberate us.

The second revolutionary war has been fully documented. I won't go into history any further here, except to say that it has been more than once amply demonstrated that mankind's proven enemy is not the Prl'oi race, but a social structure that rewarded the generals and punished the diplomats. My experience with the Blackjack Prl'oi more than amply demonstrates that culture rather than biology is the predisposing factor in deciding between a peaceful and warlike race.

In this new world, where human and Prl'oi live and work together in peace, we have much yet to learn about each other. The binding together of our two faces in friendship may well prove to be the great adventure of the age. If so, I won't be surprised. As Rogers' Rangers have proved, and as Anthony Rogers himself has often shown, more, much more, can be accomplished together than apart.

Mankind is lonely no longer.

BEST-SELLING
Science Fiction
and
Fantasy

	47809-3	**THE LEFT HAND OF DARKNESS**, Ursula K. LeGuin $2.95
☐	16012-3	**DORSAI!**, Gordon R. Dickson $2.75
	80581-7	**THIEVES' WORLD**, Robert Lynn Asprin, editor $2.95
	11577-2	**CONAN #1**, Robert E. Howard, L. Sprague de Camp, Lin Carter $2.50
	49142-1	**LORD DARCY INVESTIGATES**, Randall Garrett $2.75
☐	21889-X	**EXPANDED UNIVERSE**, Robert A. Heinlein **$3.95**
☐	87328-6	**THE WARLOCK UNLOCKED**, Christopher Stasheff $2.95
☐	26188-4	**FUZZY SAPIENS**, H. Beam Piper $2.50
☐	05469-2	**BERSERKER**, Fred Saberhagen $2.75
☐	10254-9	**CHANGELING**, Roger Zelazny $2.75
☐	51552-5	**THE MAGIC GOES AWAY**, Larry Niven $2.75